THE BILLIONAIRE'S
Dirty Little Secret

THE BILLIONAIRE'S *Dirty Little Secret*

L.J. DIVA

★ Royal Star Publishing ★

Chances is an imprint of Royal Star Publishing
www.royalstarpublishing.com.au

Originally published as *Her Secret Island of Sex And Torment* in
2014 Re-released as *Her Secret Island* in 2016
Third edition paperback published in 2019
All Rights Reserved, Copyright ©L.J. Diva 2014, 2016, 2019

Trade Paperback ISBN: 978-1-925683-88-2
Large Print Paperback ISBN: 978-1-922307-39-2
Dust Jacket Hardcover ISBN: 978-1-922307-40-8
E-book ISBN: 978-1-925683-87-5
A catalogue record for this book is available from the National
Library of Australia

Cover design: Royal Star Publishing and Odyssey Books
Cover photo: istock.com/EkaterinaSolovieva
Typesetting in Minion Pro by Royal Star Publishing

DEDICATIONS

This book is dedicated to Conrad Coleby

PROLOGUE

She stroked his penis into a long hard shaft and descended onto it with slick swiftness.

He groaned in pleasure.

She did not.

He was another one of *them*. A walking, talking penis that was just another conquest. A penis and *nothing* else. Not a conversation. Not intelligence. Not a deep and meaningful relationship.

Did he fill her completely?

Sure.

Did he *fulfil* her completely?

Not even close!

She thrust up and down in robotic motions until he was done and she was over it.

Over the men who didn't care about her.

Over the men who didn't want her.

Over the men who didn't give her the orgasm she was after.

They just wanted the one hundred thousand dollars for staying on *her* island just for *her* pleasure.

They wanted the money, *not* her.

She slid off him and he groaned again. "Good to see someone got off on it." Her Russian accent came thick and heavy.

"Oh, yeah, baby," the hunky brunet yelled. His muscular six ten frame shone with sweat in the dimly lit boudoir.

"Well," she muttered. "You are done." Leaving him tied to the chair, she headed for the doorway of her sanctuary. Pausing, she glanced back at him. The hot American with the crew cut who had failed to please her. Pleasure her. Give her the mind-blowing orgasm she'd been after. Instead, she felt empty.

And dirty.

She closed the door and pulled on the silk cord hanging beside it. It rang a bell in the hall outside, letting her men know to come and take her latest sex stud away. She padded into her luxurious dressing room, yanked off the long straight black bob she was wearing and dumped it on the dressing table, then grabbed her robe from the back of the chair.

Wrapping herself in the soft satin material, using it as a warm cocoon, she pulled a towelette from its container, rubbed her face free of make-up, and gazed forlornly at herself in the mirror. A depressed, lonely girl gazed back.

"What the hell am I doing?" she asked the forlorn figure.

"I don't know," the figure replied, "but you need to do something."

With a frown and a longing glance, she walked into her now empty room and slipped into bed.

PART ONE

She gazed down from her third-floor balcony, secluded by thick green palm trees and plants, to stare at the men surrounding the pool.

Bronzed, muscular bodies, swimming, playing volleyball, or lying on the outdoor lounges sunning themselves.

Tall, muscular, masculine bodies in teeny tiny swim briefs or trunks, all slick with sweat or dripping water.

Moving and turning and flexing.

"Ah," escaped her breathlessly. "Beautiful, just beautiful."

She laid a hand on the railing and licked her full luscious lips. Long feminine fingers trailed up her abdomen, across her chest, and onto her left nipple to find it hard. Sliding off her sheer black dressing gown, she continued to stare down at the men by the pool.

Fifty gorgeous, glorious men she would have her way with. She felt herself moisten at the sight, and the aching between her long slender legs told her one thing.

Turning on her heels and striding into the bedroom, she called down to her assistant. "I want three men sunbaking on lounges by barbeque. Now!" Dropping the phone into its cradle, she groaned. "Ugh, want, now." Keeping herself aroused, she waited the few minutes it took for her guards to bring the almost naked blindfolded men up, and watched in wet silence as all three were tied to the bed.

Barely waiting for her men to leave, she slid and licked her way up the first hard masculine body, dipping her tongue into places it wanted to go. "You are good," she murmured into his ear as she climbed on. "Very good." Rubbing him until he was stiff, she descended and lifted, continuing the motion until she was done. "Oh, good."

She squeezed his pecs and clenched her vaginal walls to keep him hard. "Oh, good."

The hard body moaned and shifted, bucking at the muscular assault on his penis.

The warmth in the darkened room was heady, making the actions even more stimulating. Sweat formed, making them slick. Hands slid over muscles, mouths slid over mouths, tongues slid over tongues as they came together, grinding away in the late afternoon heat.

With a sigh, she slid down over him. The man with the rock-hard abs and rock-hard penis that was still inside of her. "Good...good," she murmured into his chest, her body pulsating and throbbing. She drifted in and out of the heady haze, her hands doing what they wanted as they reached and stroked, rubbed and groped. Her nails left little red lines on hard toned bodies, and teeth left bite marks on muscles.

"Ugh." The hard body belonging to the penis she was holding groaned.

She squeezed.

"Ugh." He arched upward, excited by the hand around his hard dick, and groaned again as she slid off the body she'd fucked and onto him. "Ugh." He collapsed and brought his knees up. "Yes," he hissed. "Yes." Using the position of his legs, he thrust up and down, and she matched his every move with moves of her own.

"Ah, uh, oh, God, fuck me," she gasped, moving against him thrust for thrust. Sweat ran down her body, from her brow to her collarbone, down between her breasts, and pooled between her legs. She rubbed her breasts and threw her head back. "Oh, God, oh, God." Within moments she was bouncing along, thrust up by the beast beneath her before she landed back on him only to be launched upward again. It was a cross between being on a trampoline and an uncontrollable wild stallion. "Ugh, oh, ugh," she gasped as his seed flowed into her and her G-spot was pleasured. "Oh, God, oh, God, oh, God." She sucked in air as she fell against him, his heart racing beneath her ear.

His lungs expanded and deflated rapidly as he regained his own breath.

She licked the sweat from his body, rubbed her hands over it, and planted her mouth on his. "Mmm," she mumbled. "You're *very* good."

"So are you," he breathed.

She rested, lying full out on top of him, his penis still inside of her. He felt good and was better than the first, yet there was one more to go. Her eyes slowly lifted to the man beside her. The last one on the bed. Blindfolded like the others, he lay there, hands tied above his head.

She slid off number two and onto number three. "Hello," she breathed. "My, what big arms you have." She pulled the rope undone and sat on him, wrapping those arms around her. "Ugh, big arms." She groaned as he crushed her to his broad muscular chest. "You very big. More ways than one." She moved up and down against him. Hot naked flesh rubbed against hot naked flesh. Her breasts squished against muscles as his mouth tried to catch them, succeeding in capturing her nipple in its grasp. "Ugh." Arching into him she let her head fall back.

He sucked harder, and his fingers found her crotch. "Ah," she yelled, "in me, in me." His fingers probed and pushed, in and out, and she moved against them, moved against him, moved against his mouth. "More, more." She spread her legs as wide as she could while sitting on him.

He held her tight. Mouth greedily sucked, fingers greedily found their way into her *very* wet, *very* aroused, *very* ready and willing body.

She thrust and pushed against him as her climax heightened. "More, more." One hand grabbed his head to keep it where it was, and the other grabbed his hand to grind it against her clitoris as his fingers poked and prodded her innermost self, terrifying her G-spot into doing what it was told. It was a prisoner. A prisoner of his magic hand, and her breast was a prisoner of his magic mouth and tongue.

"Oh, God," she barely managed. "More." She came on his fingers, his hand. She was soaked, and so was he. "Oh, God, oh, God." Her head flung itself back, away from his mouth. Her breast was ravaged red by that mouth and its wicked tongue. She leaned backwards until she was lying on his legs and his magic fingers withdrew. "Oh, God," she muttered as his magic fingers now played with her curls and flicked her clit. "Oh, God, you…are…very…very…good."

"You don't get to lie back and relax," he growled, pulling his legs from under her so he could position himself on top, frog style. "Now it's time for me to get off." He rammed his rock-hard dick into her as far as he could.

"Oh, God," she screamed, wrapping her arms around him. He was huge and filled her in every way. "Fuck me," she cried hysterically while he grunted back and forth until a climax that sent them into slumber.

Her eyes opened in the late afternoon light that glowed red from fluttering through the dark red velvet curtains draping the French doors. The weight lying on her shifted, and she realised *he* was still on top *and* inside of her; the latest conquest that had fucked her so soundly she'd never been fucked like it before. Her arms slid around his broad muscular back, and fingers trailed up and down his rock-hard muscular spine.

He breathed. He sighed. He woke.

"Shh," she whispered, "say nothing." Hitching her legs up, she wrapped them around his waist as high as she could get them. Hands slowly groped, mouths slowly kissed, tongues slowly danced, while bodies slowly thrust back and forth. She felt him move, every inch of every muscle worked to please her, to pleasure her, to fuck her into a stupor until she screamed in orgasm.

His knees were beside her hips, so he had the strength to push, and that position, in turn, rocked her back and forth. He cradled her, containing her in the cocoon that was his arms and legs, so she barely touched the bed. She was encased in him, joined with him while his penis did what it needed to.

"Mmm, uh," left her mouth in a breath, "mmm." She plastered herself to him, tightening her arms and legs to keep him there. She tasted him, his tongue, she sucked and bit, groaning, gasping at the way he made her feel. She was on fire and burning out of control from the inside out. He filled her to an overflowing capacity, and it made her hornier, harder, throbbing like the pounding of a tribal drum between her legs with every movement.

He tilted her down, rising as he did, still moving back and forth until they climaxed.

"Ugh," she groaned, "ugh."

His mouth found her breasts, and his hands found their way down to her hips which he lifted so he was kneeling above her. His fingers squeezed her clitoris as he spilled himself into her body.

She spasmed before falling silent, and he fell on top of her into a quiet sleep.

When she woke, it was dark out, and after a few moments of tranquillity, and some tugging and pushing, managed to roll the stud still on top of her from her body.

"You don't want me anymore?" he mumbled.

She glanced at him. "I want you all night, but we must get rid of other two." She called downstairs for her guards to help the other men out of her room, and shortly after that food arrived. She settled number three back on the bed, and her hands slid over him as she nuzzled his neck. "You are very good."

"Good to hear it," he replied. "Can I take this blindfold off?"

"No." She made sure it was still firmly in place. "It stays. Beside, make it more erotic. Here, let me feed you." She picked up an exotically spiced roll from the tray on the bed and teased open his mouth. He took it, and she licked his lips for him. "You are very, very good. Where you learn to be that good?"

"Years of fucking women. I'm an escort. They tell me what to do, or show me what pleases them, and I do it. Learned quite a few tricks along the way. All of which I can use on you." His big manly hands slid over her smooth, supple body and found her ever ready hardened nipple.

"Escort?" She frowned. "You mean hooker? Male prostitute, no?"

His hand stopped and retreated. "I prefer escort.

Hooker and prostitute are only for women.”

The frown was still in place. “But you are prostitute, no? I am paying you for sex, so you are technically hooker.”

“Wouldn’t that mean we all are then?” He cocked his blindfolded head. “All fifty of us?”

She shrugged and waved a hand. “And fifty before, and fifty before, and fifty before that.”

His head turned to her. “How many men have you fucked?”

She looked back. “How many women you fucked?”

He thought about it. “Well, it’s probably in the hundreds. One, maybe more a night, but not every night, and some don’t even want sex, they just want a hot stud to go to a function or party with. I see them home and leave. Many are repeat offenders.”

She was intrigued. “How many years you do this?”

“Uh, let’s see.” He mentally counted, but his fingers moved. “Five.”

Her brows went up. “And how old are you?”

“Twenty-eight.”

She smiled. “So, young. No wonder you so good and have so much energy.”

His lips curled into a grin. “Well, I do work out and eat lots of protein to give me muscle strength. Hey!” He grabbed her hand as it closed around his penis.

“You are right,” she purred. “You do have muscle strength.” She clenched and unclenched, and he guided her. “But to keep up strength you must eat.” Releasing him, she picked up another roll, placed it between her teeth and nuzzled his mouth, so he knew it was being delivered.

He caught it, bit, and swallowed in one gulp before delving into her mouth for the rest.

Coming up for air, she wiped her mouth and took a long drink of champagne. "You are very good." She sighed in delectable pleasure.

He put his hands behind his head. "I always aim to please."

"You certainly do."

When dinner was done, she left the tray outside the door and locked it to keep the world out. Sidling up to the massive four-poster bed, three times the normal size, so it took up most of the room, she climbed on and lay on top of him, resting her head on his chest. "Mmm, good." She breathed in deeply and slowly, taking in his manly scent before slowly releasing it.

His fingers trailed their way up and down her spine, across her back, down her sides. They caressed her firm, feminine buttocks, and she lazily stretched out on top of him, purring like a cat.

His fingers slid between her legs briefly before continuing on their merry way across her bare ripe flesh, repeating the trail, stopping just a little bit longer between her legs each time.

"Mmm, you know how to relax woman."

"Massage always does the trick." He continued feeling her, his hands owning every centimetre of flesh. His body burned beneath her, her breasts, her mouth, her lower abdomen where that soft ripe flesh of a woman was. His thighs burned to move, to rise between her, so she fell toward him. His penis burned to enter her, but he waited. Waited and continued the massage his fingers were giving her until the time he knew she would be so relaxed there would be no fight.

Her eyes flew open, and she sprang up like a cat, deftly ensconcing him inside of her and surprising him with her swiftness.

He sat, and jailed her in his arms as she fucked him senseless all night long.

*****

The next morning, she called for her guards to take him away before showering. The hot spray of water pummelled every aching muscle and then some. She stretched luxuriously before turning off the water and grabbing a fluffy towel. "Today, I rest. Tonight, I fuck." She entered her bedroom to find her stallion gone and the sheets changed. A breakfast awaited her on the table in front of the open balcony doors, and she dined on her favourite omelette, freshly squeezed juice, and French toast. Once done, she grabbed her binoculars and gazed out over the island.

Her island.

Her *secret* island.

Bird here, dolphins there, ocean waves here, two men fucking there.

She dropped the binoculars. "What in God's name?" Grabbing them, she peered through again, finding them half hidden by trees on a quiet stretch of the island. Fully naked and getting into it, she watched the hard-bodied men do it. One was holding onto the tree in front of him, the other coming in from behind. Hands groped the penis in front, and both climaxed together, leaning into the tree for support.

She blinked. She stared. She recognised the two men being from the group here for her bidding. "They are…gay?" she murmured, not sure whether to be shocked or not. She watched them kiss against the tree before they eventually dressed and walked off in opposite directions. She followed both, but soon lost them.

"What…homo…here…oh?" Her brows knitted together and she thought about it. How many? How many men who have been here are gay? How many men have fucked each other here on island? She walked to the balcony overlooking the pool and saw the rest gathered there. Within minutes the two she'd seen joined them from opposite sides, but didn't acknowledge each other. "Interesting. I think I shall play with them, see what they do."

She called for the two men she'd seen and waited until her guards were gone before joining them in her room. "Gentlemen, you are very studly." She gazed at the blindfolded studs before her, flicked a whip on their backsides and watched them rise. "You are already horny just from whip? Does not take much to get you going."

She led one brunet to the chair and the other to the bed where she ripped off his loincloth and mounted him. "Come," she commanded and gyrated against him. "Come." She whipped him and felt him harden inside of her. "Come." She rode him like she was racing in the Kentucky Derby, whipping as she clung to him, bouncing up and down like it would help her win, but in the end, she didn't even cross the finish line as he withered inside of her. "You not come?" Surprised, she stared down at him, as he seemed completely uninterested in her at all. "You…not…come?"

She frowned, slumped, and dismounted, leaving him for the man on the chair. Whipping and rubbing him, she mounted, whipping and bouncing away. "Ugh, oh, ugh." He was big and good, but not as good as the one from the night before. She noticed his unenthusiastic body language and slowed to a stop, another frown on her face. "You not like sex?"

"What?" he mumbled, dazed and somewhat confused by all that was going on.

"You not like sex?"

"I um," he licked his thin pink lips nervously, "I um, like sex."

She stood and led him over to the bed before untying their hands and making them face each other. "You like sex with men?" Watching their expressions under their blindfolds, she could see guilt all over. "Have sex with each other. I watch." Sitting in the chair she'd just fucked on, legs crossed, twirling a strand of hair, she waited as they just stood there. "Well? What you wait for?"

"Um, I—"

"Um, we—"

She waved a hand. "Um you were having sex with each other this morning in palm trees, so you have sex now. I watch."

"What?"

"We weren't."

"No, we weren't."

"Stop protesting. I saw you have sex." She cracked her whip. "Now!"

"Um, I—"

"Um, we—"

Another crack. "Now!"

Male hands nervously reached for the other and finding their way, arms entangled. Mouths found each other and legs entangled. They fell onto the bed kissing, touching and rubbing penis against penis.

She was aroused. *Very* aroused.

Watching two hard and horny men roll around naked, she wanted in, and moved to the bed for a closer look. She held onto the bed's wood poster frame, slowly sliding up and down it, pressing herself to it and biting her bottom lip in desire.

Mouths mashed together and bodies embraced. Hands slid between legs and legs entwined. Grunting and groaning and rolling over the bed they briefly stopped when she joined them.

"This is turn on for me, go on."

They did, forgetting she was even there as she rubbed against them, groping and grasping.

One turned the other over and started to slide between his legs.

"Stop!" She grabbed his arm. "We do this my way."

"What?" came the drowsy reply from the stud on top.

"We do this my way, but you still fuck." Lying on

her back, she pulled the man about to *be* fucked on top of her. "Get inside of me." She led his penis in and made him lift his knees up to her waist. "You." She grabbed the fucker. "Fuck him while he fucks me."

"What? I—" He stopped and reached for the blindfold.

She cracked her whip. "Do it my way or not at all."

He relented and found his way into the man beneath him.

They moved, and she groaned.

Three bodies, weirdly joined, in a sex act she'd never experienced.

A man fucking the man who was fucking her.

Her legs came up for the easier passage, and they all moved in sync. Grunting and groaning with each other they moved back and forth. The eroticism titillated her, making her harder and wetter. She lay back and enjoyed the experience, knowing it would be the only day she'd allow it to happen. Three bodies moved into one as all three came simultaneously.

"Oh, ugh, oh," she gasped, thrilled at such an unusual act. "Oh, that is good. Very good."

The two men collapsed against her, gasping for breath.

"Clearly not first time for you two, but first time for me fucking men fucking each other." She looked at them, slick with sweat and shame. "Do not be scared to express yourself in this room, gentlemen. This room is all 'bout sex. Who you fuck, who you fucked by, first time for threesome like this, though. Definitely turn on."

The stud on top slid out and the one beneath followed suit.

"As long as I join in, you fuck as much as you like today. Tomorrow, you go home." She got up and grabbed the champagne bottle from the ice bucket on the bedside cupboard.

"Go home?"

"But I…"

"You here for month, but you not straight, no point being here." She poured rich cold golden liquid down her parched throat and watched the two men. "Like I say, stay here today and fuck all day. We play games. You cannot say no. Drink?"

Sitting on the side of the bed the men accepted drinks and thought about it.

"I give you extra fifty thousand each to fuck me and each other all day." She stood before them, running her fingers through their golden-brown hair and her breasts against their faces. "We fuck each other."

"Well, I…"

"For fifty thousand extra."

"Should I…?"

"Why not?"

She picked up a box from the bedside cupboard. "Just as well have extra condoms," she muttered before sitting on the hot hunk of man meat to her right. "Good. Fuck me while your friend fucks you. We very free sexually on island, we fuck whoever, whenever." She shrugged nonchalantly and kissed him. "Fuck me now."

He pulled her to him and kissed her back.

She pulled the hot hunk of man meat on her left into the mix, and they landed on the bed in a tangle of arms, legs, tongues and penis.

They spent all day fucking each other from both ends. Her on top, them on top, fingers, mouths, tongues and penises probed and poked and pleasured each other as all three fucked until dawn.

She then rested the day away while they were flown home, and then asked for the men she had not claimed. Five men were brought to her, and she chose two, whipping them into a frenzy as she rode them all night, one then the other, not stopping, not resting.

"Ugh, harder," she yelled, flicking the whip back and forth. "Faster."

"I'm," grunt, "moving," grunt, "as fast," grunt, "as I can."

Her breasts jiggled furiously with his thrusts. He was holding himself up, thrusting from the hips and not using his leg strength in any way. She sighed. "For God's sake, get your legs into it."

"I, uh, I, uh, oh, oh, God, oh, God, oh, God." He spasmed and collapsed onto her, gasping for air and almost suffocating her.

"What…was…that?" she muttered beneath him and shoved him aside. He sprawled across the bed. Leaning up on her elbows she looked at him. "What *was* that? You could not wait for me to come? You are disgrace."

"A disgrace? I was fucking fantastic!" he gasped, sucking in air as fast as he could, lying there like a limp wet fish.

"For *you* maybe, but *not* for me." She turned to the hard body on her right in the warm dimly lit room and slid her fingers over his chest. "What about you? You ready to please me?"

"Climb on."

Sliding and grinding she found he was just right, and ground her way to a very happy ending. Falling against him, she relaxed. "You are good. Better than him." Glancing his way she found him snoring his head off. "Ugh, he snores." She stretched and promptly fell asleep.

*****

The next evening, she called down to her assistant. "I want one I had few days ago. Big muscles, one who is escort." She reclined on the bed and waited for the man she would have all night. *Maybe we do in shower?* she thought as he was escorted through the door that closed behind him. "Darling." She went to him and removed the cloth that covered his precious package. She stroked it. "I have missed this."

"And it has missed you." Picking her up, he headed for the bed, directed by her until they fell onto it a writhing tangle of human flesh.

"Mmm, mmm, darling." Hands groped and grabbed. "Mmm, mmm."

They came together with loud grunts and groans before collapsing.

"Good," she gasped. "Very good."

Half an hour later, she came to and called down for

a dinner tray full of exotic and spicy foods. She fed him a spiced meat roll. "So. We do in shower?"

"Mmm." He licked his lips. "We can do it anywhere you want to."

"Anywhere?" She thought about it.

"Anywhere, anyhow, anytime." He stretched out on the bed and crossed his legs.

"Then we do in shower, come." Dragging him from the bed, through the dressing room, and into the spacious floor-to-ceiling glass-walled 270 degrees white circular bathroom, she turned on the hot water. "Come, get wet." She pulled him into her arms, and they stood under the spray, soaping each other into a slow hot frenzy.

"Ugh, fuck me," she whimpered, and he lifted her onto him. Her legs wrapped tightly around his waist, and she locked her ankles, and by flexing her leg muscles was able to move up and down on him. Suds made everything slippery, and they slid against each other as they moved.

"More, more," she groaned, hanging onto him like her life depended on it. She came in an explosion of convulsions, and he waited for them to subside before getting off.

Carefully lowering her to the floor under the spray, he had his way. Groping breasts and sucking nipples, biting soft wet flesh, he played with her clitoris while moving inside of her.

She arched her back against the pummelling water and his onslaught. "Oh, God, what you do me. Digging her nails into his arms and spreading her legs even further. "Oh, God, oh, God, oh, God."

The second orgasm was better than the first.

Hours later they lay in bed, barely taking up any space in the massively oversized four-poster. A rich, luxurious red spread lay over them, and she was comfortable in his strong masculine arms. Her fingers drifted casually across his hair-free chest, and she felt better than she had in years. Decades even. Her right leg slid over and planted itself between his, moving so her knee lifted his penis and rubbed against his testicles. Her right hand slid down and grabbed it.

"I clearly don't need Viagra," he mumbled, left hand under his head, right arm around her.

"Clearly not." Rubbing her cheek against his chest, she marvelled at the smooth silkiness of his skin and how there was not a flaw on him. "You very fit, Mister Escort. Very fit indeed."

"Mmm." He enjoyed her hands on him, cradling his penis with care one moment and roughness the next. It was a complete turn on. "Need to be, Ms Fuck Me Senseless. I gotta say, though, I've never had this experience before. Fucking someone almost 24/7. Usually, it's only once at a time."

"But how many you fuck at night?" Her tongue slid nonchalantly.

"Usually one, sometimes two, maybe three. Depends."

"On what?"

"On whether I worked in the office or freelance."

"Office? You have office for prostitution work?"

There was a slight pause as he made some sort of

sound. "Escort agency office. Women come in, buy an hour, get fucked. I did that for two years before going solo and running my own business. I was fucking ten or more women a night."

Her fingers trailed. "Well, you are very fuckable. Were you popular?"

"Most popular guy at the agency."

Her hand moved on. "Must be your muscles that turn on?"

"Well, one muscle, in particular, I'm sure. Hey!" He grabbed her mischievous hand and rubbed it over his testicles. "Squeeze." She squeezed. "Oh, again. Oh, God." He moved her hand all over his crotch, and she didn't seem to mind. "Oh…God…"

"Stop!" she commanded, and he did. "This must not go to waste." Sitting on him, she moved, and he pulled her close while he got off.

"Tell me 'bout fucking women. What you do?"

"Ugh," he grunted. "Not now, not while I'm fucking you."

She wrapped her arms around him and clenched her vaginal muscles until he stopped. "Tell me now while we fuck. Could be good."

"Ugh, okay. Ugh. There was this one woman, ugh. Who had a really hairy pussy, ugh. And she expected me to go down on her, ugh. I couldn't, and ugh, she demanded her money back, ugh."

She guided his hand to her own pussy. "You like mine?"

"Babe, ugh. I love yours, ugh. Not too much hair and ugh, nice and wet."

"Not too wet?"

"No, no, ugh, not wet enough, ugh. I had a woman who didn't get wet at all, ugh. Needed to use lube and even then, ugh, it wasn't enough."

She rocked back and forth, clenching and unclenching. "You had some women do things you did not know how to do?"

"Ugh, yeah. I, ugh, had a forty-two-year-old, ugh, who was incredibly adventurous, ugh, had a trapeze set up in her bedroom, ugh."

She slid up and down, clenching and unclenching. "You have sex on trapeze? How you do that?"

"We didn't, ugh. Tried to get both of us on it, but it wasn't strong enough. Ugh, damn thing broke, ugh, God…coming."

She rotated in circles, clenching and unclenching. "Did you break anything? Did she pay you?"

"Ugh, God. Didn't break anything. Still had sex, though, ugh God. Still got paid, coming, oh, God, coming."

She pumped up and down until he released. "We must try trapeze."

He slumped back against the pillows gasping for breath. "Do you have a trapeze? It would have to be wide, not a thin bar, and bloody strong to hold both of us."

She stretched out on top of him and drifted off. "I do not have trapeze, but could get one made up. It is idea to think about."

When she awoke to a warm, dark room, she rolled over and reached for a box of matches. After lighting the candles on the bedside cupboard, she lay on her back and watched the light dance across the bed's red velvet canopy.

"Mmm." He moved beside her, shifting in his sleep. He had been the best fuck of her life, and she did not want to stop. But her migraine told her otherwise. "Mmm," she whimpered, rubbing her temple. "Go away."

"You want me to go away?"

Her head moved slightly toward the direction of the voice. "Mmm? What? Not you, migraine in back of head."

"Well, I can fix that." He flung the sheet back. "Let me give you a massage. It might make the pain go away." He knelt and slid her body down on the bed getting a squeal in reply. "Spread out, like an eagle."

She settled, "uh, okay," and flung her arms and legs out wide.

He started on her left foot, massaging, poking, and prodding, working his way up her soft white calf to her knee and onto her luscious thigh up to her groin, but he left her crotch alone. Shifting to her right leg he did the same, kneading the soul of her foot, her ankle, calf, knee, thigh and groin.

"Ugh, is good." She sighed, eyes closed, contented.

His magic fingers worked their way across her abdomen, her sides, bypassed her breasts and moved to her right arm and then her left. Her hands and wrists, all the way up to her shoulders. He massaged her collarbone, neck, jaw, the back of her ears, her scalp and temple.

She groaned in absolute pleasure. "Good, good. But no breasts? No pussy?"

"When I'm done." His lips and tongue trailed across her face, her lips, her jaw and neck, down to her breastbone and then her breasts, teasing and tormenting her rubbery nipples.

"Oh, God." She reached for him, but he pushed her arms away.

"No." His lips and tongue trailed down her abdomen into her curls and between her legs. Tasting, licking, sucking.

She arched her back and bent her legs. *"Fuck, good, good."*

Ending with a big suck, he withdrew, and she collapsed. Rolling her over, he laid her out and started again. Right leg then left leg to the groin, her back, sides, spine, shoulders, arms and hands. His fingers slid into her hair and massaged her scalp, gently probing the base of her neck.

"There, there," she muttered into the bed.

His fingers worked their magic and so did his penis, lightly dragging back and forth across her slender white back.

"Ugh, what is that? Feels good." She revelled in the sensation.

"My dick."

"Ugh, so good for lots of things," she replied half-jokingly.

"Certainly is." It stroked its way down her back and between her buttocks, gently prying them apart until it gained what it sought.

She lifted herself for him to enter, and groaned again in pleasure when he slowly slid inside.

He moved against her, towered over her, and grasped her outstretched hands.

Rocking back and forth against him, she breathed hard. "Ugh, good." He finished, and they lay there, breathing in sync. "I should keep you as sex slave forever. Pity you cannot stay."

His lips left a blazing trail of kisses. "Why can't I?"

"Because men only stay month. Easy to deal with."

"You can make an exception for me can't you?"

"I could. Maybe you come another time."

"I won't need to if you let me stay." His lips blazed in another direction.

"Mmm," she sighed into the softness of the bed her face was mooshed into. "I wish I could, but there is plan in motion. Plan must stay in motion. Plan must not leave motion."

"Can I be added to your plan?" Tongue tasted.

She sighed again. "Wish you could, you very, very good. All these years of being hooker come in, how you say, handy."

"If I go home tomorrow will I ever see you again?"

"Probably not. I never see men again. Once been here never come back." She shifted underneath him and he slid his arms around her. "So we must end this night with bang, because I not see you again." She clenched her muscles and he sprang into motion, riding her like she'd ridden him. Hard and fast, long and short, endlessly for the rest of the night.

*****

It was ten o'clock by the time she rolled out of bed. "Ugh," she groaned when the sunlight hit her face. She padded into the circular bathroom and showered, gazing out at the ocean and the waves rolling by. The birds flew from tree to tree, and the fluffy clouds floated past.

She sighed. *Maybe I should be cloud,* she thought. *Or bird. Free to fly anywhere anytime and not worry about finding mate, that special someone, that person who makes your heart tremble and jump and do that little dance called love.*

She sighed again and came back to reality with a cold hard snap. Turning off the faucet, she grabbed a towel and wandered into the dressing room. Picking up her wig, she sat it on its head next to all the others. Black, red, brown, blonde, different lengths, different styles. Each had a name, and last night's was Cleopatra, her favourite, worn with a pure gold gem encrusted crown.

She thought about her exploits and knew in an instant what needed to be done.

PART TWO

Chapter 1

I was awoken from my deep slumber by the ringing of my phone, and after a few minutes of one sided discussion, I hit the shower and dressed before going downstairs to face the day and the usual morning ritual of our staff meeting.

The staff gathered in the main office. There were twenty couples plus four singles in all. The women did the cooking and cleaning and made sure the guests had everything they needed, and the men took care of keeping the island neat and tidy and flying her men in every month. Some worked in the spa to rejuvenate the guests after a long night, some in security and acquisitions. We have a resident medical staff in our doctor, nurse, chiropractor, physiotherapist and naturopath, plus we have our pilots and yacht crew. I am the personal assistant and manager of the island we get to call home, and am responsible for anything and everything that happens on it.

"Alexi, did the Queen enjoy herself last night?" Dimitri asked quietly as he sat his huge six foot five Russian frame into a chair beside me.

"No," I replied, "and she realised why." I looked around at the employees. "She wants new men. She's bored with the ones that are here and wants new specimens. So we need to find some." Dealing with the usual checklist first, we moved on to finding new men to accommodate the Queen's island. "We need to find fresh meat," I said, "celebrities, sportsmen, anyone interested in spending a month on our little old island simply for the pleasure of a rich woman."

Dimitri smirked. "Wouldn't most men want that?" As head of Security and Acquisitions, he knew all about the Queen and what she wanted, as well as her insatiable need for men and sex. He was also one of three loyal workers she had kept after her husband died.

I smiled back. "Yes, you'd think they would for a hundred thousand dollars tax free." That was the way it had been set up, so the conquests could get away with not having to explain where they got that much money from to their wives or girlfriends. Or the tax department.

I turned to John, our computer guru and internet hacker extraordinaire. "Dig up anyone. Find photos of eligible men, do background checks, the usual, in the meantime, Captain," I looked at our yacht commander, "can you get the boat ready to send the current lot home?"

"Ma'am." He wrote some notes on the paper in front of him. "About an hour?"

"That's fine. Mattie, can you get the men's things together and start cleaning their rooms. They can lounge outside until it's time to go."

"Of course."

I looked around the room at the humble servants who served the Queen and thanked them for their time. "Meeting adjourned." I tidied my papers and was stopped by Dimitri as he stood.

"Alexi, is the Queen all right?" he asked softly in my ear.

I waited until everyone had filed out of the room before answering. "No," I replied just as softly, "she's not." I gazed imploringly up at his big brown eyes and sturdy face. He was the Queen's only confidant and knew so much of the pain and angst she had gone through. "But she will be." I smiled again and squeezed his hand. "Can you make sure the men get on board and leave for me?"

"Of course." He squeezed my hand back and left the room.

The moment he was gone I clutched the table. Dizziness overcame me, and I breathed slowly. "Oh, God, I need to get out of here." I ran upstairs to my room and shut the door tightly behind me. Leaning against it, I felt my knees buckle. "How can I keep doing this? How can *we* keep doing this?" I muttered before my knees gave way. I caught a glimpse of my reflection in a wall mirror as I slid to the floor and did not like what I saw.

*****

The Queen stood on her balcony, watching the yacht sail off with its passengers on board. Brushing a strand of hair aside, she wondered who would arrive next and what sort of slaves they would be. Would they pleasure her the way she wanted? The way she *needed.* Would she finally find the one that could give her *what* she wanted? *What* she needed. And would her servants do her proud with the choices they made?

*****

I walked into the mansion's large spacious office with its ocean views looking for John, and found him staring at the three large computer screens around him. "Any news yet? Pictures, details, bait, man meat?" I joked.

He barely glanced up. "There are a few potentials," he muttered. "But by the time I narrow it all down to milady's requirements, there aren't many left. She's been through most of them."

"I highly doubt that." My hands moved in my pockets. "What about Aussie men? The good old land of Australia? I know there are some pretty hot men there considering I'm from there, grab a list of them together for me. Pics, bios, background check. Celebs, non celebs, there *has* to be *someone*?" I scratched my head then straightened my short brown hair. "Think outside the box…find some *blond*…actors."

John caught the second last word, and his head shot up in shock. "But, but, but…"

"Think outside the box, John," I repeated as I walked toward the door. "But she doesn't like blonds…" was all I heard as I headed for the kitchen.

*****

The Queen sat in her large dark red dressing room and stared at the person looking back. It was dark out, and the only light was the lamp glowing softly next to her on the dressing table. "What do we do?" came from her in her Russian accent.

"I don't know," came the Australian reply. "Haven't you had enough of this yet?"

"Not yet." She thought about her days in Russia and the pain she had endured. "Not until I find the man who killed my husband."

"I thought you wanted to find the man who was your soul mate so you could spend the rest of your life playing happy families?"

"No," she said, glancing up. "That is you."

*****

"We have some candidates," John said the next morning at the daily meeting.

"Show me." I reached for the files he was holding.

"There's only five so far," he added, "unless she wants more."

I scanned each bio carefully and studied their faces. All good looking men. Brunet, blue-eyed, tall, muscular, masculine. I felt nothing, like I always did, until I flipped to the last photo.

He took my breath away.

My heart started its dance of love, unless it was a rhumba or samba. I couldn't breathe, couldn't move, I could only stare at his blue-eyed blond looks. Six five, muscular and wide. Wide, wide, ever so wide shoulders that had wide muscular arms attached to them that could envelope me and never let me go. No chest hair, just smooth, soft looking skin that I wanted to slide my fingers over and have the muscles below ripple under them.

"Alexi?" Dimitri called. "Alexi?" He frowned at my silence.

It brought me out of my raunchy scenario to see everyone in the room staring at my face, which I'm sure was beet red, with dilated pupils. "Um," cough, "um, what?" I squeaked.

"Looks like we've found a winner," John said as others tittered and giggled. "Are those five enough for now as that's all I could find?"

"Um," I muttered and cleared my throat. "Um, sure. I'll just um, keep these and um, show the Queen when she's up." I slammed the bios to my chest so no one could take them. "Dismissed." I gulped down a glass of water as everyone except Dimitri walked out.

He waited until they were gone. "Looks like you may have found one you like yourself." He waited for my reply, curious and suspicious, yet angered by my reaction to the man in the photo.

I slipped another glance at the blond hunk in the photo. "Oh," I breathed, "maybe. Do the usual, meet them on Sunday, give them the week to decide, then fly them out on Friday. Make sure they understand the confidentiality agreement before signing. And make sure they have the time to come." I looked at him as I handed over the folders, with one particular bio on top. "Make sure *he* is treated with absolute care. I don't want him forced."

He glanced at the photo and frowned before a hard smile crossed his lips. "Of course. Anything for my little Alexi."

*****

"We have some new candidates," I told the Queen as I stared at her reflection in her dressing table mirror.

"How many this time?" She stroked her hair until it shone.

"Five. They're good looking, tall, muscular. The way you like them."

"Show me."

I handed over the duplicated folders and waited.

"Mmm," she muttered. "He looks good, *he looks delicious*, he looks boring, he looks…blond…" Her head slowly turned to me and she gazed up in shock. "Blond!? I do not do blonds! I only do brunets. What is this, this blond?" She brandished the folder in front of me.

I tried to placate her gently. "Just read his bio. He's an Aussie actor who's been in some of Australia's biggest shows and movies. He's still young enough, and except for the blond hair, he fits the bill perfectly."

"He has no chest hair," she muttered, frowning as she examined his photos. "But he does look blemish free. Smooth skin…soft…" she sighed, "all right…keep him." She shoved the folders back at me. "But that does not mean I will use him."

I sighed inwardly. "Whatever you want, the choice is yours."

She looked up with her steely gaze. "Yes, Alexi. And don't you forget that."

I looked down and matched her steely gaze with my own. "No, Natasha. I won't."

*****

"All set to go?" I asked Dimitri and his men on Saturday. It was several days after the last lot of men had been sent home, and Dimitri was off to find some more.

"All set." He adjusted his briefcase before putting it on the seat next to him.

"Okay, good. Make sure you follow the directive." I nodded. "And come back with fresh bait next week."

He nodded in return. "Of course."

I left the plane and walked over to the hangar, waiting while they taxied to the end of the runway. Once they had taken off for Sydney, I sighed, stuck my hands in my pockets, and decided to clear my head.

A walk around the island always did that. Clear my head. It was something I did every couple of days as exercise and was a way to make sure everything was kept up to scratch.

A tiny little island in the middle of nowhere, warm all year round, a gorgeous, tropical setting, and one hell of a place to live.

I walked along the path and passed the small huts

the workers lived in, the sheltered cove for swimming and snorkelling, and the fresh fruit and vegetable gardens that made the place liveable and sustainable.

I rounded the curve to come across the huge kidney-shaped pool with its big barbecue pit, covered and uncovered lounge areas, and huge fun park waterslide. Palm trees swayed overhead, and I slowly breathed in the salty sea breeze. It always cleared my head. I glanced up and caught a glimpse of *her* in a window. Sighing, I wondered what the hell we were going to do.

*****

"Natasha, my dear. I want you to entertain my friends tonight. Wear your best lingerie and make sure to get your pussy waxed for me. There's my dear Natasha."

She felt sick to her stomach. It was going to be another one of those nights. A night where she was forced to be degraded and humiliated just because her husband could make her. She looked at his retreating back and mentally threw daggers, a million a second, hoping one might actually find its way into the base of his skull so he would drop dead instantly.

There was no way she was going to continue enduring this life.

No way in hell.

*****

Saturday night was luau night. While it may have been a Hawaiian tradition, we had adopted it for the island.

The men set up the fire pit; the women prepared and made the food. We went all out, regardless of whether we had guests or not. And there were times when we had *many* guests. The Queen's harem we called them. For her to use when, where, and how she wanted.

"Alex," Jenny called. "Is the Queen joining us?" She placed a bowl of potato salad on the table.

I joined her and took in the deliciousness of the evening. "No. You know she never does."

"No, she doesn't," Jenny continued. "Why is that? I've never even met her in all the years I've been working here."

"Neither have I," Mattie chimed in, gathering napkins.

"Me either," Megan added, laying out a container of cutlery.

"I don't think any of you have," I said. "She keeps to herself and makes me and Dimitri deal with everything."

"Why is that?" Jenny asked again, popping a cherry tomato into her mouth.

I shrugged and tried to diffuse the subject. "That's just the way it is. We all have jobs to do and we, I mean all of you, don't need to know anything besides when your pay goes into your bank." I grabbed a plateful of succulent meat and salad. "Let's eat, I'm starved."

Afterward, I wandered upstairs with a plate of food to find the Queen on her third floor balcony overlooking the barbecue below.

"I am bored, Alexi," she said, taking the plate. "Bored and tired."

I sighed and ran my hand through my hair. "So am I, Natasha, so am I."

"What are we going to do about it then?" She gazed at me.

I stared back at her. "You're going to find the man who killed your husband, and I'm going to find the man I want to spend the rest of my life with."

"Let's hope we do that, Alexi."

"Let's hope we do, Natasha."

*****

I tracked down John the next day to see what he had dug up on the death of a Russian billionaire. "Found anything else yet?" I leaned against the desk.

"Still tracking the shooter. No sign, no nothing. If he's KGB or something he'll be so buried underground we may never find him."

"That's *if* he's KGB." I thought about it. "What if he's," I waved my hand, "I don't know, just someone who wanted to kill a Russian billionaire arsehole for the hell of it?"

John sat back in his seat and stared at me, a million thoughts apparently passing through his mind. "So… you're saying what? It was just some random shooting, possible mugging, a robbery gone wrong?" He slowly stroked his chin in thought.

I saw those thoughts pass behind his eyes and stopped leaning against the desk. "Could be, John, could be. Either way, we need to find out where he is." I called Dimitri on my phone as I walked out the door.

"What's happening?"
    "We are 'bout to contact first potential…client."
    "Good. Behave yourself."
    "Of course, Alexi, of course."

Chapter 2

Bang, bang, bang.

The freshly painted white door flew open to reveal a six foot hunk of brunet man meat.

"Mister Dashiel?"

"Yes?"

"My name is Dimitri Yurogov, and I have proposition for you. May we come in?" He waved a hand at his black leather clad colleagues.

"Um, what kind of proposition?" Mark Dashiel gripped the door tighter at seeing the three big, bulky, sunglasses-wearing men before him.

"A proposition where you live on tropical island for month and get paid one hundred thousand dollars."

Mark's eyes bulged at the amount, and all worry slipped away. "Are you serious?"

"Yes, Mister Dashiel."

"Then come in, come in." Mark held the door open and waved the men in, closing it behind them. "Please, sit down." He motioned to the couch in the living room. "Tell me all about it."

Dimitri and his men stayed standing, and only he removed his dark shades. "I'll get straight to point, Mister Dashiel. There is very rich lady who owns island and loves men. She likes to use them as her plaything. You will stay for one month, get paid one hundred thousand dollars tax free, and to be held in secret bank account while you spend it, so tax man does not find you, and you *may* be chosen by her to be her sex slave on any given night."

"Um," Mark gulped. *"Her what?"*

"Her sex slave. If she wants sex with you, you do her bidding."

Mark stood staring at the imposing figures before him. *FBI? CIA? ASIO? KGB with that accent,* he thought. *Mobsters? Are they going to kill me? Cut off my head and bury my body somewhere on that island, so I'm never seen again?*

"Mister Dashiel?"

He came out of his reverie. "Um, yeah?"

Dimitri sighed inwardly at the stupidity of it all. "Do we have a deal?"

It's a hell of a lot of money, Mark thought. *And I do love sex!* "Hell yeah," he replied.

Back in the car, Dimitri rang Alex. "One down, four to go."

I picked up the folders and drew a big red tick next to Mark Dashiel's name.

Sergei started the car, and twenty minutes later pulled to a stop outside a block of apartments. "This is address," he said.

They alighted just as victim number two ran up to

the door dressed in shorts and a tank.

"Ugh, runners," Vladimir mumbled. "Who wants to get all hot and sweaty?"

Dimitri stepped forward. "Mister Pascoe?"

The man turned from unlocking the door. "Yes?"

"We have proposition for you."

Ten minutes later they were back in the car. "Where do we go now?" Sergei asked, manoeuvring through traffic after leaving Pascoe's place.

"225 Market Lane," Dimitri answered, glancing at the folder for Jake Michaels.

They found the rather posh looking mansion set back from the road with an intercom in the driveway. Sergei pushed the button.

"Yes?"

"Ah, yes, is Mister Michaels home please?"

"He is. Who wants to speak to him?"

"Dimitri Yurogov."

"And who is he?"

"He is assistant to very wealthy Russian billionaire."

"Oh," the woman said, clearly unprepared for that comment. "Come in then, come in."

The gates opened and Sergei followed the driveway around to the large double front doors.

Jake Michaels met them there. "So, which one of you is the assistant to this Russian billionaire?"

"I am, Mister Michaels." Dimitri stepped forward.

"Well, do come in." He waved them into the expansive *and* expensive-looking living room and offered drinks. "Who is this billionaire then?"

"Woman who owns island and wants you to stay for one month to be used for sex," Dimitri replied.

Jake spat his drink out. "What?" He gathered a few napkins and mopped up the mess. "Wait, what?" He sat there staring at the three men who looked so out of place in his home.

"My boss is very wealthy woman who owns island and flies men in for pleasure. One month, one hundred thousand dollars. You have medical when you get there, and sign confidentiality agreement." It was a speech he had repeated many, many, many times. And it bored him. To death!

"I, wow, I, I don't know." Jake flopped around in his chair. "It's not like I need the money…but I *do* love women."

"Of course you need money, Mister Michaels. We have done full background check on you. This is not your house; it is your father's. You have no money 'cause you gambled it away. You are not wealthy man you pretend to be, Mister Michaels."

Jake stared at the dark and swarthy man who clearly knew more than he should, and it angered him. "What are you? Why are you here? Are you some sort of henchmen of Louie's?" He leaned forward in his seat, pointing his finger in time with his words. "Well, you can tell him he's not getting any money because as you just pointed out, I have none."

Dimitri sighed. *Stupid man with stupid arrogance,* he thought. "We are not henchmen of this Louie you speak of. You have debts; we are offering one hundred thousand dollars tax free. Spend it as you wish, but you will need to sign agreement and spend one month on island."

"Where *is* this island?" Jake's suspicions heightened.

"Somewhere warm and tropical," Dimitri replied and stood. "You have until Friday morning."

They left and tracked down the fourth victim at an AA meeting.

"Mister Jacobs? We have proposition for you."

"Yeah, yeah, whatever," Todd Jacobs said, waving a hand at the mess he had to clean up. "I'm busy right now, just leave your details, and I'll call."

"This is something that has to be done in person, Mister Jacobs. I have proposition for you."

"I don't really have the time…" Todd started, but stopped when Dimitri mentioned money and a month long stay on an island. He turned to the three imposing men. "Who did you say you were?"

"I didn't," Dimitri replied and pulled an envelope from his jacket pocket. "Read this and have answer by Friday morning."

They left the meeting hall and Todd Jacobs, who was wondering if a month long stay on an island would help him get away from the ever increasing temptation of the devil. *And* alcohol.

After tracking down the last victim on their hit list, it wasn't until five o'clock that Dimitri finally knocked on his door.

The door of the blond man Alexi had taken a fancy too. *It not like her to act that way—* His thought was cut off as the blond man answered the door.

"Hey, what can I do for you?" he asked the big

frowning man and his two equally big cohorts in front of him.

Dimitri stared hard at the man before him, trying to understand what had made Alexi react the way she did. What had she seen that he could not? Baggy pants called cargos, huge white t-shirt, oversized blue shirt hanging open, well-worn sneakers.

"What can I do for you?" the blond hunk repeated, now puzzled by the situation and the three huge men standing in his doorway staring at him and saying nothing.

"I have proposition for you," Dimitri said. "How would you like working holiday on reality show for one month, and get paid one hundred thousand dollars."

The blond man frowned. "What?" Suspicion swept over him.

"May we come in?" Dimitri gestured. "I can explain it better."

"Um, sure." He waved them in and shut the door behind them, before walking into the kitchen area. The apartment was small and open plan. He picked up his coffee and wondered what the hell he'd just let himself get into. "So…from the beginning."

Dimitri still couldn't figure out what this man had that Alexi wanted. "My employer is making reality show of sorts and is inviting celebrities, ordinary people, and business people to come on show. It's on tropical island, you stay one month, get paid one hundred thousand dollars, you may or may not have to work, there may or may not be challenges. You sign agreement, and money is yours tax free to do whatever you want with."

The frown was still in place. "What sort of reality show?"

Dimitri didn't react. "My boss does not know that yet. She will make up mind as she goes along." He had to be delicate and reel this one in.

"What will be in the agreement?" The blond had signed enough TV contracts to know the question was worth asking.

Dmitri was unblinking. "The usual. You do not talk about, mention, sell story to magazine or TV show. You do not mention where it is, what you did, who you met."

The blond cocked his head. "You do know I've been on TV for many years and made movies too? This is rather vague for a reality show idea."

Dimitri was unmoving. "We know who you are, what you do, and that you have not worked in seven years. That is why you have been chosen."

The blond shifted at the man's knowledge when he had none of his own. And that made him even more suspicious. "How many others will there be?

"Four more this week. Who knows how many will come and go?" Dimitri shrugged. *This is harder than expected,* he thought. *And it is boring me.*

The blond thought about it. "Do you have a write-up of the show so I can read about it before deciding?"

Dimitri handed over a manila folder. "You have till Friday morning to decide. My boss thinks you would be perfect, and won't let me come back without you."

He looked at the contents of the folder. "It looks

like a great place for one month…and such a big amount of money."

Dimitri clamped his hands together in front of him. "My boss thinks you worth it."

The comment aroused far more than just suspicions, it also aroused curiosity, and the blond looked up from the papers. "Why? Why am *I* worth it?"

Dimitri shrugged nonchalantly. "I do not know, she did not tell me. I just fly around and find people."

The blond man sighed. "Tell her I'll think about it, once I've read through this a few times, of course." He gestured at the open folder.

"Of course." Dimitri nodded, *so* over the whole situation. "We will be in contact and show ourselves out."

"Great," Chris Cameron, actor of stage and screen said, watching the three big brutes walk out and close the door behind them. *Why the hell have I just been lied to, and what is really going on?*

Downstairs, Dimitri settled into the car and made a call. "We made contact."

"How'd it go?"

"All right. I think he suspicious, but I did my best."

"Good. Don't harass him, let him decide."

"Of course. I still do not see in him what you do, Alexi."

I sighed. "Neither do I…he's blond."

<h1 style="text-align:center">Chapter 3</h1>

All five men stood on the tarmac at Sydney's airport waiting to board the private jet that would fly them to destination unknown.

Dimitri had contacted them all that morning and told them to bring nothing but the clothes they were wearing and a small cabin bag or backpack with a few essentials. Everything else would be supplied. "I need you to sign agreement before you board plane," Dimitri said. "Please do not talk about what it is you doing, where you going. In fact, do not talk to each other at all."

The five men looked at each other, eyeing off the rivals they would be competing against, and one by one signed the agreement Dimitri shoved into their hands.

"Good, all done," he said when Chris finished signing. "Please board." *This was going to be a difficult one,* he thought, *since I lied to him about what would happen.* He followed him up the stairs and found the others sitting in the cabin. "Please, you do not mind, you are to separate and placed into small rooms, so you have no further contact. Is all part of rules. Sarah," he called to one of the flight attendants, "please escort men and make sure they buckled up."

"Of course."

Dimitri watched them go and then settled himself into his own seat. He looked at Sergei and Vladimir and sighed. *How many more times do we have to do this?* He picked up his phone.

I grabbed my cell from my pocket. "How'd it go?"

"Good. They all on board."

"All?"

"All."

I heaved a sigh of relief. As long as he doesn't find out until he gets here, there was no way he could leave. "Thanks, Dimitri."

"Anything for you, Alexi."

I hung up and scurried around yelling orders. "Get the rooms ready, make sure the doctor's ready, get lunch ready." I stopped and took a breath.

He was coming.

*****

It is Friday, and I have men coming tonight, she thought, stepping out onto the balcony, the sea breeze gently lifting her hair. She gazed out over the island and its ocean view and thought about what would happen. The new men she would have, the new men she would conquer, the one blond man that was amongst the group. He is not my type, but the others…they look good. She preened and smoothed her jet- black hair. I am the Queen, and this is my night.

*****

The plane made a smooth landing four hours later and taxied to a stop near the island's hangar where Dimitri escorted the men down to the doctor who was waiting.

"Gentlemen," gorgeously brunet Dan the doctor said. "We need to check you for bugs and insects, take your blood, do swabs, and make sure you're clean." He paused. "Everywhere."

The men silently looked at each other with mixed expressions, then reluctantly followed the doctor. They said nothing, as Dimitri had instructed them, and let the doctor swab, inject, examine and take blood. After showering and changing into the shorts and tank tops provided, they were escorted to their rooms in the mansion.

"Whoa, dude!" Jake Michaels exclaimed. "Posher than my house."

"My flat could fit in this room alone." Andrew Pascoe stared at the spacious living area.

"Mmm, nice," Chris Cameron muttered, still wondering what he had signed up for.

Their rooms were large, luxurious, and gadget free. No TVs, no stereos, no phones, which had been confiscated on boarding.

Chris opened the French doors to his room to see the ocean and its waves. "Nice." He poked around at the modern style furniture, looked in the bathroom, and decided to check out the rest of the island, coming across the pool half an hour later where the others had taken up residence.

"Dude, come in, the water's great," Mark yelled out.

"Maybe later," Chris replied and turned away, catching a glimpse of a woman on the third floor balcony. *Now, who is that?* he wondered.

I lurched back against the wall and freaked out a little. Chris had just spotted me staring at him. "Oh, God," I gasped. *Why him? Why does he make me feel this way?*

Natasha was beside me and rolled her eyes. "Get grip, Alexi, he is just man. Blond man at that."

I shook my head vehemently. "No, Natasha, he's much more than that." I glanced at her. "Much, much more."

*****

It was seven p.m., and I pulled a surprised Mark aside as he ambled through the house after dinner. "The Queen wants to see you tonight, so you need to get ready." I waved a hand at the two women hovering nearby, and they took him to prepare. I went up to the third floor into the dressing room, and an hour later Natasha walked out in her black bob and a sheer black ankle-length caftan.

"Send him in." She reclined on the bed.

Mark was brought into the room, blindfolded, hands tied behind his back, and wearing nothing but a brief loincloth wrapped around his hips.

"Darling, look at you." Natasha rose and all but ran for him, greedily grabbing at his muscular hair-covered chest. She bit, and kept on biting, every inch of his torso and arms. Ripping off his cover-up, she reached for his burgeoning erection. It had been *far* too long.

"Whoa, steady on," he gasped.

"Do not speak," she commanded. "Not unless you are spoken to." She pushed him toward the bed and sat him on the corner, getting on top of him, mounting him, riding him for all he was worth. "Uh, uh, uh, uh," she groaned, timed with her bouncing up and down. "Oh…my…God," tore from her throat as she pushed him onto his back as he grunted, and bounced harder, faster, using the bounce of the bed to make it go further, digging her nails into his chest, his stomach, grabbing his arms as she climaxed.

"Uh…uh…uh…" She gasped hard before throwing herself onto him and rubbing her bare breasts against his torso. "Oh, darling…you are good." She sighed and relaxed, glad to finally have another man beneath her.

After a refreshing nap, a bite to eat, and some French champagne, she was at it again. This time Mark was flat on his back and tied to the spacious bed. Slowly, moving up and down, she ground against him.

"Oh, yes…that is it…good…good…very good…" She rubbed her breasts into his chest hair, moving back and forth. "Oh, yes, good, oh, yesss," came out like a hiss. She dug her nails into his shoulders and arched her back, pushing down on his erection. "Yesss…ahh…" came out as she climaxed, shuddered and collapsed.

*****

Saturday morning dawned bright and early, and I really didn't want to get out of my soft and fluffy bed. My body was on fire from the dream I'd been having about Chris, after spying him by the pool, and I didn't want it to end. But it did, and I had to get up and get to work.

Ugh!

"How did it go last night?" I asked Natasha as I stared at her reflection. I was up in her room seeing how she was after her first night with a man in a week.

"Very well," she muttered, a satisfied and smug smile on her face.

I scratched my head, not really needing to ask. "So…he was good then?"

She gazed at herself in her dressing table mirror. "*Very* good. I might have him again tonight. Use him up before I move on. So make sure he gets plenty of rest and lots of protein. He will need his strength."

I sighed at the drudgery. "Of course."

*****

That night, Mark was once again led into the Queen's boudoir.

"Hello, Mister Dashiel, we meet again." She ripped off the skimpy material covering his manhood and smacked a whip across his backside.

"Ow, what the hell?" he cried, and tried to move out of the way.

"Do you like it rough, Mister Dashiel?"

Another crack.

"Hey, stop that." He moved again, but Dimitri and Sergei grabbed him, taking him over to a contraption that was part bed, part bucking bronco. "What are you doing? Hey," he cried as he was tied down on his back.

"We're going for a ride, Mister Dashiel." She jumped on him as Dimitri started it up. "Hold on tight, Mister Dashiel, we will be here all night."

She rode him hard like the bucking bronco he was…for hours.

*****

"Natasha, my dear, come and meet my friends, make sure you give them what they want," Grigor told his wife.

"Yes, husband," she replied, following him out of the bedroom and down into his office, wearing nothing but a see-through negligee.

"Well, what do we have here, Grigor?" the heavy-set man said. "Entertainment?"

"Of course," Grigor replied. "My wife is here to entertain you. To entertain all of my friends."

Their laughter made her sick. She knew what was coming, but she had made her bed and needed to lie in it because there was just no way out.

*****

Mark stumbled out of the house and over to the pool, falling into a lounge chair next to the others who all stared in shock.

"Dude, what happened to you?" Andrew asked.

Jake took his sunglasses off and added, "looks like you got used *and* abused."

"I did," Mark muttered. "I was. *All night.* For the last two nights, she's used me and whipped me and tied me to some machine that wouldn't stop." He rubbed his eyes. "I hurt," he whined. "She broke it, and I hurt."

"Dude, she broke what?" Andrew was on the edge of his seat.

Mark slowly turned his head to look at them. "My penis."

The others cracked up laughing except for Chris who sat silently by, listening, and frowning.

"Your penis? Dude, *seriously?*"

"Seriously!" Mark was hurt now. "That's what we're all here for you know, so we can be sex slaves for a month. If she broke mine, she can break yours too."

Raucous laughing followed, but not from Chris who sat up and faced Mark. "What do you mean; we're here to be sex slaves? I was told we're doing a reality show."

Jake stared at him. "*Are you serious?* You were told *that?*" He looked at the others. "What about you lot?"

"Sex slave."

"One hundred thousand dollars."

"One month on a tropical island."

"What?" Chris exploded. "What the fuck!? Why was I told something different to all of you? What the…we'll see about that." He stormed up the tree covered path and into the cool shade of the house. "I want some answers," he yelled. "Who's in charge here? I want the person in charge."

"Sir, please, stop yelling." Jenny came running

from the kitchen.

He whirled around. "Are you in charge? I want the person in charge, and I want them *now*!"

"Mister Cameron," Dimitri's voice boomed.

Chris jumped at the sound then spun around to face off with the man who'd brought him there. "*What the fuck is going on?*" He waved his arms around in emphasis. "You told me this was some sort of reality show. Challenges, work, but now I find out the others were brought here to be sex slaves for the month, so what the fuck is going on? I want answers, and I want them now. I did *not* agree to come here for sex, with *anyone*." He stuck his finger in the Russian man's face.

Dimitri put his hands up in surrender. "Mister Cameron, things are different for you, you are, how you say, special."

"Special!" Chris spat, his face bright red, and his hand on his hips. "Special!" He shook his head in disgust. "I'm out of here." He started for the front door.

"You cannot leave, Mister Cameron, we are on island," Dimitri boomed.

Chris kept walking. "Then tell the person in charge I want to see them. Now!"

"*What is going on here?*" I ran into the room and skidded to a halt. "Dimitri?"

He pointed.

I turned my head and saw Chris Cameron do a u-turn at the sound of my voice and stalk toward me. All breath left my body, my lips parted with exhalation, and swelled like they had been thoroughly kissed. My eyes widened, my heart pounded, my body became aroused.

"Are you in charge?" he stormed, pounding up to the brunette woman standing next to the big Russian bruiser. "I was lied to. *Why* was I lied to? I did *not* agree to be some rich woman's sex slave. What the fuck is going on? I want to leave, get me *off* this island." He paused at the look on the woman's pale face, and the wide pupils in emerald green eyes. "What the fuck is wrong with you?"

I couldn't breathe. I couldn't talk. I could only stare into those big blue eyes.

"Are you all right?" he asked, his voice softer now as he realised the woman in front of him may not be feeling well.

Dimitri noticed the problem. "Mister Cameron. Why don't you retire to your room and someone will be in to see you shortly?"

Chris slowly backed off a step and calmed down. "Um, yeah, sure." He glanced at Dimitri then the woman. "Mmm," was all he managed before walking away with a few backward glances.

Dimitri waited until he was gone and grabbed me as I sagged into his arms. "Alexi, what is it, what is the problem?"

My head slowly moved from left to right in jerky motions.

"Alexi?"

Faster now, my head flew back and forth, and the rest of me shook. I raced out of his arms and up the stairs to my room, slamming the door shut and racing for the bed before bursting into tears.

Chapter 4

An hour later, I walked downstairs and was met by Dimitri. "Has he said anything?"

He took me into his arms and hugged me. "No. Are you all right?

"No." My reply was muffled against his chest.

"Alexi," he said gently, pushing me away. "What is wrong? What happened?"

I shook my head. "Nothing. *Everything.*" I shrugged. "What do I say to him?" I rubbed my head, hoping to get rid of the migraine that had set in.

"What do you want to tell him?"

"I don't know." I kept shaking my head. "That I will try and convince her to leave him alone and just stick with the others, and to please don't worry, he can stay and still get the money and just see this as a holiday." I spread my hands. "What else *do* I say?"

Dimitri shrugged. "That is all that needs to be said."

"Okay. Then can you go and tell him that? That he'll be left alone?" I gave him my puppy dog look that I knew he always fell for.

He fell, but with a sigh. "Of course."

I smiled brightly. "Thanks, Dimitri."

"Anything for you, Alexi."

I wandered outside and followed the path to the other side of the island. I needed air, I needed space. I needed to sort my bloody shit out.

*****

"I want that one." Natasha thrust a picture at Dimitri.

"Yes, my Queen," he reluctantly replied.

She lounged on the bed until Andrew was brought into the room. "Well, look at you." She walked around him, admiring the view.

"I, um, don't feel comfortable doing this," he muttered.

"Darling, you wanted to come, you had choice and you made it."

"Yes, I know, but," he shifted nervously, "Mark said—"

"Do not worry about him," she snapped, cutting him off, "just worry about pleasing me."

*****

Monday morning the sun radiated through the house, and I needed sunglasses to stop the blinding migraine that still pounded in my head. I fled to the relative darkness of the third floor. "How was your night?"

Natasha straightened her hair in the mirror. "Fine."

"Just *fine*?" I watched her.

"Not as good as other one. Bit, how you say, dismal, really."

I took my glasses off and rubbed my eyes.

"Migraine?"

"Migraine."

"We really need to do something about those, Alexi."

"I know."

*****

"So, Grigor, is your wife up for anything?" the bald man asked.

Grigor smirked as Natasha stood there, shivering in her nightie. "Oh, she likes to think she isn't, but I know she is."

The five men in the room laughed and fear like she'd never known gripped her stomach.

"Darling, come and say hello to Nicolai."

*****

I stumbled out of bed Tuesday morning. I'd dreamt about Chris all night and woke up in a sweat.

Why did I want him there?

Why did I *need* him there?

What was I going to do about it?

Ignoring him helped, for now. But since he was going to be there for four weeks, I had to come up with a plan. And fast.

I spent the day staying out of his way, and that night I pulled a very eager Jake aside, telling him he'd been chosen.

"Yeah," he yelled and walked off with the servants.

I went to help Natasha, and she was ready an hour later when he walked in.

"Hell, yeah," he yelled again. "Let's do this, babe!"

"Quiet," Natasha commanded. "You will be quiet unless I want you to speak."

"Not on your life, babe. I love women, and I love sex, so let's get this party started." He started dancing.

"What are you doing?" Natasha had never seen one of her conquests disobey orders so blatantly before.

"Yeah, baby, come on." With a blindfold, a skimpy cloth covering his manhood, and his arms tied behind his back, he couldn't really dance and looked quite ridiculous.

She moved him over to a straight-backed chair. "Sit," she commanded and sat on him. She rubbed herself all over him, but did not descend onto his manhood. It wasn't that big, and she wanted to feel his body against her.

Her nipples rubbed against his, and his mouth reached for one. "Ugh," she groaned as he sucked. She kept moving up and down as he fed on her breast and she felt the rubbery sensation of his skin. Hot and naked against hers.

"Ugh, ugh, ugh." She shuddered in pleasure at the climax and fell into him.

"Babe, why didn't you fuck me? I wanna fuck you, too."

She waited until her focus became clear. "It is not always about the fucking." She stood. "Leave, I am done."

*****

"Aw, yeah man, we fucked all night. She's hot, she's wet, and she's fucking horny man. It was fantastic."

I stopped behind the bushes lining the pool and listened to our new guests talking.

"Aw, man, she was hot. Fucked me all night, rode me hard, I was bloody exhausted and need to rest today just to recover."

My left brow flew up so high it hit my hairline as I bristled at his lies. I knew what had happened and it certainly *wasn't* what he was describing.

"Dude, really?"

"*Really!* I had barely calmed down before she was getting me up again. I'm surprised she didn't break it she was riding it so hard. Fuck, my dick is sore."

"Mmm," I mumbled, frowning at all the lies being spread. I walked inside and found Dimitri. "Get the pilot to get the plane ready, you're taking Mister Michaels back to the mainland." I turned and walked back the way I'd come.

"And why is that?" he asked, following me and falling into step.

"Because, Mister Michaels has been a *very* naughty boy." I stopped long enough for him to call the pilot, then we walked toward the pool. Sergei and Vladimir appeared out of nowhere and joined us on the way.

"Mister Michaels," I called as we approached the men by the pool. I thanked God I had my sunglasses on as I spied Chris, who was only wearing shorts, which meant his lean, mean torso was on full glistening display, lounging on a bed.

I swallowed…hard.

God, sooo hard…so, so hard…

"Yeah, babe?" he said when he saw me. "Well, hello. After last night I don't think we've been properly introduced yet."

"Mister Michaels. I hear you've been telling lies to our other guests."

"Lies? What lies?" He adjusted himself and pushed his sunglasses up on his head.

"The lies about what happened last night." My hands were in my pockets as I tried to look casual, but they were sweating up a storm. "You've been bragging about your exploits…or should I say…lack thereof?"

"I don't know what you're talking 'bout love. Jealous are you? Want me to take *you* for a ride too, do ya?" He guffawed, and the others joined in except for Chris who looked disgusted.

Dimitri stepped forward, but I put my hand out to stop him. "Mister Michaels, part of the agreement you signed was that you keep your mouth shut about your nights here. The other part is that the Queen hates liars, *and you*, Mister Michaels, have been lying about your exploits from last night. I know *for a fact* the Queen did not have sex with you, I'm her assistant, I know all, I see all. In fact, she barely got off on you before sending you away, and yet here you are, telling all kinds of stories to the other guests. That's not on, Mister Michaels."

He was looking green around the gills and gulped as the others stared at him.

"Dude, seriously? None of that happened?" Mark asked.

"Geez dude, I hate liars." Andrew turned away to settle back on his lounge chair.

"Mister Michaels," I said. "You will now have to leave. The Queen does not want your type on her island." I waved at Dimitri and his cohorts. "Please escort Mister Michaels to the plane; he'll be leaving as soon as it's ready."

Dimitri stepped forward and hauled Jake from his seat.

"Hey, wait, I didn't mean it," Jake cried, trying to get his footing as Dimitri held onto one arm and Sergei the other. "I didn't mean it; I was just having some fun. I didn't want anyone to think there was something wrong with me because she didn't fuck me last night. Hey, ow, that hurts…" his voice trailed off as he disappeared from view.

I started walking back to the house, but was stopped.

"Hey, hi." Chris touched my arm, and I jumped ten feet. "Hey, sorry." His hand recoiled. "I didn't mean to startle you. You okay?"

I think my mouth was flapping open and closed as his touch had created a billon bolts of power in my body and I was tingling all over.

"Um, *are* you okay?" Concern was all over his face as he reached the hand that had sent that billion bolts of power through me out to take hold of my arm.

"Ugh," I gasped, a look of horror on my face I was sure, and I spun around and ran, terrified of what would happen if he touched me again.

"Dude," Mark called out. "What did you just *do* to her?"

Chris shook his head and put his hands on his hips. "I have *no* idea."

I didn't stop running until I had fled up to the third floor. A sanctuary in my time of need.

"What is it, Alexi? Why have you disturbed me?"

I was gasping hard and leaning against the door in the dark dressing room.

"Alexi? Are you all right?"

I took a few deep breaths to calm my pulse and managed a tiny, "no".

"What has you upset?"

"It's nothing, I…" I slid to the floor. I'd never felt that way before, at a man's touch. What the hell is going on? Why does he make me do this?

"Alexi, if you do not want to talk, then leave."

I glanced at her. Why were we there? How did we come to be here and what the hell were we doing? I slowly got back on my feet and walked out the door.

*****

She walked over to the man in the chair and her husband's outstretched arm.

"Nicolai, this is Natasha, here to do your bidding."

She looked at her husband, terrified at the implications of his words. "Grigor," she started, crossing her arms over her chest as some sort of barrier.

"Quiet," he snapped, his grip on her arm tightening. "You say nothing, and you do nothing except what my friends ask of you." He leant in to her

ear. *"Do you understand me?"* his tone menaced.

She whimpered. "Yes, Grigor," she whispered, so afraid of her husband and what he might do.

"Good girl," he muttered and thrust her into *Nicolai's dirty outstretched hands.*

*****

"Which one do you want tonight?" I asked Natasha as I helped put her wig on.

"Which one haven't I fucked yet?" She brushed her fringe out of the way.

"Ah, Todd Jacobs, I think." I grabbed the red lace nightgown from the drawer.

"Then he will come…hopefully." She smiled wickedly.

Half an hour later Todd came in her boudoir.

"Would you like a drink, Mister Jacobs?" Natasha purred, sliding her fingers over his tanned torso. All that sunbathing had given him a healthy glow.

"I, um," he stuttered and moved uncomfortably. "I, um, don't drink, um, anymore."

"At all? Just a little sip?" She nibbled on his ear.

"Um, I'm, um, stop that!"

Her hand slid to his crotch.

"Oh, hey, um, stop that, what are you doing?" He stepped away, but couldn't go far since he was blindfolded and his hands tied behind his back.

"No, Mister Jacobs. I will *not* stop that," she purred as she knelt and took him into her mouth.

Chapter 5

With Jake gone there were only four left and one of those was Chris Cameron.

I stood staring at his photo and wondered if I should try and talk to him at all. "God, what would I say?" I threw the photo down on my bed and wandered onto the second floor balcony. The soft breeze ruffled my hair as I leant on the railing. Closing my eyes, I breathed slowly and tried not to think about the blond bombshell downstairs.

The splashing water brought me back to reality, and I saw Mark and Andrew bombing in the pool, Todd lounged on the sidelines, obviously worn out from the night before. Chris was nowhere to be seen.

"Damn it," I muttered and walked back into the bedroom. "What am I going to do?" I asked the room. "Well, do you know?" I turned to the comfy lounge chair. "Do you?" I asked the side tables. "What about you?" I asked the bed. "What am I gonna do?" I flopped down onto the bed and pictured his big blue eyes. "What the hell am *I* gonna do?"

I spent the day in my room trying to figure out the

answers to those questions until Dimitri got back when I finally emerged. "Did Mister Michaels understand the fine print of his contract?"

"I think he did," he muttered as he straightened the leather jacket he wore regardless of where he went or what the climate was.

I knew Dimitri well. *"What did you do?"*

He shrugged nonchalantly.

"Dimitri?" I jammed my hands onto my hips and faced him.

He shrugged again. "I, *we*, made sure he understood all clauses in contract." There was no trace of any expression or emotion on his face. That is what made him so good at his job.

"Your job is not to beat him up, Dimitri." I feigned anger and shook a fist at him.

He smiled faintly. "Of course not, Alexi. Would I do that?"

"Mmm," I mumbled. "Yes, *you* would. You know we don't want him harmed because that will give them more reason to talk." I tugged on his lapels. "And we don't want them talking, now do we, Dimitri?"

He stared down into my eyes. "No, Alexi, we don't."

I stared up into his big brown ones. "No, Dimitri, we definitely don't."

*****

I walked around the island, stopping to smell a flower here, listen to a bird there. I caught sight of the waves at the back of the airport and the flat glassy surface of the cove. I stopped and stared out at the small cut-off area. There were shark nets and concrete partitions sunk to form a barrier against the elements which is why the water was so smooth and flat.

The breeze caught my hair, and I allowed myself to drift off into a light meditation, just listening to the breeze and the birds, the waves off in the distance, feeling the warmth of the sun filtering through the palm trees swaying overhead.

I took a deep breath and let my muscles relax on the exhale. After another, I slowly opened my eyes to the sight of Chris emerging from the water. Slow motion, like that moment in the *James Bond* movie where Daniel Craig emerges, and the water slowly slides off his perfect body, *this* was that. *That moment.* That moment where actor, Chris Cameron, was slowly emerging from the water, millions of drops running in rivulets from his blond hair, and down his muscular chest to his long, lean legs.

I stood still, unable to move, unable to breathe, unable to think.

He made his way up to a lounge chair parked on the sand under a beach umbrella and grabbed a towel from the back of it.

That towel travelled to places and did things my hands ached to do, and my lips ached to follow.

He gave his hair one last rub and threw the towel over the back of the chair, and reaching into the bucket beside it, pulled out a bottle of chilled water and cranked it open. That liquid slid down his parched throat like a river of sweet surrender. Capping the bottle and throwing it back in the bucket he glanced my way, saw me, and straightened.

He stared.

I stared back.

He smiled.

I stared back.

He started walking toward me.

I stared back.

He made it to about twenty-five feet from me when I got into gear and turned, dashing away along the path, sweating profusely, my throat as dry as all of those parchments from that Nancy Drew book.

"Hey," he called and grabbed my left arm, pulling me back toward him.

I spun around to face him, smacking into his chest with the momentum as he grabbed me with both hands.

The shock from touching electrified both of us. His hands on my arms, my hands flat pack on his chest, our eyes staring into the others.

I have no idea what it was, those few seconds that lasted a lifetime. The sensation that we knew each other from a life long lived, a life long gone. Emotions and brainwaves capturing and remembering memories from a bygone era.

His eyes are so blue, wandered through my mind, *so…blue…*

The moment was gone, and I snapped from my delusions.

"Hey," he said softly, slowly releasing his grip, but letting his fingers trail down my arms. "You…you okay?"

"I..." I breathed hard and quickly unglued my hands from the hard muscular, masculine torso lightly covered in soft blond chest hair. *Oh, where did that come from, he didn't have that in his photos, so soft...so blond...so soft...so...* "I." My hands turned into fists and launched themselves into my chest. "I..."

"I just wanted to talk to you." The words flowed deeply, smoothly and softly from between his lips. Lips I wanted to kiss, lips I wanted so desperately to lock onto mine.

"I..." I swallowed. "I," I croaked. "I..." I stumbled backwards away from his hands, his arms, his fur-covered chest, and oh so masculine body that towered over me, overwhelmed me with its hot manly... muscular...masculine...scent... "I..."

I swayed like a palm tree being felled by a man.

"Hey," Chris yelled, catching the woman in front of him before she smashed into the ground. "Hey!" He slapped her face, but she didn't open her eyes. He checked her pulse. "Damn it." He lifted her into his arms and made his way back to the house. Step after step he raced as fast as he could, looking for anyone to help him.

He spied a man in uniform in one of the gardens. "Hey, can you call for help, this woman's collapsed." The gardener got on his walkie-talkie and Chris continued his way to the house. As he sped up the path, the main door opened, and out rushed Dimitri with several people wheeling a stretcher.

"What happened?" he thundered, grabbing for me.

"She fainted, I think," Chris replied, laying me down

on the bed.

"Quick, get her into the medical room," Dan the gorgeous doctor said.

As they wheeled me away, Chris followed. "We were talking by the cove, well I was talking, and she was turning white, and then she stumbled and weaved and just collapsed like a sack of potatoes."

Dimitri stopped him at the room, standing in the doorway with an arm across it, his big meaty hand plastered against the doorjamb. "No, not you," he said, shutting the door in Chris's stunned face.

The jackhammer pounding away in my head got louder and faster and harder. It just wouldn't stop. I reached up and grabbed my head, hoping that would stop the pain.

It didn't.

I groaned and moved my head.

Tried to open my eyes.

Tried to roll over.

All to no avail.

"Alexi, stay still."

"Ugh, God," I mumbled. "What happened?"

"Shh, you rest, just rest."

I came out of my REM state and breathed deeply. I stretched my left leg then my right. My left arm, my right arm, stretched them above my head as I stretched my back and neck. I relaxed and opened my eyes.

Gorgeous Doctor Dan leaned over me. "How does your head feel? Any better this morning?" He held a light to each of my eyes and checked my ears.

I gazed up into his big green eyes. "What time is

it?" I looked for a clock on the wall, but didn't see one.

"Ten."

I blinked and thought about it, then screeched, "A.m.? How long have I been here?" I flung the covers back and planted my feet on the floor.

"Take it easy," Dan said, trying to stop me. "When you were brought in you had fainted, then briefly woke and mumbled something about your head. I gave you some painkillers and pumped you full of saline, so just take it easy."

I rubbed the spot at the back of my head where it met my neck. "I think I need to see Mark." Our resident chiropractor kept us all in tip-top shape.

"How about you freshen up and get some food into you first," Dan said.

"Mmm, food, mmm, shower," I sighed. "Sounds so good."

Up in my bathroom, the water pummelled its way over my body as I twisted and turned so it could work its magic. Hot water always soothed my aching muscles, but not today. Today they still ached and burned from Chris's touch. His manly hands. His masculine chest. That soft furry fur *on* his chest that was so…so…soft... All burned into my muscle memory like a brand on a horse's butt. Or was that a cow's butt?

"I have brunch."

My head turned towards the sound, and I turned off the water and wrapped a big fluffy towel around me before walking into the bedroom. I saw the tray of food Jenny had placed on the table by the balcony doors. "Looks good."

"Your favourite," she said, laying out cutlery and napkins. "Two egg omelette with chicken and cheese on a soft multigrain roll. A small bowl of fruit, and ice-cold tropical juice. Do you need anything else?"

"No, thanks, I'm fine."

"Good to know since you were as white as a sheet when that hot blond hunk of spunk carried you in. We all heard the call, and Dimitri flew into a panic and rushed to the door." She popped a piece of kiwi fruit into her mouth while I took a bite of my omelette burger. "We all freaked out because you *never* get sick, *never* faint, *never* keel over. And if *anything* happens to you then we're all screwed, because that means *we'll* all have to deal with *her,* and it's much better if *you* deal with her. Try not to faint again because *none* of us wants to deal with *her.*" She grabbed a strawberry and headed for the door. "I'll come and get the tray later."

I finished off my burger and was sipping my juice when Dimitri burst in.

"Alexi! Doctor just told me he let you out," he thundered. "They should have kept you in, you are not well. You were white as ghost when man brought you to house. What is wrong? What happened?" He threw himself into the chair opposite me and grabbed a berry from the bowl of fruit. "You eat this?" he asked, holding it out as he waited for my answer.

I half-heartedly laughed. "Munch away." I put my juice down and sighed, deep and slow. "*I* don't know what happened. I was walking along and stopped at the cove, and there *he* was, walking out of the ocean like James Bond and up to his chair like it was some kind of movie. All *I* could do was stare." I grabbed the last of the kiwi. "Next minute, he's walking toward me, and finally I manage to hightail it out of there, but he chased after me and grabbed me, and I'm plastered against his chest, and he's touching me, and I'm touching him, and we're looking into each other's eyes and then I'm stumbling and bumbling and bang I'm down for the count." I got up and paced around the room. "I don't get it. I just...don't understand this connection I have to him. *With him.*" I stopped and faced Dimitri. "I just don't get it." I shrugged and plaintively held out my hands.

"Alexi." Dimitri moved over to me. "For you, *of all people,* to feel this way 'bout man after everything that has happened." He placed his hands on my shoulders. "There must be something special 'bout him."

I hugged him tight, and he hugged me back as I sighed. "I don't know, Dimitri, I just don't know." I finished off breakfast and left to meet up with Mark in the spa area of the house. "Do I get a massage first or do I see you first?" I asked.

"Well, since I'm about to crack your back, you might want the massage after."

Tall and good looking, like all the men on the island who worked for her majesty, Mark Trundle was sadly already taken, being married to Jenny.

I climbed on the bed. "All right, crack away. Ow. What the bloody?"

Ten minutes later I was face down again, but this time on Owen's massage table.

That was the good thing about working here, even though this house and island were privately owned, it was still run as a luxury hotel with its own medical staff and spa area, a gym, playroom, den, library, lounge, games room. Anything that would please the men of the Queen's choosing, they got what they wanted, and we enjoyed it too.

Owen placed heat packs on certain muscles in accordance with Mark's notes. My muscles relaxed under them as he slowly worked on other areas, leaving me feeling loose as a goose when he was done.

"Damn, you're good." I sat up and blinked a few times. "Pity you're married!

He grinned. "We all are, except for you and your three man mafia squad."

I giggled. "Not sure they'd want to know you call them that."

"I think they already do," he whispered conspiratorially.

I leaned toward him and whispered back. "Yeah, I think they already do."

Chapter 6

Nicolai's greedy filthy hands grabbed her and groped her, and she squealed as one went between her legs and into her private area.

"Grigor," she squealed, slapping the pig's hands away. "Grigor, help."

"I told you to say nothing and do what they want," he snapped, stopping at the door. "I will see you, my friends, later."

"Grigor," she yelled at her husband as the door closed behind him. "Grigor, ow."

The men closed in on her as Nicolai's fingers pinched and pulled.

"Nooo."

*****

I walked into the office looking for our tech head. "John, have you found any more men yet?" I stopped and stared at an empty room. "John?"

"Here."

I looked. "Where?"

A hand flew up. "Here."

I walked over to the pile of boxes in the corner of the room. "What are you doing?"

He was sitting on the floor behind them, with an open box in front of him, and papers strewn all around. A sigh came from him. "Well, I *was* searching for something, but I can't remember what." He scratched his head and shook it. "I don't know."

"Well, ah, okay. Have you found anything else on that billionaire yet?"

"Um, yeah." He got up, walked over to a pile of paper on his desk and handed it to me. "Here's some printouts and photos and stuff. All say the same, though. As for the other thing, I really *was* serious the other day. She *is* running out of men able to come here."

I looked up from the papers. "Yes, I'm sure she is. Thanks for these." I smiled and walked upstairs.

"Well?"

I stared at Natasha in the mirror. "John found some more details. News, pictures, some of it's just repeated from before."

"Does not matter, show me."

I handed her the files and waited while she went over them, reading every word of every line and studying every picture.

"All the same. It is all the same," she muttered and flung some papers away. "Why is it all the same? Why is there *never* anything new? Anything different." She slammed the rest down on the dressing table.

"Well, it *was* a while ago and clearly no longer news.

Too much other stuff in the world to write about and report on." I picked up the papers from the floor.

"We must find him." She balled her hand into a fist. *"We must find him."*

"I know."

"Do you?" She spun to face me, her eyes shining with daggers of anger and hatred. *"Do you? Do you* understand *why* we must find him? To *avenge* his death."

"Yes, Natasha," I said quietly, accepting those daggers with anger and hatred of my own. "I do."

*****

I didn't want to face Chris that night, so Dimitri did my dirty work for me.

"Gentlemen," he boomed, standing in front of the four remaining racks of meat who were just finishing up their evening meal. "You are all invited to Queen's quarter's tonight."

"Hell, yeah!" Mark exclaimed.

"No," Chris said quietly, elbows on the table, hands together in front of him.

They had barely heard him, but stared anyway.

"You have no—" Dimitri started.

"Yes, I do," Chris snapped, eyes flashing. "You *never* told me what I was actually coming here for, and just the other day you said I would be exempt from the Queen's shenanigans." He slammed his hands onto the table and stood. *"Now* you want to invite me into her quarters. *No. I won't go."* He started moving away from the table, but Sergei and Vladimir appeared from nowhere to stop him.

Chris stopped in surprise. "What is this? You're going to strong-arm me into doing it? Force me?" He looked from the men to Dimitri. "What about that woman, the brunette? I want to talk to her, go and get her."

Dimitri bristled slightly at the mere mention of Alex. "Alexi does not make the orders, the Queen does."

"Queen," Chris spat venomously. "Who the hell *is* this woman you all run around after, being lapdogs and henchmen for? Who the hell *is she* to order *me* around? Ow, hey…" He stumbled, and Sergei grabbed him and pulled the syringe from his neck.

"You need to calm down, Mister Cameron. Just because the Queen has called you, does not mean she wants you. She passes on many men." Dimitri watched intently as the drug had its effect.

"Hey…I…" Chris swayed on his feet.

"You will be all right in minute, in meantime, gentlemen, why don't you go get ready." Dimitri nodded at Chris. "Help him to his room, Sergei."

*****

"Well, well, well," she purred, pacing in front of the four men in front of her. "You were very good, Mister Dashiel." She ran her fingers over his chest.

"Baby, I always am," he crowed, swinging his hips.

"And Mister Pascoe, you were…" she ripped off his loincloth. "Ordinary. *But your penis is extraordinary.*"

She playfully tapped it with her whip, and it responded instantly.

"Mister Jacobs…" He shifted nervously. "Your years of drinking have done you disservice. Next time we use Viagra."

"But, I, um…" He fidgeted, clearly embarrassed at having been called out in front of the others even though they were all blindfolded.

"And here is one man I have not had yet." She stood in front of Chris, who was swaying slightly behind his blindfold. He was like the others, hands tied behind his back, and just a teeny tiny cloth covering the one thing she wanted to see the most. She ripped it off.

"Hey," he grunted, swaying forward with the momentum, and still feeling the effects of the drug Sergei had shoved into him.

"Well, well, well," she purred again. "You are fine specimen of man." Her fingers lightly slid over his chest, his arm, and as she circled him, his back. She slapped his arse and scratched at his lower back before coming around to the front again. "I do not fuck blonds, but with dick like that," she bent down to measure it, "I could certainly make exception." She straightened. "But, I told Alexi she could have you. For some reason, she see something in you that attract her, and now I see what." She flicked her whip at him, and he cringed.

Alexi? he thought vaguely. *There's that name again. Is the brunette that fainted, Alexi? Alex? I need to find her…*

"I will leave you for Alexi." She pointed to the

others. "But I will have all of you. On the bed, cuff them, tie them so they cannot get away," she commanded Dimitri, Sergei and Vladimir.

They grabbed Mark, Andrew and Todd, pushed them down onto the bed and tied their arms and legs to the posts.

"What? All three of us?" Mark asked. "You mean, *together*? *All three of us together?* And how come blondie gets an out?"

"Quiet," Natasha commanded. "You will shut up and say nothing while I do what I want to you." She waved her whip at Chris. "Take him with you. I have no need for him."

Chris was taken back to his room and placed on the bed.

"God…" he groaned. "What did you give me?" He struggled against his bonds. "What the hell is going on in this place? So much for being left out of it. Clearly, promises don't count for anything."

The door closed on his words.

"Ugh, God, gotta get out of this, out of these, out of, God, why am I so tired?"

*****

I sneaked into Chris's room to see him still naked and lying on his side. I turned the bedside lamp on and cut the ties that bound his hands.

He groaned.

"Shh," I whispered. "Go back to sleep."

"Alexi?" he mumbled. "Alex?"

I froze. He'd never said my name before, and the sound of it escaping from between his lips electrified me. "Shh." I grabbed the throw across the end of the bed as he rolled onto his back. "Oh." I froze again, this time at the size of his huge, glorious manhood. "Oh…"

"Alex?" His hand was slowly reaching for the blindfold, ready to remove it.

"No, shh," I rushed, quickly covering him with the blanket and moving his hand back down to his side. "I'm sorry, I'm so sorry. I tried to stop her, told her to leave you alone. I'm sorry. I'm so sorry." I took one last look at the man lying before me, the man I so desperately wanted to kiss, flicked the light off, and ran out of the room.

*****

"So, who is ready to go next?" Natasha asked after a brief respite from her sexcapades. She had already had them once each before stopping for sustenance of champagne and oysters.

"I, no…" Todd mumbled. "I couldn't…"

"I could!" Mark piped up. "Jump on and ride me, whore, yeah."

Whore?

He called me, whore?

Natasha bristled at the insult and climbed onto the bed. "Whore?" she spat at Mark who was in the middle. "Whore? You dare call me whore?" She whipped his leg.

"Ow." He cringed. "I didn't, I thought, it was

appropriate since you called us names."

She sat on his chest, grabbed a handful of his hair and yanked his head back. "Nobody," she hissed, "calls me whore and gets away with it." She sat on his face. "Ride this, whore," she yelled and whipped his penis hard.

*****

"No," she cried. "No, stop, what are you doing? Let me go. No."

Two men were holding her arms while Nicolai shoved his fingers into her womanhood.

"Shut up, whore," he sneered, grabbing her legs, spreading them and pulling her toward him, so she was sitting sprawled on his lap.

"Stop it," she cried before her mouth was covered to muffle her.

Nicolai lifted her to his mouth and sucked on ripe young pussy.

"Mmm, mmm," her cries were muffled, but no less full of terror. She thrashed her legs, but two other men grabbed her while Nicolai had his fill before releasing her to unzip his pants.

"Hold her," he said, pulling out his withered old cock and giving it a rub to get a good hard-on. Once it was up, he pulled her toward him, and with the help of the others, slammed her down on top of it.

A set of arms went around her and lifted her, then slammed her down. They were moving her up and down on top of him because he couldn't do it himself.

She struggled against the arms that held her, all to no avail.

*****

"Don't, you, ever, call, me, whore, ever, again." Natasha whipped Mark in time with the words she spat. She ground into his face until he passed out and then dismounted. "If you other two wish for whipping, then I more than willing to give you one. Just call me, *whore*."

"No, no, not me," came muttered replies.

She stormed into the bathroom and turned on the hot shower tap. She needed cleaning after that episode. To wash away the filth and memories that came with it.

The water scalded her, but she didn't care, she just needed to scrub away all reminders of that night.

*****

She was sobbing uncontrollably as the men pulled her off Nicolai.

The old man sat back in his chair while his cock shrivelled back into its flesh. "That was good," he muttered. "Very good."

"I'm surprised you got it up old man," said the one still holding her. She struggled, but he held on tight.

"So am I," Nicolai replied.

"Stop struggling, you little whore," the man hissed, "I am Yuri, and I am next." He carried her over to the pool table, and she flailed her arms and legs. "Stop it,"

he yelled, throwing her face down and half bent over the table. "Hold her," he told two others and tried shoving a pool ball into her mouth.

"Mmm." She twisted her head back and forth, but the men had a hold of her arms and were holding her tight.

He jammed the ball into her mouth, and she gagged. "That will be one of my balls soon." He tied a handkerchief around her mouth and head so she couldn't spit it out.

She breathed hard, dizzy from a lack of oxygen and the treatment she was receiving. How could Grigor do this to me? screamed through her head. How could he do this when I am his wife? Why would he do this?

"Hold her," Yuri told the men as he jammed his dick into her hard and fast.

"Mmm," came her muffled screams.

He spread her legs and lifted her body up to his level, thrusting harder and faster.

She sobbed into the pool table, unable to move, unable to fight, unable to defend herself, unable to do anything.

When he stopped and pulled back, she thought it was over.

"That was good," he said. "This will be better." He shoved his cock into her anus.

*****

Natasha entered her bedroom and saw the three men tied to the bed. *Why do I do this,* she pondered. *Why do I seduce men? Why do I fuck them stupid? Why do I get off on it?* She stood there, staring.

Mark had come to, but his penis looked like it needed an ice pack.

She gathered some ice cubes from the champagne bucket into a towel, and after tying a knot in it, threw it onto his penis.

"Ah, fuck, what the hell?" he stuttered.

"It look like it needs cooling down," she said, lying across the end of the bed. "That will teach you to never call me whore again."

"Well, if that's what it's going to get me, then no, I won't be," he said. "*Fuck, man,* no one's *ever* done that to me before. I don't even think I'll be able to use my dick again. *Fuck,* I bet you destroyed it, not to mention fucking suffocated me."

She lifted the ice pack and studied it. "It look all right to me. A little red, but not how you say, mincemeat."

"*Fuck you,* you..." He clenched his jaw. "Mmm." He so desperately wanted to say it after the whipping he'd just received.

Natasha knew. "All right," she sighed. "You get to say it one last time. Go head. Tell me I am whore."

"You fucking whore. You cock sucking, vile whore, slutty fucking bitch."

She bristled and crossed her arms. "Feel better now you got that off chest?"

He let out a deep sigh. "Yeah, yeah, I do."

"Good. Because that is last time *anyone* call me whore!"

Chapter 7

I woke up the next morning wet, horny, and hungover, even though I hadn't drunk because I don't drink. It was a very hard heavy feeling in my head.

The sight of Chris's hot, amazingly smooth, and very naked body laid out on his bed had set my imagination off and running and doing its own little naked dance in my head.

"Oh, God." I rubbed my eyes and rolled over, my body weary from the night before. I hadn't slept much and felt like a bloody punching bag.

My phone buzzed, and I jumped at the sound. Peering at the clock, I saw it was ten o'clock already and grabbed the phone. "Natasha?"

"Um, no. It's me, John. I have some more stuff for you."

"I'll be down soon. Don't show anyone."

"Okay."

I hung up and ambled into the shower, got out and dressed in my own time, before meandering down the stairs. I came to a halt in the office, and John turned and handed me a folder.

"More stuff. I'm not sure what you're after, but there's a pile there."

I flicked a quick look through it, and something caught my eye. Quickly slamming the file shut, I thanked John and ran back upstairs. After locking my door, I sat on the bed and read through everything in the file, laying aside two pieces of information in particular.

Half an hour later, I was in our meeting room. "So does everyone know what they're doing?" I looked at all the faces down either side of the long table in our somewhat late morning meeting. They nodded. "Good, meeting adjourned." I remained seated.

Dimitri waited until everyone was gone. "Alexi, you all right?"

I looked at him and gave him a half-hearted smile. "Not really."

He frowned. "Is there anything I can do?"

I thought about the number of years we'd known each other and hugged him. "You've already done so much for me. I owe you so much."

"Anything for you, my little Alexi."

I smiled. Dimitri was so much like a father figure to me. Always taking care of things when I needed help. "I know you'd do anything, Dimitri, you've already proven that."

"Anything for you, Alexi. And I mean *anything*." He brushed my hair aside.

John stuck his head back through the door and interrupted the strange moment that made him wonder if there was anything going on between them.

"There's some weather reports coming in about a storm. We need to keep an eye on it."

I turned my tired head. "Is it coming our way?"

"No. But that's not to say it won't change its mind."

"Okay. Keep an eye on it and let me know if anything changes."

"Gotchya."

A few hours later, and after a delicious lunch, I wandered around the island, checking in on everyone, and overseeing the work that always needed doing. Weed killing here, palm tree pruning there. Fixing pavers and uprooted concrete, setting water systems into garden beds. Chores that needed doing on the outside just as they did on the inside.

I stopped in at the hangar to make sure we had enough fuel and spare parts, and that the runway strip lights were in perfect working order. Once I realised I had finished everything on my trip around, I found myself back at the cove. Fortunately, Chris wasn't there, and I stopped to take in the view and relax.

I pulled up a chair and sat watching the waves past the cove. It was a weird sight to behold. Flat glassy water in the cove with crashing waves directly behind, and never the two shall meet. I closed my eyes against the afternoon sun. The warm sea breeze gently caressed my skin as it floated past on its way across the island.

"Alexi?"

There are only two people on this island who call me Alexi, and the voice doing so was definitely not one of them.

"Is it Alex?"

The voice was louder now and only a short distance behind me.

"Hi. Is your name Alex? We've never been properly introduced, so I'm not sure what your name is, but that big Russian guy calls you Alexi, so I'm wondering if it's Alex."

The voice stopped directly behind me, and my heart pounded so hard and so loud I'd be surprised if he couldn't hear it, or see it, pounding out of my chest.

A hand touched my shoulder, and the electric shock that came with it shot me out of my seat and into a standing position.

"Ah, don't touch me," I cried, spinning around to face the man I dreamed about on a nightly basis. And then some.

"I'm sorry, I—" he started.

I ran for the path.

"Wait," he yelled.

"Leave me alone," I cried back.

He grabbed me and spun me around. "What the hell is going on?" He was breathing hard. "I don't understand this, this power, this electricity." He glanced around. "This place, these people. *What the hell am I doing here? What the hell are you doing to me?*"

"I," squeaked out of my throat. He had me by the arms and was shaking me in time with his words as his eyes bored into my soul.

"*You!* What are *you* doing to me? Why do *you* make me dream of you every night? Think about you every day?" He stared into my eyes as if he'd find the answers he was seeking.

My breath came out in shaking gasps as I gazed back and realised what he'd said.

"What are you doing to me," his voice was a whisper as he leaned toward me.

I was shaking. With fear, excitement, panic, nerves, passion, pain, the drop in the temperature…

"What are you doing to me?" barely escaped his lips before they planted themselves on mine.

Crash…

We jumped ten feet apart.

"What the bloody?" My head moved a million miles a minute looking for whatever had made the loud crashing sound. Whatever had, it had ever so rudely interrupted a most magical moment.

"I, um, don't see anything," Chris said.

I got on the walkie-talkie. "Did anything fall over, crash, break, blow up? What was that noise, and where did it come from?"

A chorus of 'nothing here', 'not here', 'it's okay', came through.

Then what the bloody!?

I shivered, and that's when I noticed the change in temperature. "John, can you get me a weather report? It's gotten cool all of a sudden."

"Give me five."

"Alex?"

I looked up as Chris took my face in his hands. "No, don't," I whispered as my eyes closed against the touch of his hands.

"What is going on between us?" His confusion was as clear as day.

I felt myself on the verge of tears, or an emotional breakdown, either way, I was going to end up a blubbering mess on the path at his feet. My eyes slowly slid open.

"Alex." His eyes implored me to answer. His lips implored mine to kiss him back.

The electric charge that was radiating from his hands into my pores was making me dizzy, and my eyes closed again, fighting back the feelings that surged through me, threatening to overwhelm and overload me to the extreme.

"Alex. That storm I told you about this morning has turned around and is heading our way by nightfall. Looks like it might be nasty, so that sound may have actually been thunder you heard."

I very reluctantly pulled away from Chris, took a deep breath or two, or three, and answered. "Okay. This is Alex. This is *not* a drill. Everyone meet in the office in ten minutes. Stop what you're doing, and meet in the office in ten minutes. *This is not a drill.*"

"What's going on?" Chris's hands were now on his hips.

"Um." I couldn't look at him. "There's a storm coming this way, and we need to evacuate to the storm shelter in the basement." I waved a hand toward the house. "Let's go."

We met everyone ten minutes later in the long spacious meeting room.

"It's a category four at this stage. Was heading

away from us, but has now done a big fat u-turn and is heading straight for us," John said.

"Right, okay," I replied, facing everyone and gathering my thoughts. "That means we need to get everything packed away, all the windows shut and boarded. Electricals removed. Girls, pack up the food and take it downstairs. Dimitri, make sure all the generators are working and full of fuel, David get the plane underground. Guys, pack away all the outside furniture into the underground storage sheds, remove garden equipment, lights, mowers etc. John, get all the computers downstairs and set up to monitor the storm. Take all necessary electricals downstairs and store them. You know the drill," I took a breath, "okay everyone, let's get to it."

We all headed off to our chores with Chris following me into the foyer.

"I want to help, what can I do?"

I stopped for a second and thought. "Uh, you can help shut all the windows."

He nodded. "Okay, let's go then."

We went room for room, shutting windows and then closing the inside metal wind covers that hid in the wall cavities of the window frame. Think of Will Smith in *I am Legend*. What he had on his windows to stop the zombie things from getting in. Although in the end, they didn't work either. Meanwhile, some of the crew were doing the same on the outside. We finished the ground and first floors and moved up to the second.

I reached the steps of the third floor and had to

stop Chris. "No. No one's allowed up here during the day. I'll do this."

He looked confused for a moment. "Her Majesty doesn't want help?"

A small smile crossed my lips. "I can deal with her. You take those big muscles of yours and go help anyone who needs it." I left him standing at the bottom of the stairs looking somewhat annoyed. "Natasha, we need to get you downstairs." I grabbed a bag and started putting jewellery and other valuables in it.

"What did you wake me for?" she mumbled, glaring at me.

"There is a storm coming, and we need to evacuate to the basement."

"Storm? Evacuate? Basement? *I am a Queen*; I *do not* want to be held in basement." Her indignation was incredibly evident.

"Well, if you want to be blown away then, stay up here." I finished packing another bag. "Coming?"

She sighed at the contemplation of being blown away and mumbled, "If I must." She dressed quickly and grabbed her crown, placing it over her black hair.

I watched her until she walked toward me, and then pushed a tile on the wall. The wall slid aside, revealing a hidden lift. Stepping into it, we went down to the basement where I got her comfortable in the royal quarters. "See you when it's over." I went back up, locked her room and went down to my own.

I stashed all the files John had printed for me in a folder and stashed that into my backpack. I gathered clothes and personal belongings, and zipping up my case, grabbed my bag and went down to the ground floor. "Has everyone finished?" I asked Dimitri.

"Yes, just 'bout." He marked off a piece of paper on a clipboard.

I grabbed my walkie-talkie. "If everyone is finished their parts of the evacuation plan, then get to your own abodes, pack your things, lock up and get downstairs. John, any news?"

He crackled over the receiver. "All set up down here, and the storm is still category four, due in four hours."

"Okay. Go and get the rest of your things, and once everyone's in, we'll head downstairs."

"Gotchya."

"Dimitri?"

"My things are already downstairs." He didn't glance up from his folder.

"Good."

"Alex."

I turned to see Chris.

"I'm done, and I don't have anything to pack besides this." He gestured to the backpack in his hand. Andrew, Mark and Todd walked up behind him with their own bags.

"Um, okay. I'll um…" I glanced at Dimitri. "I'll take you downstairs and show you the guest quarters." I started walking for the basement door rolling my case behind me, but Chris removed it from my hand.

"I'll take it. Much easier for you." His face showed no expression.

I stared into those big blue eyes. "Um," I gulped, "okay." I led them down into the shelter and showed them to four rooms off one of many hallways. "Here are your rooms, you get one each. We have solar and generator power, and stored water so we won't run out of those, although you will be on timers. The kitchen and dining are down there," I pointed to my right, "the rec room after that, and the main lounge after that. This place is in a grid pattern, with each main corridor and offshoots clearly labelled and colour coded so you won't get lost regardless of which way you go."

"Cool."

"And you?" Chris asked while the others picked their rooms.

"Um, I'm, that way," I muttered, aware that I was more than likely beet red and really hot. I mean, *really* hot. I mentally fanned myself. *Why is it so damn hot down here...?* "I'll just take my case and um—"

"No." He held on tight to the case. "You lead, I'll follow."

"I..." came out in a sigh. "Oh." I saw the determination on his face and gulped again. "Okay," came out in another sigh and I turned and walked down the corridor, turning right then left before stopping at a door. "I'm here. I'll take my case now."

"I'll take it in for you." He stepped toward me, making me back up against the door.

"Oh," I breathed, feeling dizzy. *God, this is so ridiculous...he's coming toward me, his lips, his eyes, his heady hot hunk of man meat aroma...*

His hand slowly snaked out past me and landed on

the door handle beside my hip.

I felt his breath on my cheek and neck, creating condensation, and violent pounding sensations throughout my body. My eyes slowly closed in the hot, heady intimacy of the storm shelter and all it meant, and my breath silently left my body before silently filling it back up.

He turned the door handle slowly.

The door opened, and I stumbled backwards, quickly coming out of the sensual paradise I'd just been in. "Whoops." I righted myself, breathed to get my heart to stop pounding, and turned on the light. It was a small neat lounge room all cosy and comfy. Lounge, TV, desk, enough for a night's stay of evacuation. "Right, um—"

"Where's the bed—"

"Never mind," I quickly cut him off by grabbing my case and shutting the door on his surprised expression. After locking it, I took my stuff into the bedroom and stashed them in the large walk-in closet. The bed was large and spacious, just right for hot passionate, fiery sex with Chris. Wait, what? *Get those thoughts out of your head!* I went into the bathroom and splashed cold water on my face which, as usual, was bright red.

"Storm is three hours away," John crackled.

I stared at my face and took a few deep breaths before pulling the walkie-talkie from its clip on my belt. "All right everyone, get to the bunker now." I opened my door and saw that Chris was gone, so I headed back up to the ground floor and marked off each staff member and checked over their report sheets. "All done and accounted for," I told Dimitri. "Let's do one last check of the ground floor, Sergei, Vladimir, stay here in case someone comes up."

"Of course." The two men stood like sentinels on either side of the basement door.

Dimitri and I quickly went room for room, checking bathrooms, windows, and the fridges and freezers in the kitchens. No piece of food had been left behind. Satisfied, we returned to the basement and locked the doors behind us.

"Everyone to the mess hall." We met there five minutes later. "John, report."

"The storm is two and half hours away. The winds are getting worse, so we locked up in time. It's going to be bad. All cameras are currently working so we can keep an eye on the outside."

"Jenny?"

"All food is stored, and meals are done, all beds are made, TV's up and running."

"Dimitri?"

"Everything is locked and bolted. We are as you say, snug as insect in blanket."

Everyone laughed, and I snorted. "That's snug as a bug in a rug," I told him.

He shrugged. "I'm from Russia, same difference."

My smile grew wider. "Okay, let's get some food and then we can settle in for the night."

The girls rounded up the meal they had prepared, and we all sat down to eat. After conversations about the storm, what was on TV, and who would beat who at WII, I got an update from John.

"One hour."

"Okay, everyone, let's get this place cleaned up. Make sure nothing is left out, rubbish is in the disposal. For those who want to retire, do so. For those who want to beat each other at WII, please don't use all the power." I pointed at some of the men who laughed. "Yes, I'm talking to you lot. Take monitoring in shifts. John first shift, Mark second, David third. Make notes of any damage, and if there's anything major, let me know. I'm buggered and off to bed."

There was a chorus of good nights followed by, "and what do we do?"

I turned and saw Mark, Andrew and Todd standing behind me, with Chris casually leaning against a wall to the side, arms crossed, trying to look disinterested in the conversation.

"You guys can join in any of the games, watch TV, have an early night."

"Um, you-know-who's not going to want one of us, is she?" Mark casually adjusted himself.

I smiled wryly. "No, she's not."

"Oh, good," he said, relief clear in his voice. He motioned the boys down the hall.

I walked around to my room, only vaguely aware of my surroundings until I stopped at my door. I glanced behind me and saw no one, even though I had felt that weird sensation of eyes boring into the back of my head. "Mmm." I walked into my lounge room and shut the door firmly behind me then went into the bedroom.

I heard a click. I froze. Another click. I spun around to see Chris in my doorway staring intently like an animal on the hunt. In a few steps, he was in front of me, taking my face in his hands and planting his lips on mine, his tongue desperate to delve into my mouth.

And this time, there was no way in hell I was going to stop him.

Chapter 8

"Ugh."

"Ahh."

"Oh."

Hands greedily slid over rock-hard muscle.

"Ugh."

Tongues delved into mouths that were not their own.

"Ahh."

Bodies thrust back and forth, and hot flesh scalded hot flesh.

"Ugh."

"Oh, God," escaped in a whisper.

Legs wrapped around legs, locking onto and into each other like a maze of connected Lego pieces.

"Ugh."

"Ahh."

The climax blew a million bolts of electricity that lit up a billion sets of fireworks and set off a fire that raged out of control…

I sighed. Deep, slow, calm. A sigh that allowed my muscles to relax, my stomach to unclench, and my heart to stop pounding in my chest. I lay staring at the ceiling in the soft lamplight.

I sighed, stretching my legs one by one. My back, my neck, my arms over my head, and left them on the pillow above me.

A male hand snaked over my body under the sheet, feeling every inch it came across until it found my left breast.

The hand enveloped it.

Moulding and moving, groping and pinching.

"Mmm," I murmured in content, my eyes closing to savour the feeling.

A leg found its way between mine, and lips found their way to my right nipple, suckling like a hungry newborn piglet.

I arched my back. The feelings of sexual awareness, and my body's response seemed both natural and unnatural.

Hands held mine above my head as a male body slid fully onto me.

I wrapped my legs around his waist, high so he could have access to where he wanted to go.

He didn't.

He moved back and forth, his hand squeezing my breast, his tongue plundering my mouth before taking a trip down my neck.

He thrust.

I felt him and arched for him to enter. "Please," I whispered. "I want you."

He ignored me and continued his merry way down over my collar bone to my breast that was thoroughly worn out by his hand. He sucked harder before releasing it to continue across my ribs to my belly button, across my lower abdomen and into the curls where his tongue did very wicked things indeed. For hours on end…

"Mmm, no, get out of the way. Oh, my God."

One eye opened slightly to find Chris mumbling in his sleep.

"Move, no, out of the way, no, tried to stop. No," he shouted, sitting bolt upright in the semi-darkness, breathing hard and wiping his face.

Both eyes flew open as I sucked in air. "Hey." I touched his shoulder, and he flinched. My hand retreated. "Sorry."

"No." He looked at me. "No, don't be. *I'm* sorry, I…" He sighed and bowed his head before spinning to sit on the side of the bed. "It's not *your* fault, I…" He shook his head sadly before walking into the bathroom.

I heard the tap run for a few seconds and figured he was washing his face. I fluffed the pillows behind my back and waited for him to return.

A few minutes later he did. All six foot five and gloriously fit and naked, he slid into the bed beside me, staring at the ceiling with a hand behind his head.

"Do you want to talk about it?" I slid down beside him and rested my hand over his heart.

His half-hearted sad smile said it all as he took my hand in his.

I rested my forehead against his shoulder and closed my eyes.

*****

I awoke feeling incredibly relaxed and happy, but after checking the time, I bolted out of bed and dressed before Chris had even opened his eyes. "John, status report." I walked into the shelter's small and now very crowded office.

"Mmm?" He looked up from the three computers. "Still hanging around. It seems to have passed us, made a square u-turn and is heading back."

"Hasn't it abated yet?" I asked looking at the screens connected to the islands' cameras.

"Seems to be just as strong. Picked up some power as it went through then slowed down, but decided to change its mind and come pay us another visit." He sat back and looked at me. "Clearly once wasn't enough."

I pointed to the monitors. "So, what's the damage?"

John turned to them and picked up a clipboard. "Damage to the hangar, trees down, beach washed away, some tiles off the roof. Lost one camera here," he pointed to one monitor, "another out here, and some bushes blown away." He looked at and pointed to another screen. "Damage to all staff cottages, but nothing major. We should have the tools and bits and piece to fix it."

I sighed. "Well, that's good then. As long as the house doesn't blow away, or the basement suddenly floods, we should be okay."

He nodded. "We should be."

"Good, keep me up to date," I called as I walked

out the door and down the hall. I ran into Dimitri. "And how'd you sleep last night?"

"Like dead baby in coffin," he mumbled before realising what he'd said.

I winced at his turn of phrase. "Not good, huh?" I tugged his leather jacket lapels.

His smile was grim with apology as he took me into his arms. "Not good. You know I claustrophobic. I do not like underground."

"Yeah." I hugged him. "I know, but it can't be helped unless you want to be blown away. The storm seems to be coming back, so we'll have to stay another night." The fluorescent lights did nothing for the pallor of his thick Russian skin.

"Mmm," he mumbled. "And how 'bout you, Alexi? You sleep well? You look like you did. You also look…happy." He playfully pinched my cheeks.

A huge smile spread across my face. "I'm *very* happy, Dimitri. Very happy indeedy." I tugged on his jacket in emphasis with my words.

"You did not sleep alone last night?" He did not like the prospect of what that might mean.

My smile got even wider. "Nope!" was all I said before turning on my heel and walking into the mess hall. I found Chris at a table, and after getting a plate of food from Jenny, I joined him. "Morning."

"Mmm, morning." He pulled my chair out and then pulled me close when I sat down. "And how did *you* sleep?" He nibbled on my ear.

I giggled and swatted him away, noticing quite a few eyes staring. I gave them all a raised brow and evil eye before they went back to what they were doing and I got stuck into breakfast. "Mmm, yum." I swallowed, drank some juice and answered his question. "Very well *after* your nightmare. You okay?"

He pushed his plate away and glanced around the room. "Um, yeah, nothing I haven't had before. Don't worry about it, it's just a nightmare." He slid his arm around me and pulled me closer. "So, what are we doing today?"

"Well," I took another sip of juice, "we could go for a walk around the island, stop at the cove for a private swim, then lunch on the front porch, watch some TV, go for a skinny dip, then spend the night up in my room. How does that sound?" I scraped up the last of my food.

"Seriously?" He frowned at me. "You...wanna..."

I grinned. "Of course not."

"Oh, joking, right." He shook his head. "So, what *are* we going to do? Besides spend all day in bed where I can have my wicked way with you."

I stared into his blue eyes and smiled softly. "I wish, but I can't."

He frowned and his bottom lip extended past his top. "And why not?"

"Don't pout," I chastised before kissing the pouting lip. "I run this place and need to make sure we are okay *at all times.*"

"Mmm, fair enough. So what *can* we do today?" He pulled me onto his lap.

"Whoa," I giggled, "Mmm, well..." I kissed him again and wrapped my arms around his neck. "We obviously can't go outside, and I do need to check in with John who's monitoring the storm and island for damage." I looked around and saw many curious glances. Except for Dimitri who was boldly staring, a scowl on his face, his hands locked in front of his face, elbows on the table. I turned back to Chris. "There's TV, games room, books, internet *should* be working." I ruffled his hair. "I'm sure you'll find something to occupy your time today. Besides me that is."

"Aw." He pouted again. "I was happy to have you all to myself."

"Not today." I pulled out of his arms and stood. "Gotta go check things out." A quick kiss and I was out of the room. We spent the rest of the day crossing paths as I went back and forth from the office to the kitchen, power room and mess hall. I met up with him in one of the hallways just before dinner.

"Um, hey." He leaned against the wall and crossed his wide muscular arms. "Your pit bull pulled me aside before and gave me quite a talking to."

I frowned. "My what?"

"That Russian attack dog that follows you around." A scowl covered his blond face.

I bristled and scowled back. "Dimitri is *not* a pit bull *or* attack dog. He's a bodyguard as well as a good friend. I consider him family." I crossed my own arms.

"Yeah, well." Chris shrugged. "He's so much family that he warned me off you before I hurt you and told me that if I did, it would be the last time anyone ever saw me alive." He straightened and lowered his voice. "I don't like being *threatened*, Alex. The pretences I was brought here under were bad enough, but to be *threatened* with death if I hurt you. *Who the fuck* does he think he is? The Russian fuckin' mafia?"

"Stop." I didn't want to hear any more and put my hands up. "Dimitri's just looking out for my best interests as I've been badly hurt before, and since I haven't known you long, he's clearly worried and concerned. This *has* happened fast, so, *of course,* he's going to be concerned." I waited a few moments before putting my hands on his arm and giving him a small smile. "I'm sorry he approached you and threatened you; he shouldn't have done that. But he won't hurt you because he knows that will only hurt me." I paused. "Unless, of course, *you do* hurt me and then he *will* have to kill you." I stared into his eyes until he got that I was joking and then lightly laughed. "Come on, let's go eat."

*****

Natasha drifted awake when she was turned over on the pool table. "Mmm, mmm." The pool ball was still trapped in her mouth, and the men either side of the table were still holding her arms down. The men at the end of the table pushed her legs up and apart. "Mmm." She struggled, but the men beside her greedily put their hands on her to hold her. "Mmm."

"Don't worry, Natasha, this won't hurt a bit," Yuri said before the two men between her legs shoved the small end of a pool cue into her vagina and the fat end into her anus.

*****

After a very lengthy session of luxurious lovemaking and a peaceful rest, I was awakened by Chris mumbling in his sleep. I touched his arm and called his name.

"*No, no,*" he shouted, sitting bolt upright. "*I didn't do it; I didn't mean to do it.*"

"Do what?" I asked, sitting up and grabbed his arm. "*Do what?* What did you do?"

With sweat pouring from his brow he turned to look at me, and after a few heavy moments answered. "I killed a man."

Chapter 9

I blinked. "You what?"

He bit his lip and glanced away, turning to sit on the side of the bed. "I killed a man. I don't want to talk about it."

I blinked again, clutched the sheet to my chest, and waited. "Was it an accident?"

His hands went through his hair, and he sighed. "Yeah, doesn't matter, though, does it? I still killed a man."

I moved to sit beside him. "If it was an accident then why does it still affect you?"

He sighed again and looked at me. "Because killing someone does. Accident or not."

I took his hand in mine. "Will talking about it help you?"

He shook his head sadly. "I don't know...I just don't know."

"Ah, Alex? We have a problem," crackled over the walkie-talkie. "Alex, you there? Are you awake? Alex?"

I grabbed the squawking box from the bedside cupboard. "Yes, John, I'm awake. What's wrong?"

"Uh, we have a building down, one of the workers' huts, and it looks like it may damage another one."

"Okay. I'll come have a look, be there in five." I rested the walkie-talkie on my lap and looked at Chris. "Do you want to come, or try and get some sleep? It's only," I glanced at the clock, "one a.m."

He looked up. "Uh, I might come with you, if that's okay. Get my mind on other things."

"Okay." I smiled and squeezed his hand.

"Ooh, another one down," squawked the walkie-talkie.

"I'm on my way, John." We dressed quickly and made our way into the office. "So, what's going on and how bad is it? And why are you still here at this hour?" I aimed at John.

"I traded shifts with David, here look." He pointed to two monitors showing bungalows where the workers lived. "Number one is down, roof off, and on top of number two. Windows blown out and a wall down."

I leaned in for a better look and screwed my face up. "Ew, that's bad. I thought they were stronger than that." I straightened and stretched my back. "Looks like we'll have a lot of damage to repair, so we'll have to get a working bee together. Get those buildings redone and fixed."

"I'll help," Chris said, from his position against the wall.

"Yeah, well, all of you will have to. No time for a holiday now," I said.

"Who said this was a holiday?"

I glanced at his scowling face and baulked a little. He was here under false pretences, and I felt guilty. I also had some explaining to do about his being sent to Natasha's room. "Guess it really hasn't been that for you, has it?"

The scowl didn't abate. "Nope! Not at all. But I'm all for getting in and helping. Give me something to do instead of lazing around waiting for the world to end."

That's when I definitely knew we needed to talk. I turned to John. "Let me know if anything else happens."

"Sure, Boss." He watched curiously as we walked out of the room.

We walked into my lounge, and instead of continuing into the bedroom I sat on the sofa.

"What are you doing?" The scowl was replaced with a frown.

"I think it's time we talked." I gestured for him to sit.

"I told you I didn't want to talk about my nightmares." He sat in the chair next to the sofa.

"It's not about that." I got comfy. "It's about this, here, this place, why you're here, what's happened since."

"I was wondering if I'd get an explanation." He watched me intently.

I rubbed my legs. "She...enjoys men...and in needing men...we find them for her." I waved my hand at him. "In cases like yours, we tell you it's for a reality show. The others get the truth."

He cocked his head and stared stonily at me. "In

cases like mine? Why am *I* so special? *Why lie to me?*"

I bit my lip. "We know," cough, "from past experiences, that some men don't want to come when they find out it's for sex. Regardless of the money, they just," I took a breath, "aren't interested in sex on an island with a strange woman."

"So, you lie to us, get us on a plane, signing an agreement that is also lying to us, and wait until we get here with no way off the island before telling us what's *really* going on. *No one bloody told me when I got here.* I had to find out from the others."

I rubbed my legs again and bit my lip. "Um, yeah. I know. Sorry."

"You told me you would fix it so I never had to go to her, yet your thugs drugged me and took me anyway." He thrust himself up and paced the small room. "What the hell, Alex? What the hell *is* this? I don't appreciate being used, being lied to, being treated like a sex slave against my will." His pace quickened, anger breaking into his stride. "I don't give a fuck about the money, although it will come in handy, but that's not the point." He stopped with his hands on his hips. "I don't like being lied to, Alex."

"I know." I stood, unable even to look at him. "I'm sorry. I did what I could, and in the end, you haven't slept with her..." my voice trailed off as I realised how stupid that really sounded.

He simply stared back. "Doesn't mean I'm not pissed at what's happened. Or humiliated."

"I know, I'm sorry. I..." I didn't know what to tell him, so I rubbed my forehead. "Please don't hate me,"

I whispered, close to tears.

He softened and pulled me into his arms. "I don't hate you, Alex. I don't understand what's happened between us, or where it's going, or what to do with it, but I don't *hate* you. I don't understand what the hell is going on, or why I feel what I feel for you, but you're amazing." He stroked my cheek and shook his head slowly. "I've never met anyone like you. The way you reacted to me was the same as I reacted to you. I don't hate you…" His voice trailed off and his lips met mine.

*****

Natasha was hauled off the billiard table. Her legs were like jello, and she couldn't breathe, let alone stand or walk.

Yuri pulled off the handkerchief and removed the ball from her mouth. "Time for the real thing," he said and thrust her toward a man who was sitting. "Meet Victor." She splayed into his naked lap, and he grabbed her by the hair, ramming his cock into her mouth.

"Mmm." She tried to move, to breathe. She was faint and weak and wanted it over with. Wanted to die.

A dick was rammed into her from behind, and she tried to scream, but Victor held her there, pushing her head up and down for his own pleasure while the cock from behind thrust for its own.

*****

The next morning, we all met in the mess hall.

"It seems the storm has abated." Everyone cheered. "Okay, okay. What it means now, is we all need to go up top, check out the damage, and get to work repairing. Now, from the reports, the bungalows are the worst off, so we will concentrate on getting them done first. Any major damage, especially to the power and water, needs to be fixed and things like gardens and leaves and whatnot, can be left till last. Let's hope we can get it all done in a few days, but in the meantime, we will need to stay down here until everything is safe enough for us to go back upstairs. You all have your lists of chores and what to do, let's go."

Two by two we filed up the stairs and into the foyer, splitting into two parties, with one going out the front door and one out the back door.

I stared at the pool. Leaves, dirt and bits of wood floated in the dirty water. Some of the plants and shrubs were gone, but they were no big deal. "Okay, let's check the outside of the house." We walked around it and found no major damage, then headed in the opposite direction of the other group.

Except for trees and shrubs, damage to the island itself was limited. The plane hangar was missing some of its roof, but that had been found stuck in a tree. It was the bungalows that needed the most help.

I organized the men to make sure they were all safe to walk into before setting the chore of rebuilding. With plenty of supplies in storage, we were able to re-brick the bungalows, roofs were retiled, and the surrounding area cleaned up.

With seventeen men doing the job, even Dimitri took his leather jacket off and rolled up his sleeves, the bungalows were done quickly, leaving them to dry in the humid air.

We called it a day and headed downstairs for hot showers and hot meals.

*****

"I've been inside you, whore, now suck it." He pulled her off Victor, turned her, so she was still on her knees in front of him. "Suck it. Taste your own cunt, whore. Suck Alexander's cock, whore. Do your job and suck," he screamed at Natasha who was weak from the treatment she had been receiving. "Suck it," he screamed again, pissed off that she just knelt there and didn't do anything.

When she didn't do anything, he held her head and thrust back and forth. When she didn't do anything, he left her mouth and slapped her hard.

She fell on the floor and lay there.

Let me die, please God, let me die. Why are you doing this to me? Why is Grigor doing this to me? Why are these men doing this to me?

"Get up, you whore. Get up and suck my cock." Alexander pummelled her with his fists. Her face, her breasts, her stomach.

"Easy, Alexander," the last man left said. "I don't want you to kill her before I get my turn."

Alexander didn't hear him.

The man grabbed him, and the others followed

127

suit. "Stop it," he commanded. "Stop it now, or you will kill her."

"Isn't that the plan," Alexander screamed. "To fuck her to death and do what we want, just like all the other whores we find for each other."

The man slapped him hard, and he stopped. "Get a hold of yourself. I have not had my turn and the night is still young. We haven't finished with her yet."

*****

"Man, my muscles ache," I complained the next morning at breakfast.

Chris finished his meal and rubbed my neck. "Well, when today is over, I'll give you a nice massage to relax you."

"Mmm, that's good…hopefully we'll be done with the buildings today and can finish off the garden."

"Mmm, then we can take that romantic walk and dip in the cove?"

"Mmm." I kissed him. "We can."

"Alexi?"

I sighed at the intrusion and turned my head slowly to Dimitri.

"Time to head off now. Many chores head of us."

I drank the last of my juice. "Yes, Dimitri, there is." I caught his unnerving stare at Chris and stood up in front of him. "Stop it," I muttered near his ear. "Okay, everyone," I called out, "let's go."

With ten of the workers finishing off the bungalows, the rest of us found the hanger roof and tidied up as we went. Dirt was pushed back onto gardens, plants straightened or replanted, leaves picked up for mulch.

At the end of the day, all that was left to be done was replacing windows, opening up the main house, and getting everything back in order.

After another long, arduous day, we greedily ate the meal the girls had prepared, and all tumbled into bed.

I reminded Chris of the massage he'd promised, and he promptly rolled me onto my stomach and sat on me so his hands could work their magic.

"Ugh…so…good…" I mumbled into the bed and threw my arms above my head. "So good…"

He worked his way up and down my spine, over my shoulders, around my buttocks before spreading my legs and lying inside of me.

"Uhhh…my God that's good…so good…"

Chapter 10

"Okay, if you guys can give the bungalows a quick coat of paint, we girls will go and open up the house," I told everyone before leading the girls upstairs.

After opening every window in every room of the opulent island mansion, which took a good while, we soon found minimal damage. I went up to the third floor alone, while the girls opened up the outside windows as none of them had ever been on the top floor before.

That was the way Natasha wanted it, for privacy and solitude. Not to mention so no one saw her sexual escapades.

I dusted and vacuumed and sopped up the wet floor from a leak. Roof tiles had blown off, and even though the roof was as rain and waterproof as possible, water had still leaked into the huge dressing area and closet. "Well, not a lot I can do about that." I stood and surveyed the floor. A big wet patch remained after I had pressed rag after rag into the thick, luxurious carpet. "It will just have to dry out with the air." I called some of the guys to come and get up on the roof and fix it.

I walked down to my own room and tidied up. I wasn't sure about Chris, and where he'd now stay, and figured since he didn't have much with him, he might move into my room. I changed the bed linen, quickly vacuumed, and cleaned up the bathroom before heading downstairs.

After checking in with everyone, we all packed up and met in the basement.

"Oh, thank God that's finished," Mark groaned, flopping into a chair in the mess hall.

"Hallelujah to that." Andrew sat beside him. "What happens now? Are we finished or what?"

Everyone crowded into the room and grabbed a chair, waiting for my reply.

"Give me a minute to check, and I'll let you know." I sat down and leafed through all the paperwork while everyone grabbed a drink. Since we were on an island, the paperwork was overwhelming. Absolute precise documents had to be kept, and I needed to keep them. A few minutes later I spoke up. "All done." A round of applause and cheers followed my answer. "All right, all right." I motioned for them to quiet down. "We'll stay the night here and move out tomorrow, in the meantime, boys, help the girls get some food and then we can relax or hit the sack. Either way, we are done."

John wandered up to the table after dinner. "Alex, I have some more paperwork for you."

"Can it wait? I'm buggered and want to go to bed." I pushed back from the table and stood, stretching my back as I put my arms over my head to try and stretch out the kinks in my shoulders.

John leant in. "No, it can't. This is stuff you had me looking for."

I realised what he meant. "Where is it?"

"In the office."

"Show me." I followed him to the room and locked the door behind us as he bent down to unlock the safe. "You locked it up?"

He glanced up. "Well, I didn't think you'd want anyone else seeing it, so I kept it out of harm's way."

"Mmm! Good idea. When did you get these?" I took the manila folder from him and opened it.

"During the wee hours I spent looking at the storm. I needed *something* to do." He turned and started packing leftover things into boxes for the move.

I read through the articles. They were exactly what I was after. Exactly what I'd been after, for years. Exactly what Natasha and I needed to let go. "I'm surprised the internet was still working during *that* weather. Thanks, John." I unlocked the door and quickly headed for my room, only to be cut off by Chris.

"Hey, ready for bed?" He playfully grabbed me and spun me around and I lost my grip on the folder while its contents went flying across the floor.

He bent down. "Bugger, I'll get these."

"No," I cried and scurried around, picking them up in a panic.

"I just want to help," he said after I snatched a paper from his grasp.

"Can't, confidential." I rammed the last piece into the folder, slammed it into my chest, and spun around, looking for any leftovers that might have missed my eye.

"Okay." He slowly rose and put his hands up. "It's okay, I get it. Not for anyone but you."

I looked at him and realised how much I'd freaked out. I let out a huge breath I'd been holding and relaxed. "Sorry." I grinned wryly. "All papers are confidential and for my eyes only." I shrugged half-heartedly. "Unless they're also for Natasha's," I muttered and took a breath. "So, you said something about bed?"

He grinned, showing perfect white shining teeth. "Yes, let's." Holding out his arm, I took it.

Once inside the bedroom, I shoved the folder into my backpack with the others. The others that revealed information no one would even know about. I managed to close the wardrobe door before I was grabbed from behind. "Hey."

Chris flung me onto the bed and flung himself on top of me. "Hey, yourself." He brushed my hair off my forehead and gazed into my eyes. "Hey," the word escaped softly from between his lips.

I wrapped my arms and legs around him, returned his gaze and smiled. "Hey, yourself," I managed before his lips met mine.

*****

The man bent down and stared into Natasha's eyes. "Are you alive? Are you still with us?" He slapped her face. "Wake up! I have not had my turn yet."

She didn't move. Just lay there, staring numbly at the men who hovered around her, leaned over her. Peering at her like she was a dead alien or some sort of corpse, half dead, half alive. A zombie of sorts.

He slapped her hard. "Get up, you whore. I do not fuck whores on floor. That is beneath me. Get up." His hand cracked across her face again. "Get up, you whore, get up."

She didn't move. She couldn't. She didn't want to.

He stood and spat on her. "Whore. Dirty filthy whore."

Nicolai leant over her. "Boris does not fuck whores on floor."

She didn't move. She couldn't. She didn't want to.

"Pick her up and put her on couch," Boris commanded. "It wide as a bed and will have to do."

Natasha felt herself being lifted.

Four men picking her up by her arms and legs. Carrying her over to the couch and all but throwing her on.

She bounced a bit. Her breast jiggled around, her arms and legs flapped. Her head rolled to the side, her eyes empty, glazed over, staring at them as if accusing them of all the horror bestowed upon her.

"Is she dead?"

Yuri bent over to take her pulse. "Mmm, nearly."

"I had better get in before she dies then," Boris replied, unbuckling his pants. He walked over to the couch, dropped his pants and briefs, climbed between her legs, and thrust his way inside. He moved her head, so she was looking at the back of the couch and

placed a pillow over her head. "I do not like way she looks at me." He took his time. He had to, considering keeping his dick up was a problem. Viagra helped, but not a lot, so he kept stopping to catch his breath. Hands and mouth, fingers and teeth, grabbed and groped and bit and sucked her body, her breasts, and when he finally did come he was thrusting so hard and fast to keep going that he slid out and spurted over her instead of inside of her.

"Fuck, Boris. Your pills not working anymore," Alexander griped sarcastically. "You can't even come inside woman anymore. You are getting too old, old man." His raucous laughter filled the quiet hate-filled room.

Boris stood, and pushing his soft cock into his briefs, buttoned up his pants. "I would like to see you do better."

"Oh, I will. Again," Alexander crowed, dropped his pants, mounted her, and rode her as hard and fast as he could in his old age. Which wasn't very.

*****

"No, no, get out of the way. No, get out of the way. No," Chris shouted as he bolted out of bed.

I sprang awake beside him and watched as he paced the room. "You okay?" My heart was racing from the rude awakening, and I groggily rubbed my eyes.

"What? Um, no..." He rubbed his face and kept pacing.

"What time is it?" I yawned and looked at the bedside

clock. Two a.m. I fell back onto the bed. "You going to do that till it's time to get up, or you want to work off that energy doing something else?" I flung the sheet back. My eyes were closed, but I heard him stop. Moments later the bed moved, and he climbed on top.

"I'm in love with you," he whispered. "I love you, how does that happen?"

I opened my eyes and turned to look at him. "I love you, too…and it happens every day."

*****

Natasha just lay there. Her mind had already closed, encased and cocooned itself from the horror of the event.

Man after man rode her. Animal after animal used her and abused her as she lay there, not moving, not looking, not breathing.

Her mind had taken her somewhere else while her body slowly shut itself down. Her heart had slowed. Her breath had slowed. And she was sure if a doctor had checked her he would have pronounced her dead.

I may as well be. Dead! Am I dead? I'm not there anymore. Is this heaven? I don't feel any pain. I don't feel any*thing.* I feel nothing. Am I dead? Is this what dead feels like? Like nothing? No *thing?* I am dead. I am dead, and they are fucking a corpse. I am dead, and I feel nothing. I am nothing. I am no one. I am no thing. I am dead. I am dead. I am dead.

"What do we do with her?" Nicolai asked from his chair before taking a sip of Grigor's finest whiskey.

Boris blew out smoke from his Cuban cigar and

shrugged. "Who cares? Are we done?" He took another long suck and blew smoke rings.

Yuri slipped his tie into place. "I am done. We do what we do every other time. We kill her."

"My cock hurts," Alexander added to the conversation. "I get to stab her."

"Then you know what we need to do then," Yuri replied.

*****

Morning came, and it was all hands on deck for moving back upstairs. Electricals, art objects, pieces of expensive furniture, food, computers, it all went back upstairs, and once it was all in its place we cleaned up the shelter, getting it back to being spic and span.

"Guys," I called a halt at the end of cleaning. "Go grab your stuff and get back to your bungalows. We're having the rest of the day off." Cheers went up. "We'll barbecue, and you can all relax by the pool."

After packing everything away and seeing that nothing was left behind, I gathered my things together in my bedroom.

"Need help?" Chris asked, coming in behind me.

"No. I think it's all done. The bed's been stripped, bathroom cleaned." I snapped my case shut and fell into his arms. "Just gotta get my stuff up to my room." I kissed him. "Let's go." He carried my case up to the light and warmth of the foyer, and I lugged my backpack behind him, seeing the last worker out of the storm shelter that had been our home for the last few days. I shut the door behind me, took a step and stopped. "Shit. Natasha."

"Who? What's wrong with her?" Chris asked, standing patiently by my case even though his interest had once again been highly piqued.

"No, nothing, nothing's wrong with her, I just forgot all about her and need to get her upstairs." I shoved my bag at him. "Be a sweetie and take my stuff up to my room. I take it you're moving in with me, so it's the last room on the second floor. I'm just running back to get her. I'll meet you at the barbecue. Won't be long." I closed the door behind me and fled for Natasha's room. "I'm sorry I kept you waiting, but it's time to go upstairs. Storm's over."

"About time, Alexi. I thought you had forgotten me."

I packed her bags and got her dressed. "No, no, let's go." I shuffled her out of the door and over to the hidden lift. Pushing a wall tile so the doors would open, I felt a chill down my spine and quickly glanced to my right. There was no one there. No one in the whole basement except for us. It was empty, and every sound, no matter how big or small, echoed painfully and suspiciously in my head. I felt myself begin to freak out at the absence of other people. The bell rang. "Here we go, let's go back up to civilisation. Quick now, hurry." Something was telling me I needed to get out of there and back up to real life. Ghosts maybe.

"Stop rushing me, Alexi. A Queen *cannot* be rushed."

Chris came out of hiding to peer around the corner. Curiosity had gotten the better of him, and he'd followed Alex downstairs. Hearing her speak to a Russian woman, he'd assumed it was the woman they all worked for and had wanted him as a sex slave. He only caught a glimpse of Alex as she entered the lift, but no one else, even though he'd heard two voices.

Once the doors shut, he raced down the hall to the place the lift was, but all he saw was a wall. "What the hell?" he muttered, hands sliding over the embossed tiles, wondering what was going on, and if what he'd just seen was even real. But all he saw was a wall full of tiles.

Chapter 11

"So, Alexi... How do you find your blond man then?"

"He's fine." I settled Natasha into her bedroom. I didn't want to elaborate too much and quickly rushed into the dressing room to put her things away. I wanted to get downstairs a.s.a.p.

"Alexi, I have known you many years now, what are you keeping from me?"

"Nothing, nothing," I called. "I, no—" I saw her out of the corner of my eye and tried to stop her from coming in so she wouldn't see the water-stained carpet, but she saw it anyway.

She pointed. She stared. First at the floor then at me, then at the floor again. "What? What is? What is this?" she all but shrieked the last word.

I tried to placate her. "It's okay; it's just water damage from the rain. The roof leaked and it came through. But we fixed the ceiling and roof and now just have to wait for the carpet to dry." I glanced up and waited.

"To dry?" She bristled. "To dry? I do not wait for things to dry—"

"Natasha," I firmly cut her off. "Calm down, cut the dramatics and deal with it, it's only water, and there's nothing we can do about it unless you want people up here."

She stared wild and wide-eyed.

I raised a brow in steely defiance and pursed my lips at her.

She calmed down and relented. "All right, Alexi. I do not want anyone up here besides the men I conquest, and I want one tonight."

Alarm bells went off in my head. "Is that such a good thing?" I hastily asked. "We've only just come back up top. Breathe the air, enjoy a spa, and luxuriate in your own room."

"How is your sex life, Alexi?"

"My what?"

"Your sex life? With the blond one."

Now *I* bristled and rushed from the room. "What makes you think I have one? Have a shower, Natasha, and I'll have lunch sent up. Here," I flung her French doors wide open, "enjoy the sea breeze."

"Alexi?"

"Natasha." I turned to face her.

"Is he the one?"

I took a moment before answering. "Yes, I think he is."

*****

Unable to find the lift, or figure out if what he'd seen was even real, Chris raced back upstairs, deposited

Alex's belongings in her room, and took a quick look around before going downstairs, meeting up with her at the barbecue.

"Hey," I said, catching up with him outside, "hungry?"

He stopped, and blinked before smiling, hoping she couldn't read his mind about what he'd just done. "Starving."

They joined the others for a relaxing afternoon of poolside fun, grilled meats and salads with chocolate cake and fruit for dessert.

I lay on my back on a sun lounge with a full stomach and a big smile, which grew bigger when Chris plonked down beside me.

"Need sunscreen?"

"Mmm, I have some on, but I know that won't stop you putting on more." I flashed a wicked grin and caught his eye, wiggling my brows at the look on his face.

"You got that right." He squirted into his hand, and rubbing both together, worked on my right leg, then repeated for my left. His hands worked their magic on my right arm and shoulder then my left, leaving my torso for last. His hands were big and manly and knew their way around a woman's body. Mine in particular.

"Mmm." I slid down the lounge chair until I was flat and Chris's hands were all over me. My fingers caught the flesh of his muscular side and slid up and down over his ribs. My nails lightly scraped over hot naked man meat, and my nipples hardened. I moistened and wanted him urgently, which I tried to convey with my eyes. He sensed my arousal and wanton desires, and I saw movement in his shorts, a clear indication that he wanted the same thing.

"Oh, for God's sake you two, *get a room*," Jenny called out.

I looked up to see she meant us as everyone else noticed. "We might just do that!" I leapt up, and dragging Chris behind me, we ran inside to catcalls and whistles, barely making it up to my room before lust and desire took over.

"Ugh, oh, ugh, God."

We melded together as material fell away and we splayed onto the bed as one, writhing and groaning in pleasure and desire until sleep fell upon us…

I awoke late afternoon and stretched every muscle in my body. I turned my head toward Chris who was spread-eagled across the bed, his left arm and leg over me. My eyes travelled the length of his hard ripe body and landed on his erection. "Well, we can't let that go to waste, now can we." I gave it a quick rub, which made him stir and mumble, then sat on top of him.

I slid down the hard thickness of him, revelling in the size and goodness of his manhood. "Oh, God." I flung my head back.

"Oh, God, indeed," he murmured and thrust upward, grabbing my hips and hanging on while I bounced up and down.

"Fuck me, fuck me," I cried, hanging onto his arms like they were reins as I rode hard and fast, moving up and down like there was no tomorrow. I pulsated inside, throbbing with every beat of his strokes.

Strokes that sent me over the edge.

"Harder, harder," my voice rang louder now. "Oh, God…more…" I was riding him like my life depended on it. Riding him away from the bad guys in a cowboy and Indian movie. Riding him away from all the bad things that happen in that movie. Riding him like I would never stop.

"Harder, harder, fuck me, oh, God, fuck me, oh… God…fuck…me…oh…God…oh, God…" My head flew back with my last gasp of breath before collapsing onto his heaving naked chest.

"Oh, God," he gasped. "Oh, fucking God, indeed."

*****

Natasha was violently yanked onto the cold marble floor. Her lifeless body landed awkwardly. One leg bent, one arm twisted.

"What do we do with her?" Nicolai wrung his hands together. "I don't have much energy left."

"Don't worry, old man." Yuri produced a gun from his coat pocket. "You can use this."

"And I'll use this," Alexander added, pulling an old, long, sharp gemstone encrusted dagger out of its black leather case. "My usual weapon of choice."

A crackling sound made the men look. Natasha's body was being electrocuted by Boris' Taser, her arms, legs, breasts all jiggling and thumping around on the floor.

"Stop it! Not yet," Yuri yelled. "You will not start without us."

Boris stopped and the crackling dissipated. "You are no fun, my friend."

The five men stood around her body.

"I have my bottle. Grigor's favourite vodka." Victor held it up. "I stole it from his cabinet. The one he doesn't think we know about." He chuckled.

"What are you going to do with it? Drink it?" Nicolai asked.

"No, stupid. Pour it down her throat. The police will think she was alcoholic."

Yuri slid a small metal cylinder out of his suit jacket. He flicked his hand, and it extended into a lethal metal rod.

"Nice," murmured Alexander appreciatively eyeing the cylinder.

"Just right for bashing whore's skull in." Yuri displayed it for them to look at.

"All right," Boris said, setting his Taser to full blast. "Let's do this; it's nearly time to go."

*****

I was summoned to the third floor the next morning.

"Alexi!" Natasha stormed around her room, pacing back and forth and turning in circles.

I knew from past experience not to say too much. "Nat—"

"Do not interrupt me, Alexi." Flowing chiffon waved around as her arms gesticulated wildly. "You have *never* disobeyed an order before. You have *never* not answered my call before. You have *never* not answered *me* before. What is going on, Alexi? Is it that man, that blond that you brought here? Has he distracted you from your duties? Has he made you forget me and your priorities? Your duties to me, *to us*, to finding the truth?" She stopped to stare me down.

"No," I raised my voice. "Of course not, but I also have my own life."

"Your life is with *me*." Natasha stormed around again. *"With me!"*

"Not for long."

She stopped dead, face ashen, eyes wide, lips parted. "What…what…what do…you…mean...?"

"This can't go on forever," I said quietly, crossing my arms. "You know that."

She softened. "I know, Alexi. I know." She moved toward me, arms outstretched. "But we, we must stick together till the end. We must see it through, finish it, together. No matter how long it takes…together."

I sighed and rubbed my eyes. "I don't think it's going to be too long. Another week or two, maybe, not long now, and then it will *all* be over." I felt my body sag. "It will finally be over."

"Yes, Alexi. It will finally be over."

When I caught up with Chris an hour later, I had some energy back. "Okay, my duties are done for the day, I've asked Jenny to pack us a lunch and grab some towels because we are *finally* headed off on our day out." I threw my arms around his neck and planted a big wet kiss on him.

He kissed me back with the same amount of

vigour. "You mean we finally get to spend the day together away from everyone else?" he asked, spinning me around. "Just you and me, the birds in the tree and the deep blue sea?"

"Yep." I kissed him again. "Just us."

Jenny came waltzing into the foyer with a huge wicker picnic basket in her hands. "Here's your lunch, towels as well, and don't forget the sunscreen."

"Ohhh, I'll take that," Chris dropped me and reached for the basket.

"Hey," I protested at being dropped for a basket of food.

"Hey, what?" He looked at me, reached out, and turned sheepish. "Sorry, here, take my hand, and we'll go off on our adventure."

We walked down the path and around to the cove which was shipshape after the storm. A huge lounging bed and shade tent had been set up for us, and we wandered across the yellowish sand, our toes sinking through the warm top layer into the cooler layers below. Stopping beside the lounge, we took in the calm water, colourful birds and frolicking dolphins.

"God I love this place." I stretched my arms above my head.

"Don't you get lonely here?" Chris had already stripped off his top and was reaching for the sunscreen.

"Yeah. I don't love the *island*, I love this cove. It's peaceful, serene, quiet." I pulled my tank top off. "I love coming to this spot and just relaxing. Being one with nature, I guess you could say." I melted into him as his hands rubbed in the lotion.

He massaged my muscles as he went across my shoulders and down my arms, my back and long, lean legs.

I groaned. "Okay, stop, coz if you don't you know where it's going to lead."

"And what's wrong with that?" He swept me into his arms and onto the lounge.

I giggled. "What's wrong with that is, is that people might see us. Stop that!" I swatted his lips away and then tried to pry his fingers from my shorts.

"Well, considering what this island is all about," he grinned, "what does it really matter?"

"Stop it," I coughed, "stop it, ah…" He caught my lips with his and held the kiss while he climbed on top. "Mmm." I wrapped myself around him, my fingers dug their nails into his back muscles like their life depended on it, and my tongue delved deep into the depths of his mouth. "Mmm…"

We bumped and ground our way into a high-pitched orgasm in the hot tropical sun…

I'm not sure how long after that it was, but I woke to splashes of cold water being thrown on my hot flesh. "Stop it," I grumbled, coming to. I opened my eyes a slit against the afternoon sun to see Chris dripping wet and shaking himself off…on me. "You been swimming?"

"Yep. You should come in, it's beautiful. In fact, you should come in now." He bent down, and in one fell swoop picked me up and started for the luxurious aquatic ocean.

"What, no." I struggled. "I don't want to go in now,

no, Chris, put me down, *put me down.*" I struggled harder. "For the love of God put me down."

He stopped.

I stopped. "Put me down," I demanded. "Now!"

He grinned. "No." He ran the last few metres and dropped me into the warm salty liquid.

I came up sputtering. "I told you to put me down."

The grin was still on his face as he pulled me further into the depths of the cove. "I did."

"I didn't mean in the water for bloody God's sake." I allowed myself to be pulled further along, gliding into his arms as they slid around me. I sighed. "This is nice." My arms wound around his neck, and I lay my cheek upon his. "Very nice."

We floated. Every muscle relaxing, every care drifting away, every thought floating off on the warm tropical breeze.

I sighed again. A relaxing sigh. A relieving sigh. "Very nice," I murmured before feeling him between my legs. I opened and allowed him to enter, feeling him there. Not moving, not needing to. The two of us joined together in the only way a man and woman could be. The only way I wanted to be…with him.

Chapter 12

"So," I rubbed sunscreen into Chris's back and kneaded his muscles with it, "it's almost time for you to go home, only a week or so."

"Mmm, can't wait," he murmured from his face down position on the lounge.

I stopped, unsure what to say after his comment.

His head popped up. "Wait," he turned and sat beside me, "I didn't mean that. I didn't mean that the way it *sounded*."

"No," I shook my head and shifted on the lounge, "it's okay. I get it, I do."

"No, I don't think you do." He reached for my hand. "I can't wait to get the hell off this island because of the way I was brought here. Lies, manipulations. Sure," he gestured, "I need the money, but it's not worth the bullshit I've gone through getting here. First being a sex slave, then meeting you, the storm…" He ran his hand through his hair, and I pulled mine from his other. He noticed. "Alex. I…I don't want to leave you, but I don't want to be *here* either."

"I get it," I snapped at him. "*I do*. I don't want to be

here either, but I am." I saw his expression and softened. "We're both here for different reasons, and we're both here for the same reasons, but either way, neither of us *wants* to be here." I shook my head, sat back, and pulled my knees up to my chest, hugging them to me, desperate to cling to something.

"Alex." He moved closer. "I don't know why and I don't know how, and I sure as hell don't know what we're going to do about it but, I, I love you. I've *fallen* in love with you. I want to be with you, but *not* on this island." He looked around and shrugged. "I don't want to be here. I want to go home, take you with me, and start a life with you." He pulled me into his arms, and I went from clinging to my legs to clinging to him. "I don't know why all of this has happened, and I hate the way I was brought here, but, it means I met you. I've never met *any* woman like you. You're strong and smart and take charge of everything." He brushed my hair aside and gazed into my eyes. "As much as I hate being here under false pretences, I'm also glad I am, because I met you, and I think you're amazing, and I want to spend the rest of my life with you, and make love with you, and make babies with you." He wiped away the tears from my cheeks.

I crumpled and burst into tears, sobbing against his hot hard naked chest.

"Hey, hey," he said softly, rubbing the back of my neck trying to release the tense muscles. "What is it, what's wrong?"

"Nothing. Everything." I sniffed and wiped my face. "It doesn't matter. Look, I," I touched his face, "I'm sorry it all happened this way, but I'm a big believer in everything happening for a reason, so clearly, we were meant to meet for a reason."

"Clearly." He smiled softly.

I returned it with one of my own. "Please don't hate me." I stared at him earnestly. "Please."

He shook his head in confusion at my mood. "I don't hate you. I hate the pretences, but I don't hate you."

I sighed and looked away. "I don't want you to hate me," I barely said above the crashing waves in the distance. "I couldn't stand it if you hated me."

He was puzzled and confused. "I already said I don't," he frowned, "what's going on? I'm sensing there's some deep dark secret you're keeping from me."

His words alarmed me, and my head snapped around. "Why would you think that? What makes you think that? Why would you say that?"

"Whoa, calm down." He put his hands up in protest. "It's okay, I was just kidding, well, only half kidding…"

"Why would you—?"

"Stop it," he said firmly. "The more you protest, the more I wonder if there is. Calm down."

I took a deep breath and realised he was right. I needed to calm down. *Now.*

"Considering how I came here, I'd say there are *plenty* of secrets. An *island* full of secrets," he said.

I cast a sideways glance and felt guilty. "Yeah, I know."

"So, what are we going to do about *us* then?" He

settled back on the lounge and pulled a bottle of water from the hamper next to him.

I settled beside him. "Well, *your* time's nearly over. I'm hoping *my* time is nearly over, and when it is, I'll be free to do what I want and go where I want."

"How much longer?" He took a swig of water.

"I don't know." I grabbed the bottle and drank. "Not much longer. A few weeks, a few months. I don't want to be here for the rest of my life."

He took the bottle back. "How did you come to be here and do this job anyway?"

I froze. "Long story."

"We've got the rest of the day and another week."

I smiled weakly at him. "It's a long story I don't want to tell."

"Not even to me?" He dripped water across my stomach.

I grabbed the bottle and took another drink. "Not even to you."

"Ever?"

"Never."

We lunched on chicken and salad sandwiches, ice-cold cans of soda, and mixed berries for dessert. We walked every step of the island hand in hand to find ourselves back at the cove just before the sun hit the horizon.

We oohed and aahed at the brilliant reds and oranges that turned to pinks and purples as the sun slowly slid beyond the edge of the world to light up the other side of the planet.

As the stars came out to play, we wandered slowly

inside the dark, quiet house, since the staff had their bungalows, and hand in hand we walked up the stairs to my room at the end of the hallway on the second floor. Hand in hand we slid into bed and made love all night, never once breaking apart.

*****

"So, is everyone finally settled back into their bungalows and routines?" I asked at our morning meeting. A chorus of yesses flew around the room. "Good. Then it's all back to normal then."

"What about our guests?" Dimitri piped up from his usual spot beside me.

I looked at him and shrugged. "I don't care anymore. They can go home if they like."

A hush descended over the room.

"You what?"

"They what?"

I glanced at everyone and shrugged again. "I don't care, and they can go home if they like."

Murmurs sped around the staff, more than likely because they'd never heard me talk this way.

"Alexi?"

I turned back to Dimitri. "If they want to go home take them, and give them their money. Everyone dismissed." I gathered my papers as they slowly wandered out of the room, casting furtive glances back at me.

"Alexi?"

"They're probably wondering if I've gone mad," I

quipped and stopped what I was doing. "Hell, *I* don't even know if I've gone mad. I probably have."

"Alexi." Dimitri took me into his embrace and held me while I cried.

Sobbed, really. For all the years wasted. For all the years taken. For all the years I would never get back.

"Alexi, what is it? What is wrong? Has that blond done something to hurt you?" He pushed me away to look into my eyes.

I shook my head sadly. "No, he hasn't done anything to me." I shrugged half-heartedly. "Except make me happy."

"Then why do you not look happy?" He gently touched my chin.

"Because I'm on this bloody God forsaken island and I don't know *when or if* I'll ever get off it." My bottom lip quivered with anger and dismay before I burst into tears again. "I don't want to be here," I wailed, clinging to Dimitri. "I'm sick of being here, so sick of being here. I don't want to do this anymore. *I can't* do this anymore. I want it to end, I want it to be over with and finished. I don't want to do this anymore, I *can't* do this anymore, I *won't* do this anymore." I pushed away from him. "I love him. For the first time in years, if not decades, I've found someone to love, to *be* with, to maybe have a future with, but we can't have that future with me being here, we just can't. I know we can't, *he* knows we can't." I gazed into his eyes. "Hell, even *you* know we can't. We can't have a future while I'm still here, while he's still here, while I'm tied to this place and all it holds. All it means…" I sagged, and he caught me, helping me into my chair.

"Alexi, what is going on? You are worrying me. What has brought all of this on?" He sat beside me, holding my hand.

I slowly shook my head and rubbed my eyes. "It's time for this to be over, Dimitri." I sighed and looked at him. "It's time for this to be over."

We finished talking, and I wandered upstairs to freshen up before for my daily island inspection. Everything was still in tip-top shape after we'd fixed it, and the trip around did me good until I needed to go and see Natasha that is. I gathered the folders from my backpack and slowly trod the stairs to the third floor, feeling every ounce of weight and pressure with every step. I dragged my feet to her door and stopped, sighed, and opened it to find her residing in her dressing room, admiring herself in the mirror as she often did. The wet patch from the storm had dried and been covered with a decorative mat to hide the stain.

"Alexi. For what do you disturb me?"

"I have more information." I held out the folders.

"Is it what we are after?" She seemed disinterested, lacking her usual energy.

"For the most part." I put the folders in front of her.

She sat there, arms crossed and leaning on the table, staring at the folders. "Are you tired, Alexi? I am tired."

I sighed and rubbed my eyes. "I am *very* tired, Natasha." I could also feel a migraine coming on.

She half-heartedly picked through the papers. "They are all here?"

"Yes."

"Yes, good. Very good, Alexi." She stared into the mirror, her eyes looking directly into mine. "Is it time yet?"

I tiredly stared back. "Not yet. But not long either. Very soon, Natasha, it will all be over very, very soon."

"Good, Alexi, good." She pulled out a drawer and removed a small pearl-handled gun, just right for a woman like her. "Because I am over *all* of this, Alexi. I want it all to end." She gazed longingly at her pistol. "I want it all to end."

I had frozen at the sight of the gun but now sprang into action, gently relieving her of the metal weapon in her hand. "It will all be over soon, Natasha." I checked to see if it was loaded and fortunately it wasn't. I placed it in the drawer and slid it shut. "It will all be over soon." I stared at her, her tiny frame sagging with the weight of the world and all its pain. "It will all be over very soon." I picked up the folders. "You go and rest, Natasha, just rest."

I left her to flee to my own room and spread the papers across the bed. I read them all, word for word, line for line, paragraph for paragraph, on every single piece of paper in those folders. Over and over until the ink bled before my eyes and the images were burned into my retinas, and my memory was scalded with the details, knowing I would *never* forget, let alone get rid of them.

"Alex?"

My ears pricked up at my name being called, and I hastily shoved the papers into one folder, managing to hide it under some clothes in the closet before Chris burst in.

"Alex?"

I hastened into the room, smoothing down my clothes. "Here," I said, and saw him standing there in the same clothes he had to wear every day.

"Hey, there you are. Ready for dinner?" He smiled brightly at her.

I took in his big blue eyes, wide smile, and great looking body. I was suddenly starved. "Absolutely!"

Chapter 13

After a delicious night of lovemaking, Chris woke. It was still dark out, and Alex was asleep beside him, but he needed to leave her for a trip to the bathroom. Stealthily sliding from the bed, he slipped through the closet into the bathroom. Holding his cock, he relieved himself, feeling the immense relief as his urine left his body. Shaking it off, he flushed and washed his hands and face before flicking off the lights. Sneaking back through the closet he tripped, and in his haste to grab something to stop his fall, he pulled down a pile of Alex's clothes from a shelf.

"Shit," he swore softly then stopped. Stopped breathing, stopped moving. He listened for a sign from Alex, and when he didn't hear one, reached for the light. There was more than clothes on the floor. Piles of paper and manila folders littered the carpet, and he quickly reached for them, catching bits and pieces of information here and there. One paper, in particular, caught his eye.

"Chris?"

Hearing her voice, he quickly collected the rest of

the papers, shoved them into the folders and jammed them back under her clothes, piling up the pieces from the floor on top. He turned off the light and moved to the door.

"Chris?"

"I'm here," he said softly, hastening for the bed and getting in beside me.

"Mmm, where'd you go?" I snuggled into his arms.

"Just to the loo, go back to sleep." He pulled me tight and wondered about the secret files hidden in the closet before falling asleep.

The next morning, he was up early to tidy the pile of clothes. He didn't want Alex knowing he'd toppled it over and seen the papers. He wasn't sure she'd forgive him for even finding them, considering the way she had carried on over him wanting to help pick up the folder she'd dropped down in the basement. He finished adjusting her clothes into nice neat piles, not even sure if that's the way they were. When he was satisfied, he dressed in his shorts and tank, and lacing up his sneakers, headed downstairs for a run, stopping to stretch on the front porch.

God, what the hell is going on? he thought. *Why would she have folders full of paperwork in her closet of all places? There's an office downstairs, surely there's a safe or file cabinet. What would make them so super-secret that she's hiding them in her room?* The more he thought about it, the more he wanted to run to clear his mind. He sighed, scratched his head, and set off.

*****

I approached our house guests by the pool after breakfast. "Boys. I know you have a week or so to go, but if you want to go home, you're free to leave."

Mark looked up from rubbing sunscreen on his torso. "What do you mean, go home?"

Andrew looked up from his book. "Does her highness not want us mere mortals anymore?" He turned to Mark. "I suddenly feel unwanted." He looked at Todd. "Do you feel unwanted?"

"No," he replied, his voice soft and low as he barely looked up from his iPad.

"Look," I said, "it's nothing to do with not being wanted, it's just with the storm and other things, you need to go home. So, if you want to, you can fly out first thing tomorrow." I shaded my eyes.

"Do we still get our money?" Mark asked.

I nodded. "You still get it. It will be transferred into your accounts two days after you leave. No one will know anything different."

"I'd like to go home," Todd said, finally lifting his head from his tablet. "First thing, I'm the first one on the plane."

"Does Her Royal Cuntness not want us anymore?" Mark finished applying his lotion and stood. "I don't mind sex, it was good. Probably the best I've ever had. Hot, adventurous, wild. Can we get one last fuck before we go?" He pulled his dick out of his swim briefs. "Charlie here wants another fuck before he goes home."

"Put it away and stop being disgusting," Chris growled as he walked up beside Alex and the sight of Mark waving his cock around. "None of us needs to see that old piece of crap." He crossed his arms which made them bulge with strength and power.

Mark quickly adjusted himself. Chris was not someone he wanted to get into a fight with as he'd read the articles in the entertainment magazines about the bigger muscles and martial arts training Chris had from all the TV shows and movies he was in. "Is big Mister Actor Dude going home tomorrow, or do you plan on staying for Lady Muck's wench?" He nodded at me.

My eyebrows flew up as far as they could go.

Lady Muck's wench?

What the fuck?

Chris remained steadfast, staring the smug thug down. "I'm staying until *Alex* is ready to leave."

That surprised me, and I gaped at him.

"You what?" Andrew piped up.

Chris looked at me. "I have no reason to head home early, so I'm staying until Alex is ready to leave and then we'll go together. No point wasting jet fuel."

My lips slowly turned into a huge smile, and I quickly kissed him then turned back. "So, *you're* all going home tomorrow?" I waited for the three yesses, two of them rather reluctant, and then walked inside with Chris. I removed my sunglasses and rubbed my eyes before sighing. "Damn migraine, bloody had it for ages and it's not going away."

"Here, let me." Chris stood in front of me and

kneaded my shoulders and neck.

"Mmm, that's good." I leaned against him and wound my arms around his waist while he massaged my tight muscles.

"How long have you had this one?"

"Years," I mumbled against his flesh, breathing him and his hot hunk of man meat scent in.

"No, really?"

I sighed again and raised my head. I felt so exhausted all of a sudden. "Days. But I've been having them for years. They can get really bad. In fact, I might take a pill and go lie down in a dark room." I reluctantly pulled out of his manly hands and walked into the kitchen to grab a painkiller and juice, as I hated swallowing pills with water.

He followed me. "Do you want me to come? I can keep massaging you."

I grinned at his words and swallowed the pill. "I always want you to *come*. And a massage might help." I pointed my finger at him. "But no sex! Just massage, dark room and rest."

"Party pooper. You *do* look tired." He pouted, put his arm around me and pulled me close to kiss me on the forehead. "Come on then, I'll get you upstairs and have you feeling better in no time."

We traipsed up the stairs, and I threw myself onto the bed. Pain shot through my head. "Ow, shouldn't have done that," I mumbled into the pillow. "Can you—?"

"Already doing it." He flung the curtains together, and the room went dark.

"Good boy," I murmured drowsily.

"Yes," he said, getting on the bed. "I'm a *very* good boy." His hands moved up and down my spine. "I'm such a good boy I'm not going to take advantage of you."

"Mmm, good boy…" His hands did their magic, and I was soon out like a light.

*****

"So, who goes first?" Boris asked. "Should we do it in order?"

"Let me stab her," Alexander begged.

"How do I use this gun, Yuri?" Nicolai asked.

"Do I electrocute her first or last?" Boris added.

"And when do I drown her?" Victor cradled the bottle of Grigor's vodka.

"I want to go first," Yuri said.

"No, it should be me."

"Should we do it alphabetically?"

"The oldest should go first."

"Enough," Boris shouted. "We will do it like this. We stab, we shoot, we bash, we drown then we electrocute." He looked around at his companions. "Agreed?"

"Agreed."

"Alexander, start proceedings."

Alexander crouched beside Natasha, clasped his dagger with both hands, raised them above his head and plunged it into the spot under her ribcage.

"Haaaaa," breathed out of Natasha's body as it jerked and settled and blood formed.

"Ahh." Alexander stumbled back in surprise.

"Get up, you moron," Boris said, "and remove your knife."

"It's not a knife." Alexander moved toward the body. "It's a dagger." He grasped and pulled, sliding it out from between her ribs, leaving a wound for blood to flow freely from. He stood and displayed it. "A very old dagger. Centuries old, my friend." He glanced at Boris. "Just like you."

"Enough," Yuri said. "Nicolai, your turn."

The old man stepped up to the body, pointed Yuri's gun, and pulled the trigger.

Natasha's body moved with the impact, but not like it had with the stabbing.

Nicolai sagged and handed it to its owner. "Here, take it. I'm done. I think I'm getting too old for this." He stumbled backwards onto the couch they'd had their way with Natasha on. "Too old."

"You are right, my friend." Yuri put the gun into his pocket. "You are getting too old." He stepped forward, raised his right arm and brought the baton down upon the body of his friend's wife. Beat upon beat he did not stop until she bled from her now disfigured face, broken teeth and shattered jaw. He straightened, the baton dangling at his side, dripping blood in time with his gasps for air. "Good job if I say so myself." He straightened his tie. "Which I do."

"Yes," Victor agreed. "You did such a good job I may not be able to get vodka down her throat."

"Try it anyway old man and stop complaining." Yuri cleaned off his baton on Natasha's negligee and

dropped the stained rag on the floor in disdain at the blood that came off. He closed it and put it away.

Victor crouched down. With one hand he held open Natasha's now badly broken jaw and used the other to pour the vodka in.

The alcohol gurgled with the blood in her mouth and throat, causing a bubbling effect as it ran down her face onto the floor. He finished pouring the whole bottle in and stood. "One more," he said, watching the diluted blood of their latest conquest and victim spread across the marble floor.

"Yes," Boris added. "One more." He stepped away from the alcoholic blood and warned the others. "You may want to back away." He aimed the Taser, and they hastily moved.

A billion bolts of electricity shook Natasha's body for what seemed like an eternity, but only lasted ten seconds. Boris retracted his weapon as her body kept shaking, jerking, flopping around.

"What is wrong with her?" Nicolai fidgeted. "Why does she keep moving? Why does she not stop?"

"It will be reactions to liquid and bullet in body," Yuri replied.

Natasha slowed down. Her head stopped, her body stopped, only her right foot twitched and kept twitching.

Alexander tapped it with his own foot. "Freaky."

Finally, she lay still, and all five men gathered around for one last look.

"What now?" Nicolai asked.

"We leave," Boris replied.

"And the body?" Nicolai added as they shuffled for the door.

Yuri waved a hand. "Grigor's henchmen will do their job. They take care of it."

"Like every other time," Alexander said.

"Like every other time," Yuri agreed.

One by one they filed out through the doorway; each looked left and right then continued on their way down the hall. Nicolai brought up the rear, pulling the door shut behind him, but not before one last look at the body on the floor.

*****

The next day, I gathered the guests at the breakfast table. "The plane is being prepared for your journey. You'll leave in about an hour, and it will be a four or five hour flight. So feel free to use the inflight entertainment units. Dimitri, Sergei and Vladimir will be flying back with you to make sure you arrive safely." I pointed to the three of them standing nearby. "And your money will be in your accounts in two days to spend how you wish. Any questions?"

"How come we're being sent home?" Mark piped up from his position at the table.

"Because you need to be," I replied. "I told you yesterday things have changed and it's time you left." I checked my watch. "I'll head over with you in about half an hour. Enjoy your breakfast." I left Chris with the others to have breakfast and heard them talking as I motioned Dimitri and his men to follow me into the kitchen. "Can you see if the weather's going to be good for the flight today? I don't want you guys having trouble on the way back." I took a plate of hot steaming eggs Jenny handed to me and sat at the kitchen's island bench.

"I will do that after breakfast," Dimitri said, accepting his own plate of food. Sergei and Vladimir followed suit, sitting at the bench to eat.

I stopped shovelling food into my mouth when I saw them sit. "You haven't eaten yet?"

"No, Alexi."

"Oh," I shrugged, "okay."

"Alex," Jenny said, sitting down with her own plate of food. "What's going on?"

"What do you mean?" I was starving and shovelling eggs as fast as I could into my open and very willing mouth.

"Well," she sipped some juice, "you're sending the guests home today, a week early. Will there be more or is that it? We've all been talking, and we think not *only* is something strange going on, but you're going to shut up shop and move on, leaving us without jobs," another sip, "and money."

My mouth stopped chewing and I looked up. *Do I tell her?* I swallowed. "Um." I cleared my throat, sculled down my juice and cleared my throat again. "Things *are* changing," I told Jenny. "But don't worry. There's always a plan ready to go, and you guys will not be without jobs or money."

She sighed. "Oh, good. We were all worried."

"No need to be." I finished off the last of my eggs

and checked my watch. "Good breakfast as always. I need to see John about something. I'll be back in twenty." I rushed out of the kitchen, down the hall, and into the office. "John?"

"Yeah." Bang.

I frowned. "Ah…there you are."

He retreated from under the table rubbing his head.

"Oooh, that hurt?"

"Just a bit."

"Mmm, well, have you got anything else for me?"

"Yes." He grabbed a folder from his outbox, still rubbing his head. "And that's all I could find. Nothing else, it's all dug up, every little megabyte and terabyte of the internet has been thoroughly searched and printed. There is *nothing* else."

"Thank you, John." I took them, raced up to my room, and laid the papers on the bed. "Yes," I hissed, seeing what was there. "The last piece of the puzzle." I gathered them together and went into the closet, trying to remember where I'd stashed the others. I found them under a pile of clothes and crouched on the floor to lay them all out before realising they were messed up and crumpled.

"What the hell?" I moved the papers around. Definitely out of order, and why are some of them creased? Didn't I set them up nice and neat? I racked my brain trying to remember as I hadn't looked at them in days. My head thumped. That bloody jackhammer was pounding away at my sanity. "I know I did *not* leave them like this. I know I didn't." I quickly grabbed a stapler from my desk drawer and placed every single sheet of paper back in order, stapling each section together. There were at least a hundred pages now, and the folder was overflowing.

"Alex?"

I froze in fear, then quickly stood and jammed the folder back under my clothes, neatening them up, blood whizzing through my body, through my ears, and over my eyes. My vision blurred.

"Alex?"

The door opened.

"Here." I rubbed my eyes and walked into the bedroom to find Chris.

"Hey, it's time to go." He saw me. "You okay?"

"Ugh. Blurry vision, pounding head, the usual." I stopped rubbing and waited for the spots to leave my vision and my eyes to clear.

"You okay?" He moved to me and rubbed my shoulders, hoping it would help ease the pain.

I blinked a few times. "Um, yeah, will be." I smiled and kissed him. "You coming?"

He shook his head. "I thought I might head into the playroom and use the net. Check up on the family, see if they're missing me."

"Okay, I'll see you later then." Another kiss.

"How about lunch, on the porch, at twelve thirty?" He wrapped his arms around me.

"Okay." Another kiss, a kiss that deepened. Passionate and desirable, hot and alive, full of want and need, power and strength.

I reluctantly pulled away, breathless. "Wow… okay…wow…must…go." I weaved my way to the door.

"Wow, see you at lunch, porch, twelve-thirty…don't be late," I called before closing the door behind me.

"Same for you," he called back, his gaze swinging around from the closed door to the closet. He waited sixty seconds before walking to the door and silently opening it to see if Alex was gone before closing and locking it. He turned. "Now, time to check those papers."

Chapter 14

I ran down the stairs and into the breakfast room. "Ready to go?"

A chorus of yesses sailed into my ears as Todd, Andrew and Mark rose from the table.

"Okay, I guess you don't have luggage since you didn't come with any, and you've got your own clothes on, so let's go." I led them out the front door where two golf carts were waiting. "Hop on board gentlemen, and we shall go."

The three of them climbed onto the first one which Sergei was driving, and Vladimir and I hopped on the second one with Dimitri behind the wheel.

"And away," I called.

*****

Chris watched Alex and the others drive off through a slit in the bedroom curtains. "Now, I won't be disturbed." He headed into the dressing room and looked for the folder, finding it thicker than the last time. "Heavy." He sat on the bed, ready to see what secrets Alex had been hiding from him. Taking a deep breath, he opened the file and picked up the first stack of papers that was now strangely stapled together.

"Alexi," Dimitri said as he drove around to the airport. "Is this what you want?"

"Yes, Dimitri, it's time." I breathed in the salty sea air, and a pounding started in my temple. I rubbed it and stretched my neck, hoping to get rid of it.

"Headache?"

I sighed, and even though I had sunglasses on, I squinted. "When *don't* I have one? It seems I've had a permanent one for seven years now, and it's *not* going away."

We rounded a corner and neared the airstrip.

"Will it be gone soon, Alexi?"

"I hope so, Dimitri." I looked at him. "I hope so."

*****

"What's this…? I can't read…" Chris mumbled, leafing through the first few pages. "Mmm, is this Russian? Could be Russian." He turned a page. "Ah, here it is in English. Looks like the same article." He flipped between the pages. "Yep, same article." He began reading.

Police today found the body of billionaire, Alexander Von Blon, stabbed to death in his home office. Police could not find evidence of an intruder, so suspect Mister Von Blon had let the person in. There seemed to be nothing missing, although Mister Von Blon's wife could not tell. There were no missing artworks or displays, and the billionaire's safe was not cracked. The mad attack came only days after his niece, Natasha Von Blon, had been viciously stabbed in a robbery gone wrong. Miss Von Blon had been out partying and drinking, and when she did not return home when expected, Mister Von Blon reported her missing. Police found her body in a dark alley, her clothes and bag were gone, and she was stabbed and bleeding, but still alive. She was recovering in the hospital at the time of her uncle's attack, and so had not been home when it happened. She has lived with her aunt and uncle since she was a child.'*

Chris flicked through stories about the niece's attack. "Vicious," he mumbled before laying it down. "But what's this got to do with Alex, though?"

*****

We arrived at the hangar and disembarked. "Okay, everyone, ready to go." I herded our guests up the plane stairs and turned to Dimitri. "Hope everything goes well, and you get back tonight. I have a feeling it won't be much longer." I stepped aside for Sergei and Vladimir to enter the plane.

Dimitri watched me. "Alexi?"

I looked back. "Dimitri."

"Take care of yourself." He enveloped me in a big bear hug and didn't want to let go.

"I'll try," I mumbled into his leather clad chest before pulling out of his embrace and walking over to the side where I watched him wave goodbye. Watched the stairs be rolled away. Watched the plane close up and taxi to the end of the runway. I rubbed my head and tried to block out the noise which made my ears bleed and my head pound.

I watched the plane take speed and lift off into the air. I watched until they were in the distance and all was quiet. I took a deep breath, but all I smelt was petrol fumes. I needed peace and quiet, and I needed it now.

*****

Chris picked up the next batch of papers. It was the same as the last, full of Russian. Flicking through, he came to the English versions.

'Police today found the body of Russian billionaire, Nicolai Matuschewski, shot and dead in his home office. They suspect a mob hit as they could not find any evidence of foul play, a robbery, or break and enter. It is possible he let his killer in unsuspectingly before being gunned down execution style. Police have found no weapon or evidence to point to anyone in particular and will be questioning his family, friends and employees. The eighty-two-year-old made his money throughout Russia and owned the largest drilling company in the European continent. His empire now goes to his only child, a daughter, Natasha Marioffski, who will consider selling off her father's company as she no longer lives in Russia. She had come to visit with him for his eighty-second birthday last month and stayed to have business dealings with the company. Police do not consider her a suspect as

she was in the hospital at the time of her father's death. She had been the victim of a robbery gone wrong and had been shot. She is doing as well as can be expected and will recover.'

He took a deep breath and flicked through the stapled papers. "Both say the same thing. Billionaire, businessman, leader of many charities and groups, wow, I, wow," he muttered, shaking his head. "Wait, what date was that, mmm?" Checking with the previous story, he set the paper aside. "One week after Alexander Von Blon and two days after the attack on his daughter. Russia's clearly full of hit men."

*****

I slowly walked around the island, but it didn't do my headache any good, so I headed in to see Mark. "I have a migraine that has *not* gone away," I complained.

"On the bed." He got up from his chair as I lay on the bed.

"You're our chiropractor, crack me."

"I need to do more than that," he said, putting bolsters under my hips. "One leg is shorter than the other. Lie there for a few minutes and then I'll get on with it."

I sighed. My cheeks were squashed in the face hole of the chiropractic bed and all mooshed together. I heard Mark on his computer and felt the pounding jackhammer in the back of my head. I sighed again and felt my neck stiffen. *God, how stressed am I?* Constant migraines, stiff neck. Not even sex helps! "Hurry up," I mumbled a few minutes later. "My head is pounding."

"All right, all right." He removed the bolsters and set to work pushing me back in from the lumbar up. My neck cracked and creaked before he was finished, and I finally got up from the bed.

"Take a walk and don't sit. If you still have pain, come back."

I sighed for a third time. "What's the point in paying you if you can't fix my pain?"

He smiled. "Because your pain may not be caused by the problems in your neck. I fix those, but are you fixing your emotional pain?"

I stared at him as my heart raced. *What does he know about my emotional pain? He wouldn't know anything, how could he possibly know?*

"It may not just be physical, you know?" He opened the door and held it open while talking. "Maybe it's time to fix everything else? Everything I can't."

"Mmm," I mumbled and went off for another walk.

*****

"Okay, lucky number three," Chris said picking up another batch of papers. They were the same as the last, Russian versions on top of the English versions.

'Billionaire, Yuri Putin, was found bashed to death in his home office overnight by his maid. She had been taking Mister Putin his nightcap when she found him sprawled on the floor of his office, bloody and dead. Her screams brought the rest of his staff, including Mister Putin's valet, who rang the police. There was

no sign of a break in, robbery or intruder, and no weapon found. Mister Putin's sons were out of town, and his wife was in the hospital after being bashed in a robbery gone wrong. Natasha Putin had been coming home from one of her many charity dinners when the car was hijacked, and her driver shot. She was dragged from the car and severely beaten. Mrs Putin will remain in the hospital for some time, and police have no other suspects. This is the third billionaire to die in as many weeks, and the third relative to receive a less severe version of the crime. Sixty-eight-year-old, Yuri Putin, will be laid to rest next week by his sons, who now take control of the business.'

"Third billionaire in as many weeks," Chris repeated, comparing details with the first two victims. "Female relative called Natasha, assaulted two days before they are killed. No intruder, no burglary, no nothing. Just dead billionaires. Three dead billionaires." He read the articles concerning the wife before putting the stack aside.

*****

I walked around the island again thinking about what Mark had said. *I know he's right; I do need to sort out my emotional life because it's a bloody shambles.* I rubbed the back of my neck. It still ached. Still pounded. A pounding I'd experienced for seven long years. *Seven long years too many.*

I found myself at the cove and lay down on a lounge. Admitting the truth would be a good start, especially with Chris. But then he's got his own truth to admit, and nothing can happen until he does and that could be God knows when. If he can't admit and reveal it, then I can't get on with my life, and I need to do that. Mark's right, my headaches are caused by my emotional issues, and I need to get rid of them.

I breathed deeply, hoping to blow out some of the cobwebs in my brain. In…and out…in…and out. My eyes were closed against the warmth of the tropical sun. The breeze skipped along my bare arms and legs as it made its way along the shore. Waves crashed gently against the breach in the cove, and that damn jackhammer kept pounding in my head.

I tensed and released every muscle in my legs, every muscle in my arms, every muscle in my back. I stretched my legs, my arms above my head, I arched my back and gently stretched my head left and right, forward and backwards. The pounding persisted.

"Ah, damn it." I thrust my feet into the sand and stomped off to the water.

*****

Chris leafed through batch number four, staring at the photos of Victor Oblonsky and his sister, Natasha Oblonsky, who had almost died from alcohol poisoning after ingesting several bottles in only a few hours. Her friends called paramedics who rushed her to the hospital where Ms Oblonsky remained in a coma. Chris flipped the page and saw a headline for Victor.

'Victor Oblonsky, the seventy-year-old vodka

magnate, was found dead in his home office. Police were unsure of the cause of death until the laboratory claimed it was death by drowning. Mister Oblonsky died from drowning in his own vodka. He had started the brand, Victo Vodka, at just twenty years of age. He'd become a millionaire by twenty-one and a billionaire by forty. Police are yet to determine whether there were any visitors to the mansion, as there was a crate of Victo Vodka on Mister Oblonsky's desk, and several bottles were broken on the floor. Mister Oblonsky is the fourth billionaire in as many weeks to die, and a relative receive the same treatment just two days beforehand. Ms Oblonsky is president of her brother's company and has no children. Mister Oblonsky leaves a wife and three sons.'

"Another Russian billionaire, another relative named Natasha," Chris mused. "Why do I see a pattern forming?" He added it to the pile.

*****

I knifed through the water and swam the length of the cove, then turned around and swam back, all the while hoping whatever pressure the water was creating would somehow counteract the pressure in my head. I don't know how many laps I did to make the pressure lessen, but I walked out of the water feeling okay. I brushed off the excess and slowly trekked back up to the lounge chair. I sat down, stretched out, and pain exploded in my head.

"Ah, damn it," I yelled, quickly sitting up and

rubbing my head. "You need to get out of my head, you need to get out of my head, *you need to get out of my bloody head.*" I hurried back to Mark's office. "Help me," I wailed. "My head is *killing* me." I stood dripping as he handed me a towel and then checked my alignment.

"Hips fine, back fine, neck fine." He massaged the base of my skull. "Uh, huh, yeah, there. Back on the bed."

I jumped on face down, and he pushed my skull off my neck.

"That should help. Go get yourself a massage and seriously think about what I said before," he told me as I stood. "Maybe it's time you get off this island." His concern was all over his face.

The pain was abating in strength and ferocity, and I sighed with some relief. "I know. I'm trying, *believe me*, I'm trying."

*****

"Mmm, second last one," Chris said, pulling another stack of papers from the pile.

'Boris Yeltonson was found dead in his home office last night, possibly from electrocution. The maid claimed the lights flickered then went out, and moments later the backup generator powered to life and lit up the house again. She went to check on Mister Yeltonson, only to find him sprawled on the floor with his desk lamp broken and lying beside him. She rang the police and they found no hints of an

intruder, break in, or robbery, and so put it down to accidental electrocution. The seventy-two-year old's wife, two daughters, and two sons-in-law were not home at the time, and Mister Yeltonson's mother, Natasha Yeltonson, was in the hospital recovering from her own electrocution two days beforehand. The police believe faulty wiring in the house is to blame for both incidents and do not believe it is related to the other billionaire deaths. His daughters will take over his export company with their mother.'

Chris laid the papers down and thought about all he'd read. Clearly suspicious, clearly someone intent on killing off Russian billionaires. He rummaged in the bedside cupboard for the notebook and pen Alex kept there. Turning to a clean page, he wrote the words, *billionaire, dead in office, relative named Natasha, same assault, but ending in death. Coincidence? Mob hit? Billionaire killer?* He sighed. *What has this even got to do with me? What has this got to do with Alex?* His train of thought changed track. *Has this got to do with the woman upstairs? Is it all about her? What do they call her, the Queen? Hasn't Alex called her Natasha? Is she royalty? Does she have something to do with all of these men? These murders? They* cannot *be accidents. All in their home offices, their relative meeting the same fate only two days before. All billionaires dying on Sunday night. Does she have something to do with this and Alex is involved because she's her assistant, or is she* actually one of the Natashas *I've just read about?*

He ran his hand through his hair and sighed deeply.

Does Alex have anything to do with this and how is she involved? Is she even involved? Oh, God, I hope not. I hope she's not involved in any way because I don't know what I'd do about it. I love her. I want to spend the rest of my life with her. But if she's a killer, or involved with one, what the hell do I do?

He sighed again and looked down at the list in the notebook before writing one last word at the end with a question mark.

Alex?

*****

I trooped into the spa and threw myself down on Owen's massage table. "I've seen Mark, now give me a massage, my head is killing me, and I'm sick of the pain."

"You might want to take your clothes off first."

I raised my head to see him standing in front of me, arms crossed. "You just want me naked so you can do what you want with me, you bad boy," I retorted and got a smirk as my reward. I sighed and exerted what little energy I had left by getting up and undressing behind a screen. I wrapped a towel around me and lay back on the table.

Owen's hands were magic. They poked and pried and rubbed and tried their damnedest to ease my migraine. He put hot rocks on my back, tried cupping, acupuncture, all kinds of alternative ways.

An hour later, I rose from the table feeling refreshed and like jello, but there was still that incessant pounding at the base of my skull and around my left eyeball. It wasn't as bad as before, but still there nonetheless. I wobbled my way into the shower and stood under the pulsating water, using only the best body wash and shampoo. I luxuriated in my surroundings. I was lucky enough to be living on a tropical island, in an amazing mansion, with everything provided for, and yet, I was stressed, lonely, alone and single, with a bloody constantly pounding jackhammer of a headache.

I sighed, rinsed off, and towelled down, thinking about Chris and the way his body moved with mine during lovemaking. I smiled at the image, the heat searing through my loins. No other man had ever done that. No other man had ever made me feel this way. Like I was the best lover. The *only* lover. The *only* woman he would ever want.

My skin sizzled at the thought of his against mine, my hands remembered how they felt in his, my tongue tasted him, wanted him, and my vagina ached for his penis, and my body wanted him now.

"Thinking about someone special are we?" Marissa asked, coming in to see where I was.

My eyes slowly opened and my hands wrapped my towel tighter around me.

"That smile says it all. The hot spunky blond. We've all noticed, you know."

My smile widened, and I felt myself blush.

"Oooh, you're blushing." She held out a fluffy robe and helped me into it.

"Well…"

"Well," she replied. "I don't think any of us have ever seen you so happy, let alone *this* happy. And we've all worked together from the beginning."

I tied the strap on my robe. "Yeah," I sighed. "I am happy, and yes it's Chris that's done it. Speaking of, I'm off to find him. Bye!"

*****

Chris ripped the paper from the notebook and replaced it in the bedside drawer. Could Alex be involved somehow? He set the notepaper aside and picked up the last stack of stapled paper. Flicking through to the English version, he came across a photo of a man and woman and froze.

The face was instantly recognisable.

The features he would never forget.

The face he saw every single night when he closed his eyes.

The face he would never forget.

The face he would forever see until the day he died.

The face he would never forget.

His breath barely escaped from his throat.

"Oh, God..." He stared at the photo. "That's him. That's the man. That's the man I killed."

Chapter 15

"Chris?"

His head flew up, and he quickly gathered the papers and rushed into the dressing room, wrapping them in their folder, and tucking it away where he'd found it. "Shit, the door's locked." He raced to the door, unlocked it, and managed to rush into the bathroom seconds before Alex entered.

"Chris, you here?" I called and heard the toilet flush.

"Yeah," he replied, entering the bedroom.

"Bed, now," I ordered, ripping off my towel and robe. I threw myself at him just as he got to the bed and we landed in a mash of mouths.

"Whoa, what?"

"Sex, now."

"Okay, um, what about lunch?" He pushed me away.

"Stuff lunch, horny, now."

"Ah, okay then."

I helped him pull his shirt and shorts off and barely pulled his jocks down before I mounted him. "Oh,

God." I bounced up and down. "Oh, God, oh, God, oh, God." I moved harder, faster, up and down. I was grabbed and rolled over, Chris now on top of me.

We were sprawled on the bed sideways, but it didn't matter.

"Oh, God, oh, God, oh, God, oh, God, oh, God," I groaned as he thrust back and forth. I wrapped my legs high around him making myself available for him to do his job. I clung to him. "Oh, God, oh, God, oh, God." I felt it coming. That wonderful, amazing build-up of power and strength, of electricity and fire, of passion and desire. "Oh, God." It surged. "Oh, God." It flowed. "Oh, my fucking God." It came.

We moved back and forth as one. A cradle rocking in a swift motion as it slowly winds down until it comes to a stop. We ground to a halt as one, exhausted, hearts pounding, breath panting.

Chris collapsed on top of me, gasping for air. "What…bloody…hell…"

"Oh, God," I managed, my legs slowly falling to a place on the bed. "Oh, God."

"What was…that?" He shifted slightly.

"That," gasping, "was me," gasping, "wanting you," gasping.

"Well, you certainly wanted me bad." He nuzzled my neck as his hand casually found my breast, his fingers leaving gentle trails of burning fire.

My hand covered his. "Oh, I did," I breathed. "I saw the chiro," breath, "then had a massage," breath, "then a steaming shower," breath, "and I was thinking about you," breath, "and everything you do to me," breath, "I was horny," breath, "and wanted you."

"I want you, too." He kissed my cheek and stroked my hair, wondering if this was the real Alex. If the woman he'd just fucked so magnificently was caught up in some Russian billionaire mob killing.

A killer?

A murderer?

A psycho?

I sighed. My heart was back to its normal rate, and I shifted my head so I could look at him. "I love you." I waited, and got a smile, smiling in return. "I haven't loved many men in my life, and I *mean really* loved." I reached up and stroked his smooth, silky cheek. "But, I love you. This is different, real, all-consuming. I see myself spending the rest of my life with you." I kissed him, "having babies with you," another kiss, "growing old with you," the kiss was long, "I want to be with you...forever." I gazed into his eyes and hoped he felt the same way. So much had happened in the three weeks he'd been there, and I hoped it was going to be for the best.

His lips curled into a grin, and it reached his eyes. "I love you, too." He kissed me, "and I haven't loved many women either," kiss, "but I love you, and this is different," kiss, "all-consuming," kiss, "and I definitely see myself spending the rest of my life with you," kiss, "having babies with you," kiss, "growing old with you," kiss, "I want to be with you...forever." He gazed into my eyes and lay fully on me, lunch long forgotten as we made long slow passionate love in the heat of the afternoon.

*****

Chris jolted awake with a start. The picture of the man and his wife and all the other billionaires had been floating through his head.

I stirred. "Hey," I croaked then coughed. "Mmm, dry, need something to drink." Chris shifted and rolled off, leaving me lonely and cold without him.

He sat up and checked the clock then fell back on the bed. "Three o'clock. Can we order something, or do we need to go downstairs?"

I stretched, and he made a grab for my uncovered breast. "Hey." I swatted his hands away. "I'll call Jenny for something, and we can have a quick shower before she gets here." I crawled over his lean muscular body to get to the phone and ordered chicken salads and sodas. "Okay, she's on her way, let's have a quick shower." I almost fell off the bed my body was so relaxed, but I caught the side cupboard, and Chris grabbed me from behind.

"You right?" He slid his legs between mine as I straightened and his tongue left a trail up my spine as he stood. He nuzzled my neck gently and breathed in my womanly scent.

I smiled and leaned back into him. "Mmm, yeah, I'm, just very relaxed. Come on, let's shower." I tried to be quick, but showering with Chris was not an easy task. We managed to get out and get robes on as Jenny wheeled the food trolley into the room.

"Ready for a late lunch," she called.

We walked into the room to see huge plates of

thick chicken salad, beer steins of icy cold soda, and huge slices of chocolate cake for dessert on the table by the balcony doors.

"Mmm, yum." I grabbed a stein and sculled back the Pepsi Max floating around in it. "Good," I gasped, "cold." I sighed. "Thanks, Jenny, we'll leave it outside when we're done." I smiled and waited for her to leave before sitting down and digging into my salad.

Chris followed suit and watched me while I ate. *Are you a Russian spy?* he wondered. *Hiding from the Russian authorities for killing five Russian billionaires?* He munched on his salad and took a swig of drink. *Are you on the run? On the run and hiding out with your boss? And where is she?* Who *is she? Did she have something to do with it? The killings of the five Russian billionaires. Did you do it together? Did you do it for each other?* He watched me over his glass as I chowed down on salad, munching away as if my life depended on it. *Does your life depend on it, Alex? Does it depend on being here, hiding out from the Kremlin? From the families of those men? Those men you may have killed?* He picked up his fork and ate some chicken, thinking about all he'd read.

"Mmm, not hungry?" I had almost finished my salad, but Chris had barely touched his. "Not hungry?" I repeated when he didn't answer.

"Huh," he came to, "sorry, what?"

I nodded at his salad. "Aren't you hungry? You've barely touched it." I got stuck into the rest of mine and noticed he took a while to answer.

He looked down at his food and picked up his

glass. "More thirsty than hungry." He drank. The coldness numbed his throat and brain against the thoughts that kept floating around, threatening to spill out of his mouth into words he may regret. "I see you were hungry."

I finished off the last of my salad. "Starving. Hadn't eaten since breakfast, and I worked up an appetite with two walks, a swim, and an hour on the massage table. And then, of course," I wiggled my brows, "there was our afternoon activity."

A grin spread across his luscious lips. "Ah, yeah, our afternoon activity. We're certainly doing that a lot. Our new favourite pastime I guess you could say."

"Well, it's not like there's much else to do on this bloody island." I reached for the biggest slice of cake. Three decadent layers of the softest, fluffiest, chocolate sponge cake with jam filling and chocolate cream topping whipped till it was light and fluffy. Fresh sliced strawberries topped it off.

"True," he muttered. "True." He ate the rest of his salad in silence while watching me devour the huge slice of cake. *Why does she have details on the man I killed? Does she know him? Did she know him? Does she know I killed him? Is that why I'm here? She knows I killed him.* "Are you going to eat your cake?" cut into his train of thought. "What?" his gaze focussed on Alex who'd polished off her cake and was holding the other slice.

"Are you going to eat your cake?" I asked again, wondering where he kept disappearing to as he ate, or rather, didn't eat.

Chris looked at it, felt sick, and shook his blond head. "You have it if you can find room for it."

"I always find room for it." I put the plate down and picked up my fork. I was finished just as he polished off his salad. "Geez, you really weren't hungry, were you?" I watched him drain the last of his cola.

"Told you." He replaced the stein on the table. "Thirsty, not hungry."

"Well *I*," I rubbed my stomach, "am full." I finished off the last of my drink and placed everything back on the trolley. "Do you want to lie around, or go for a walk? Lie by the pool, go to the cove?" I pushed the trolley into the hallway and closed the door.

"I don't know," his voice faded off, "don't care..." He stared out across the ocean as he leant back in his seat, hands behind his head.

I sat back down and squeezed his leg. "Are you okay? You've been a little weird all through lunch. Are you sick? We have a doctor on staff as you know."

He was quiet. "No, I'm not."

"Then what is it?"

He turned his head to stare into her big green eyes and wondered what lay behind them. A killer? A wife, a daughter? A murdering psycho that the Russian police were after?

He blinked.

I blinked.

He stared.

I stared.

"*What is wrong?*" I asked, shaking my head

slightly, perturbed by the weirdness.

He finally shook his own head and stood. "Nothing. I'm gonna get dressed and go for a walk." He went into the dressing room and grabbed some clothes.

I bit my lip and felt tears spring to my eyes from the tone of the moment. "Want me to come?" I managed to call out.

He walked toward the door without looking at me. "No. I need time on my own." The door opened and closed and he was gone.

Behind a closed door that I sat staring at, tears welling in my eyes, threatening to fall until they did. I sat there crying, not sure what for, but the pain that struck my heart was terrifying. Not an hour or two before he was telling me he loved me and wanted to spend the rest of his life with me, and now he was shutting me out. Cutting me off, keeping me out of things.

I took a deep breath, wiped away my tears, and grabbed a tissue from the box on the bedside cupboard. I blew my nose, sat on the bed, and pulled my notebook out from the drawer. I clicked on my pen and opened the book. A small white thing fell from it. I picked it up and realised it was a small piece of paper from the spiral. Like a page had been ripped out, but a bit had stuck in the roll. That's funny, I haven't pulled any out lately. I tilted the book back and forth and noticed indentations. Grabbing a lead pencil from the drawer, I lightly rubbed it back and forth over the page to reveal words that had been written on the piece ripped out.

Billionaire. Dead in office. Relative named Natasha. Same assault, but ending in death. Coincidence? Mob hit? Billionaire killer?

I finished rubbing lead across the page and saw one last word with a question mark.

Alex?

My eyes looked up from the book to the dressing room.

I knew what that meant.

*****

Chris walked the entire round trip of the island and landed back at the cove. Settling in to a large chair on the sand, he sighed and closed his eyes against the lowering rays of the afternoon sun.

Is she a killer? God, is she? If she is, what the hell am I going to do?

She's too young.

You don't know her age.

She can't be the killer.

Why not?

Because she just couldn't be.

Because I am?

What?

I am a killer. *I* killed him.

Chapter 16

He'd picked up the last stack of papers, flipped through to the English version, and saw a face he thought he'd never see again.

The face of the man who'd died by his hand.

His hand killed the man in the photo, and now it was as fresh as it had been seven years ago.

Seven long years ago that he killed the man in the photo.

The man who stood next to his beautiful Russian wife.

He read the text.

'Russian billionaire, Grigor Yurogovnia and his beautiful wife, Natasha, photographed at a charity event for sick children six weeks before his untimely death. Natasha Yurogovnia looked resplendent in a royal blue taffeta gown, close fitting with a deep v and high split. Grigor Yurogovnia cut a fine form in his tuxedo and bowtie. The fifty-one-year-old billionaire was run down on Sunday. Unfortunately, Mrs Yurogovnia was not in the country at the time of her husband's death, so his assistant made funeral arrangements. He is the sixth

Russian billionaire to be killed in as many weeks.'

Chris came to, memories of that fateful night still too fresh in his mind. Trying to repress them all, he stripped off his clothes and ran for the water.

*****

I ripped out the page from my notebook.

I knew what it meant.

I knew *exactly* what it meant.

I placed the book, pen, and pencil back in the drawer, and then flushed the paper down the toilet. In the dressing room, I pulled the folder out of its hidey - hole and opened it to the stack of papers about Grigor and Natasha Yurogovnia.

Oh, I knew *exactly* what it meant, all right.

It meant the end of days was coming.

*****

Chris swam a few laps of the cove before floating on his back. He stared up into the changing sky, trying to get his mind to think about something else.

Alex, think about Alex.

What about Alex?

Is she a Russian murderer?

She can't be; she has an Aussie accent.

Doesn't mean she's not Russian and learned to speak English.

You're kidding, right?

No.

What the hell is wrong with you?

I…

You love her, don't you?

I…

You want to spend the rest of your life with her, don't you?

I…

Well, get your bloody shit together then and do something about it. Your time here is nearly over, and you need to do something about it. Now.

What do I do?

Tell her.

Tell her what?

Tell her what happened.

Are you crazy?

No.

Why the hell would I tell her?

Because only the truth can set you all free.

*****

I threw on some clothes and grabbed the folder. There was someone I needed to see, and I needed to see her *now*. I climbed the stairs to the third floor and entered the sacred boudoir. I found her at her dressing table brushing her hair. "He knows."

"He *who* knows *what*, Alexi?"

"*He* knows *we* know *what* he did."

She sighed and stopped brushing. "Stop playing games, Alexi, my head hurts."

"He found this folder." I slapped it down in front of

her. "And he read every single word. He *knows* what happened. *He knows* what he did."

She looked at my reflection. "Now, all *we* need is for *him* to admit it." She flipped the folder open and glanced at what I had placed first on the pile. Her face twitched. "He read it all?"

"I have no doubt he read *every single word.*"

She pulled open her drawer, removed the pearl-handled gun, plus a box of bullets, and placed them on the table. "We need to be ready, Alexi. Ready, for *anything.*"

"I don't think we need *that.*" I reached for them.

She waved me away. "Maybe, maybe not. But it is best to be prepared. How much longer do we have to wait?"

My hand retreated. "Not long now, Natasha, not long now."

She cocked her head. "Weeks, days, months?"

I stood there. "I have a feeling it will only be hours, if not a day or two."

She glanced down at the folder. "That soon?"

I glanced at the folder as well. "That soon."

"That is good, Alexi. Not much longer now. Not much longer and we will have what we want. We will finally be free of the hold he has on us...the hold he has...we will be free from the torture and the pain... the heartache and the terror..."

"The migraines," I added.

"Yes, the migraines. We will be free from the pain of the last seven years. The torture will soon be over, and we will be free to live a normal life once again."

She loaded the gun, bullet by bullet, and placed it back in the drawer. "We will soon be free, Alexi."

I worried and frowned at her actions, but didn't mention it. "Yes, Natasha, we will."

Later, I welcomed Dimitri, Sergei and Vladimir back after landing and entering the house as the last rays of the sun dipped below the horizon. "Trip go well?"

"As well as can be expected," Dimitri replied.

I cracked open bottles of their favourite Russian beer and handed them over. "Weather fine? Flight fine? *Guests* fine?"

Dimitri swallowed half a bottle of ice-cold liquid gold and sighed in contentment. "Weather fine, flight fine, *guests* safely back in homes and brainwashed with what would happen if they talk." He finished off his beer, and Sergei and Vladimir followed suit.

"Good." I sighed and deflated. "Good." Time on the island was coming to an end, I could feel it. Soon things would start wrapping up and be over and done with. I collapsed onto a kitchen stool and rested my elbows on the bench before laying my head in my hands.

Dimitri noticed my demeanour change and waved the others away, waiting until they left the room. "Alexi?"

I sighed again and swivelled my head to look at him through tired, hooded eyes. "Mmm?"

He reached out and stroked my head. "Alexi, when will it be over?"

I sighed a third time. "Tonight, tomorrow? I'm not exactly sure, but soon. I'm hoping tonight if I can push it to happen."

His fingers gently moved through my hair. "Is it close? Close enough for you to do that?"

Another sigh as I relaxed at Dimitri's touch. "I hope so. *He* knows things. *I* know things. I hope I can push him to get an answer. To *finally* tell the truth."

He leaned in and kissed my forehead. "And what is truth anymore, Alexi?"

My smile was minuscule. "I don't know anymore, Dimitri, I just don't know."

That night, I wandered aimlessly through the house.

I didn't know where Chris was, and for all I knew, he could have gone to bed ages ago.

I heard the mantel clock in the office.

Nine p.m.

Its chimes echoed lightly around the room.

So did I.

I ambled along in a dream, a fog, a haze, not thinking, not seeing, not hearing or feeling.

I floated along the hallway into the foyer and stopped.

I felt dizzy and sick to my stomach, not sure if I was going to throw up or not.

I rubbed my head, my eyes, trying to stop the pounding and blurriness. I could barely see; the light was so dim.

I took a deep breath and tried to move.

Another breath.

One foot in front of the other.

Another breath.

One foot on the bottom step.

Another breath.

The other foot on the second step.

And before I knew it, I'd reached the top of the house.

The dreaded third floor.

*****

The body of Natasha Yurogovnia lay motionless, unmoving, dead on the floor.

Well…almost.

Her mind wandered aimlessly through the haze.

She didn't know where Grigor was, and for all she knew, he'd gone to bed ages ago.

She heard the mantel clock in her husband's office.

Nine p.m.

Its chimes echoed lightly around the room.

So did she.

She ambled along in a dream, a fog, a haze, not thinking, not seeing, not hearing or feeling.

She felt dizzy and sick to her stomach, not sure if she was going to throw up or not.

She tried to rub her head, her eyes, tried to stop the pounding and blurriness, she could barely see the light was so dim.

She took a deep breath and tried to move.

There was a sound.

The sound of a doorknob turning.

*****

I drifted into the bedroom and wanted to lie down. I

stood staring at the bed, for how long I don't know. Wanted to lay down to rest, to let all of the pain go away.

"Alexi…" drifted in from the bathroom.

My head twitched in its zombie state, and I made a zombie growl, shifting my zombie self toward the sound and ambled along in my zombie walk.

"Alexi…"

"Grrr…"

"Alexi…" Natasha stared back at me in the mirror.

"Grrr…" I swayed on my feet.

"Alexi! You need to snap out of it." Her voice was barely loud enough for me to hear. "You need to snap out of it and get this over and done with. You need to make this stop, Alexi. This needs to stop."

"Grrr…" I swayed. "Natasha…" I slurred, "make stop…" I turned and threw up into the sink. My last meal came up, and I turned the tap on to wash it away before washing my face and mouth out. I grabbed a towel and dried myself, my eyes focussing on our images in the mirror.

"You need to stop this, Alexi."

I sighed. "I know. I know it needs to stop."

"Tonight, Alexi."

"Tonight, Natasha."

I wearily stumbled out of the room and across to the stairs.

I swayed, I grabbed the bannister, my right foot went down.

I swayed, I lost my grip on the bannister, my right foot flew out from under me.

I swayed, I turned, I rolled down the stairs to the second floor.

"Alex," Chris yelled, coming along the hallway and seeing me fly off the stairs onto the landing. He flew to my side. "Alex. Alex, talk to me." He slapped my face. "Alex? I need help here," he yelled and picked me up before starting down the stairs to the first floor. "I need help. Help me." He reached the first floor landing and saw several men staring up at him, launching into action when they saw him carrying me.

"What happened," Dimitri thundered, flying up the stairs to meet him as he was coming down.

"She fell down the stairs from the third floor. I saw her land." Everyone herded me around to the medical rooms and laid me on the table.

"I need x-rays and scans, blood pressure and a vial of blood for analysis, stat," Doctor Dan said, taking charge.

Dimitri turned to Chris. "What happened?" he asked again.

"I don't know." He stared back. "I only saw her fly off the stairs and land."

"And what were you doing up at that hour?"

Chris frowned and sneered. "*What* hour? It's only nine-thirty, and *I* was looking for *her*." He turned his attention back to Alex, watching as the doctor and nurse examined her. "Is she okay?" He craned his neck to see her face looking pale.

"Blood pressure low, no response. Alex, can you hear me? Alex?" Dan waited for a response. "Get me some smelling salts, and we'll get her ready for x-rays."

"Doctor." Caitlin fetched the salts, broke open a

capsule, and waved it under Alex's nose, only getting a slight response.

"Again."

She held it under Alex's nose until she twitched and gasped, moving her head.

"Mmm, ugh." I squeezed my eyes and ears shut against the world.

"Open your eyes for me, Alex." Dan waved a light in each then let my lids go. "Open your eyes, Alex, come on."

"Ugh." I forced them open a slit. "Ugh, ugh." I tried to raise my hand to my head, but I don't think it moved, even though it felt like it had.

"We're going to give you a full body x-ray now so we can see if anything's broken. Do you remember what happened?"

I felt the slab I was laying on move, and the motion made me sicker than I already was. "Uh, uh…" I tried to move.

"Don't move; we're getting you an x-ray."

The table halted, and I heard a clanking sound behind me.

"You need to lie still. We're going to strap you in so the machine can scan your body. Alex, can you hear me?"

"Ugh." My arms, legs and feet were fastened, then something was pulled over my head.

"It will only take a few minutes, and then it will be over. We'll be back shortly, we're just popping into the next room."

I heard a door close, and the x-ray machine start. I

lay there for God knows how long while it moved up and down my body, taking scans and x-rays. The sound stopped, and the door opened.

"You're all good, Alex. No broken bones, no bleeds, you're even in alignment."

"Ugh." I tried to open my eyes, but only managed brief glimpses of the room, half the staff, Chris and Dimitri.

"One, two, three."

I was lifted onto the medic room bed and tucked in for the night.

"I'll give you some strong medication plus saline. You should sleep well and be okay tomorrow, well enough to sleep in your own bed tomorrow night."

"Ugh. Uh," I cried as my hand was punctured for the drip.

"It's okay. It will all be okay tomorrow. Caitlin, is the drip in?"

"Yes."

"Good. We'll leave you alone now, Alex, but we'll monitor you all night. Get some rest."

"Ugh."

"Alexi?"

"Ugh?"

"We will talk about this tomorrow. No getting out of it."

"Ugh."

"Alex?"

"Ugh?"

"It's me, Chris. I love you, you rest and get better, and *we* will definitely talk tomorrow."

Chapter 17

Had tomorrow even come?

I breathed and felt myself slowly rising from that deep pit of sleep. I moved my fingers, my toes. I popped one eye open and scanned the pale green and blue room while the other rose at its own pace. My eyes blinked. "Mmm," I croaked and licked my lips.

"Alex." Chris moved from the chair beside the bed.

"Dry," barely made it out of my mouth before he was pouring a glass of cold water and holding it to my lips.

"Slowly, drink slowly."

I sucked greedily. I was all the world's deserts rolled into one. Parched beyond belief and in need of swallowing a whole ocean just to quench my thirst. A thirst I feared may never be quenched. "Mmm."

He placed the glass on the table and picked up my hand. "Alex."

"Mmm?"

"You okay, Alex?" He stroked my hair and gripped my hand for dear life.

"Mmm." I blinked a few times and looked around the room before my eyes landed on Chris. I smiled. "Hey."

He smiled back and moved my hand to his lips for them to kiss. "Hey, yourself. That was quite a tumble you took from her majesty's balcony. Flew all the way down, you did. You okay?"

I blinked and stared, trying to remember what had happened. I saw images float through my head. Me upstairs, me *at* the stairs, me grabbing the crooked bannister, me falling arse over tit down the stairs. "Mmm," I mumbled. "I fell."

"Yeah." He kissed my hand again. "You fell. But there's nothing broken, so you should be okay." He pushed my hair aside. "You okay, Alex? Really?"

I looked at him through sore, tired eyes. "No." A sigh escaped from my lips as Dan and Caitlin walked in.

"Ah, good, you're awake. Let's check you out. Chris, can you wait outside, please." Dan motioned to the door he'd just walked through and waited for him to leave before turning his attention to me. "He was here all night, you know. Would *not* leave your side. Dimitri wanted to throw him out so *he* could stay." He popped his stethoscope into his ears. "In the end, I had to kick Dimitri out because Chris tied himself to the chair."

The stethoscope disc was cold against my chest as I breathed deeply.

"We need to sit you up. Caitlin."

I was helped into a sitting position and breathed deeply again as my lungs were checked.

"Can you take some more blood and we'll do another scan and x-ray?"

"Sure." Caitlin gathered syringes and swabs from

the cart and took another vial of blood as I lay on the bed. "All done."

I was wheeled into the other room and closed my eyes for the scan. *No point moving around,* I thought. *May as well just lay back and let it happen.* A few minutes later I was wheeled back to the patient room, and Chris was allowed back in.

So was Dimitri.

"Alexi."

"Dimitri," I murmured.

"How is she? How is my little Alexi, Doctor?" He grasped my hand in his.

"Don't know, Dimitri. Alex," he turned to me, "I'll go run some tests on your blood and examine your scans. Depending on the outcome, you may be able to break free from this prison in the next couple of hours." He wrote some things on my chart. "Do you feel like breakfast? I'll get Jenny to send it in."

I settled back onto the pillows Caitlin had propped behind my back. "Mmm, breakfast. I am hungry."

Dan looked at Dimitri and Chris. "Get her to send in three, shall I?"

They nodded from their places beside the bed.

"Okay, see you in a couple of hours." He moved toward the door. "Caitlin, get the blood tests going, please. I'll check the films from the x-ray."

I was left alone with Dimitri, who quickly claimed the chair Chris had slept in all night, and Chris, who quickly claimed the bed.

He grabbed the hand Dimitri had let go of. "How are you feeling? You okay? I was so scared when I saw you fly down the stairs and land in a heap in front of me."

I squeezed his hand reassuringly. "I'm okay. *Now.* Just hungry and bruised and battered and sore." I shifted. "Very sore."

"Alexi, we need to talk. *Alone.*" Dimitri eyed Chris.

Chris eyed him back. "Yes, Alex. *We* need to talk too…*alone.*"

My eyes flicked from one to the other and the power play going on. "For God's sake, you two. I'm not in the mood for your macho crap ownership; I just don't have the energy. We'll talk after I've had a good breakfast and a shower. Meantime, try to get along for bloody Pete's sake. My head still hurts, and I don't need you two at each other's throats making my headache worse."

They at least had enough manners to look embarrassed, as Jenny took that moment to arrive with three steaming hot breakfasts. "Hey, Alex. Good to see you're alive." She handed trays to Dimitri and Chris before handing one to me. "We were all worried after you took a header off the stairs."

"I'm fine. Just sore," I said as she removed the lid to reveal steaming hot eggs, bacon, tomatoes and mushrooms. "Mmm, yum!"

"Enjoy. I'll be back later." She left us to our meals in peace.

I was famished so dug in, shovelling forkfuls of eggs and bacon into my mouth. "Mmm." I squeezed in a tomato and three mushrooms, happily munching away while the others ate theirs.

"Good to see you still have an appetite." Chris grinned, popping a mushroom into his own mouth and enjoying the succulent juiciness.

"Mmm." I grinned around my full mouth and swallowed. "Yum!" I drank a few gulps of fresh tropical juice and shovelled in the rest of the bacon and eggs. "Mmm." I watched Dimitri delicately cut his tomatoes and mushrooms before placing a piece into his mouth. I swallowed. "For God's sake shove it in. No time to eat delicately."

He flashed me a filthy look. "You may be starving, Alexi, and want to eat like animal, but I do not." A mushroom followed the tomato, and he chewed thirty-two times before swallowing.

I shook my head and inhaled the rest of my food, washing it down with my juice and watching while the two men in the room finished their own. I gazed out the large bay windows. "Another perfect day in paradise," I muttered.

Everyone descended on the room. Jenny came back for the trays, Caitlin came back to administer some painkillers, and Dan came back with the result of the scans and x-rays.

"Good news. Nothing's changed from last night. Still don't have any broken bones, blood clots, aneurysms. You're all spic and span."

"Does that mean I can go back to my room and take a shower?"

"Absolutely." He signed off on my chart. "Just take it easy for the next few days, and you will be fine. Lots of rest. Lots of T.L.C."

I flung back the covers. "Thanks, Dan." My feet hit the floor, and Chris helped me stand. I squeezed his hand and gave him a grin. "Let's go upstairs, I need a shower." I took a step and wobbled, flinging my other hand out for balance.

Dimitri grabbed it. "One step at time, Alexi. Just like before."

The memory came blasting into my mind. Memories long gone and long buried. I winced and stared at him, sending brainwaves to shut up and say *nothing* about *before,* so Chris didn't ask questions… *about before…*

Dimitri blankly stared back.

"I'm fine," I said quietly. "No need to worry." I felt stronger with each step, and before I knew it, I was being led to my room. "Time for a shower, and Dimitri," I stopped him at the door, "I'll talk to you later." I closed it on his thunderous expression and let Chris take me into the bathroom.

We took a long luxurious shower with Chris soaping every inch of my body and cleaning me from head to toe, which resulted in wet, slow lovemaking under the water. We came but didn't finish. Turning off the taps, Chris carried me to the bed, and we lay in an array of wet towels and sheets while we climaxed again.

"Mmm," I murmured. Time had disappeared in a haze of sex and water. Chris lay on top, still inside of me, still full, still throbbing.

"Mmm yourself," he replied, gently kissing my neck.

"Mmm, you feel so good…" my voice came out soft

and whimsical as my fingers ran across the smooth muscles in his back and over his shoulders. Such strong, wide shoulders.

"Mmm, so do you." Lips made their way across my collarbone and ribs before finding and latching onto my left nipple.

I arched into him, and a groan escaped as I felt him inside of me. He hardened and moved. "Oh." I clenched my vaginal muscles then released.

"Oh." His head flew up from sucking. "Do that again. Oh, there…" His eyes closed. "Oh, God…oh, God stop…oh, God."

"Come." My arms slid around him and pulled him close. "Release and come." I clenched again, and he released and came.

"Oh, God," he groaned, collapsing on top of her. "Oh, God." She was the woman he loved, the woman he wanted to spend the rest of his life with, the woman he'd almost lost. The woman he was clearly going to have to tell the truth to if he expected *her* to come clean with what she knew.

After a delightful dinner on the balcony, I went in search of Dimitri. I didn't have to go far as he was sitting at the end of the hall in front of the staircase. "How come you're sitting there?" I noticed the small table set up with his favourite Russian food and drink, and there was a pile of magazines and books. Dimitri was old school. The only technology he used was a phone.

He set aside his book and stood. "I am here because you shut door on me, Alexi. So I make sure you not fall downstairs again."

I stared up at him. All he'd ever done was take care of me, and yet, there were some things he just could not take care of. I hugged him and laid my head on his leather clad chest. "Things aren't getting better, are they?"

"No, Alexi." He patted and rubbed my back. "No, they are not."

I slowly pulled out of his arms and sighed. "Let's go for a walk." Arm in arm we walked down the stairs, out the door, and around the island, talking about things past and things present, and what my future may hold. "I don't know," I mumbled, stopping to look at the parakeets feeding on the lawn. "I can only hope my future is better and pain-free."

"So do I, Alexi, so do I."

We moved on, stopping to watch the waves on the beach and Brian lighting the island's torches along the path. We smelt the flowers, watched them close up for the night, and basked in the last rays of the sun as it slid over the horizon.

"How much longer, Alexi?"

"I don't know. A day or two, a week at the most."

"I meant how much longer can you go on like this?" He stopped and held onto my arms, forcing me to look at him.

I sighed and rubbed my eyes. "I don't know, *I don't know.*"

He stared hard, willing me to know. "When *will* you know?"

I sighed again and stared back. "I don't..." My

head shook sadly. "I don't think I can go on much longer, Dimitri, I just," I shrugged, "I don't think… much longer…"

He softened. "Will you get it out of him? Is *he the key*, Alexi?"

I ran my hands over my face. "Yeah, he is." I noticed the first twinkling stars.

He shook his head. "Then you must get it out of him…otherwise…"

"I know. Otherwise, *I'm* screwed. We're *all* screwed." I let Dimitri lead me inside and up to my room where Chris met us.

"Hey, there you are. Have a good walk? Looks like it took a lot out of you." He guided me to the bed and propped pillows behind my back.

I curled up and yawned. "Yeah, we did. And now, I'm buggered."

"Well, we can have an early night." Chris gave Dimitri the evil eye and threw a blanket over me. "Just snuggle up and sleep. How does that sound?" He gave Dmitri another look and noticed he had not moved.

I looked from one to the other and back again and lightly laughed at the macho antics of both of them. They looked at me.

"What's so funny?" Chris asked, crossing his arms and frowning.

"You two, standing there." I pointed at them. "Being all macho and protective."

"I *am* being protective, Alexi, of you." Dimitri stood straight and tall. "That is my job, to protect you and take care of you."

I smiled at the proud Russian man and bodyguard who had been by my side for the last ten years. "I know, Dimitri. But, now it's time for bed. So you go and get yourself some rest, and I'll see you tomorrow."

He didn't move, just stood there looking back and forth from Chris to me.

"*Go* Dimitri."

He reluctantly relented. "All right, Alexi," he nodded, "see you in the morning." He left, and Chris locked the door behind him.

"Now," he said. "It's just you and me." He climbed on the bed beside me and took me into his arms, breathing in my scent and feeling my body. The clock ticked in the room, the sound of the waves crashed through the window, and he found himself touching my warm, soft flesh, and kissing my warm, soft lips, and sliding his tongue into my mouth, and his penis into my inner world.

I groaned in pleasure.

He groaned in pleasure.

And two warm, soft naked bodies moved in sync to a climatic groan and deep slumber.

He was behind the wheel, driving, planting his foot, speeding, yelling, driving, speeding, yelling 'get out of the way, oh, my God, where did he come from, get out of the way'.

He jerked awake and sat bolt upright, sweating, dry, and gasping for air.

"It's time you told me." My hand touched his arm.

He jerked and settled, realising it was me. "Yeah, I guess it's finally time I did."

Chapter 18

We settled back onto the pillows, and I waited for Chris to tell his story.

"I," he began, and then sighed. Glancing around the room he didn't know what to think or feel, or even where to start.

"At the beginning." My voice was soft.

He looked at me and smiled. "Yeah, might be a good place," he said before turning away. "But even the beginning is hard to start."

I held his hand and rubbed his arm. "One step at a time."

He sighed again and started. "It was seven years ago…and I…was on a movie set in Russia. My career had been going gangbusters, I was on a dozen or so TV shows for over a dozen years, really well-known in Australia but I…" He licked his lips and squeezed my hand. "I wasn't *known* in Russia." Taking a deep breath, he got up and stood by the balcony doors.

After a few moments of silence, I broke it. "Go on."

"I, uh," he sniffed, "I uh, had never been overseas before. I'd done movies, quite a few of them, but not

221

big time ones like this." He walked around the room. "Nope, not me. Never been on a big movie set in a foreign country before."

"First time for everything." I watched him.

His grin was sad, and he walked some more. "Yeah. First time for everything. I had done the audition in Australia. My agent thought I'd be perfect for it and set me up. I arrived, did it, it went well, and I got a call back a week later."

He scratched his head. "I did an audition with some females they'd chosen for possible leads, and they went well, and again, I got a call back a week later." His hands went to his hips. "I did a final audition with their final choice for female lead and…" A breath in. "Two days later I got the part."

He was on the move again. "We, we flew to Moscow a week later and started filming two weeks after that. We were going to film for a month, and then move on to St Petersburg and finish off there." He stopped beside the bed and gazed down at me forlornly. "I wish I had never gone. Never taken the part. Never *been* in Russia." Blue eyes closed and his head moved slightly from side to side. "I wish I had *never* been there."

He drifted off with the memories which brought him back to reality, and he sat down. "I, um," sigh, "I had a great time. We were filming and getting through it really quickly. Sophia and I worked well together. I had won Logies and made money and was famous. In so many shows, on the cover of the TV Week, in magazines…I was famous." His mind wandered again.

"Famous…"

I waited a few moments. "Chris?" No response. "Chris?"

"Mmm?" His head moved toward the sound of my voice, but his eyes remained glazed over.

"Chris?"

His eyes focussed.

I watched the change over him. "*Go on*. Finish the story."

He deflated. All the years of nightmares had exhausted him, and he didn't want to talk about it. But maybe, maybe talking about it would release him from the burden of it. And maybe it would mean Alex would unburden herself.

"Go on," I prompted.

He looked at the woman on the bed. The woman he loved. The woman he wanted to spend the rest of his life with. The woman he really knew nothing about. He sighed. "Everything had been going so well. I had a great career, great life, great house, but…all of that disappeared that night…" He paced again. "It was our last night of filming in Moscow, and it was a technical scene where I had to drive a car and speed through the city."

He licked his lips. "Everything was set to go, it was all in order. It was supposed to be safe." His head moved from side to side, and he frowned. "It was supposed to be safe." He moved again. "I was in the car," his breath became laboured, "I was in the car for the final scene in Moscow. I was in the car and…it was all set up. It was supposed to be safe."

He wiped his face. "It was supposed to be safe. They told me…they told me it was safe and that no one was going to get hurt. The roads were blocked off, the, the car was safe to drive, that…no one would get hurt." He gasped for air like he'd been holding it in.

"Take a breath," I said. "A nice, deep breath."

He breathed in and out and stood by the balcony doors to get more air. "I feel like a prisoner sometimes."

"Why?"

"Because of the way I lived after what happened."

"What happened?" I asked, and he glanced at me. *"What happened?"* I repeated.

"I killed someone," he whispered.

"Tell me."

His face crumpled, and he threw himself onto the bed.

I stroked his hair as he lay there. "It was seven years ago. It's time to let go."

"I know," was muffled by the sheet. "I know."

"Go on."

He slowly sat up. "It was the last night of filming. I was in the car and was supposed to speed through the streets of Moscow. The car was set, all the technical stuff in place. The streets were closed, and it was only stunt people ready to dive out of the way. It was all supposed to be safe." He looked away and shuddered. "But it wasn't."

"What happened?"

"I was in the car. We started moving. The director yelled *action* and off we went. The car sped up until we were speeding down the street. It was a long street, long and straight. We were speeding. I was saying my lines, and as we passed some side streets, I saw people standing around. Onlookers, I guess," he paused, "we made it to the end of the street, and the director yelled *cut.* We were going to do a second take to get it at different angles, so the car was towed back, and we set up again. It was supposed to be safe. It felt safe. Safety harness, controlled by remote control, I didn't have to worry about braking, accelerating or even driving."

Chris shrugged, and a deep frown appeared. "It was all controlled by the tech guys. It was supposed to be safe." He inhaled and slowly let the breath out. "We started again. The last scene on our last night in Moscow. We started rolling, and the director yelled *action.* We sped down the street just like the first time. Sophia and I said our lines just like the first time. I saw the people on the side streets just like the first time," there was a long pause, "it was supposed to be safe. It was supposed to be safe because the streets were blocked off," his breath was laboured again, "it was supposed to be safe, but it wasn't. It wasn't safe because I couldn't stop. I couldn't stop the car. I couldn't stop the car because I didn't have control. I didn't have control so I couldn't stop it. It wasn't safe. It wasn't safe because he just ran out in front of me. He ran out..."

He moved quickly around the room in time with his words. "It wasn't safe because the roads were not blocked off, because he got through. He got through and ran straight onto the road. The road that *I* was speeding on. The road *I* was in the car on. It wasn't safe because he ran *right in front of my car.* He ran right in front of my car, and I couldn't stop. I couldn't stop. The car didn't stop because I didn't control it." He swallowed. "I didn't control it, so I couldn't stop it."

I moved over to his side. "Tell me, it's okay. Be calm. It's all over…tell me…"

"I," he gulped, "we were in the car, speeding down the street, saying our lines…when…a man runs straight out into," he shook his head slightly, "*onto*, the street, straight onto the street. *Straight in front of the car.* The car I'm driving. The car I'm in. The car I don't control. He ran right out into the street in front of the car. I saw him. I slammed on the brake. I turned the wheel." His eyes glazed over. "It was all split second. He was in the middle of the street before he noticed. I remember his face from the split second he turned to stare. Finally realising he was in the middle of a street and about to be run over. I remember his face. His eyes. His mouth. It was like he was saying *no*. I couldn't stop the car."

Chris rubbed his eyes and gasped, almost holding back sobs. "I couldn't stop the car no matter how much I pumped the brake, no matter how much I turned the wheel. I couldn't stop the car." He took another deep breath and looked at me. "I will *never* forget that moment as long as I live. The moment I killed a man. The moment I ran him down."

"It wasn't *your* fault," I soothed, "*you* weren't in control."

"Doesn't matter, though, does it?" He wiped his face.

"*Of course it does.* It matters a lot because it *wasn't your fault.*"

"It is. I was driving. I will always be the driver."

"What happened next?" I hoped to keep the story moving and his mind from dwelling on the macabre.

"I, uh," he ran a hand through his hair while he thought, "Sophia was screaming the whole time, and we eventually slowed down. Some of the tech guys helped us out, and I remember looking back and seeing paramedics and lights around the scene…in fact," he frowned, "a big crowd had gathered. I think one of the roadblocks had been knocked down and they were all hanging around trying to get a look. Sophia was taken away, but I wanted to look. I tried to move closer, but the director came up to me and told me to head for my trailer, and they would deal with it. I wanted to see, to look, to see what I had done, so I broke away from them and ran back to the scene…"

"You shouldn't have done that," I whispered, leaning my forehead against his muscular arm.

He glanced down at me. "I wanted to. I wanted to *see* what I had done. *Who* I had killed. I *needed* to see what I had done. I needed to know, know *who* he was, *what* he did, if he was married or had children. I needed to know. I needed to see…"

I looked up. "And did you?"

The frown was still in place. "I stopped at the edge of the crowd and slowly moved through until I stood over the paramedics, over the body. I saw him. He was an older man with eyes still wide in shock, a mouth still open in refusal that he was about to be run over."

He bit his lip and shuddered. "They declared him… dead. He was…dead," he swallowed, "he was dead, and I'd killed him."

"*No,* you didn't."

"*Yes,* I did," he looked at me, "I killed him at speeds no one can survive I…killed him." He pulled out of my grasp and paced again.

Now, *I* frowned and felt pain seeping back into the base of my skull. "Keep going."

Chris thought about it. "I stood over him, and the director came to take me away. I killed him. They declared him dead, and I stared into his eyes, his face, the faces of everyone standing around him. I killed him. I killed…ugh. I need to splash my face, give me a minute." He walked into the bathroom and threw cold water on his face several times. After washing his hands thoroughly, he stood and stared at his reflection.

Frowned at his reflection.

Turned away from his reflection.

Walking back through the closet he glanced at the pile of clothes that hid the folder on the Russian billionaires.

"You okay?" I asked when I saw him.

He shook his head. "No."

"May as well finish the story then." I rubbed my neck as I sat on the bed.

Chris stood in front of me, hands on hips, and let out a slow breath. "The director took me back to my trailer and told me to stay there until he fixed everything. I think I stayed there for hours before being allowed to go back to the hotel. The man had been taken away, and the crowds dispersed. Filming was finished." He shrugged a shoulder. "I was told that I was going to need to talk to the police, but since I was not in control of the car and it was a movie set, I was not going to be charged with murder. Can you *believe* that?" He waved a hand. "*Me...charged with murder.*"

"It was an accident," I said, "plain and simple."

"Yeah, well, the cops didn't think so." He walked again. "They questioned me down at the station *for hours*, almost a day. Kept telling me because I was driving it was my fault. Thankfully the lawyer, not to mention director and producer of the movie, were all good friends of the chief of police and got me out of it because I was not in control of the car, so they couldn't charge me. Jesus, they may as well have, considering I did it."

"It was *an accident*," I said with more force than needed, trying to make him understand. "It was *not your fault*, it was *his*. *He* ran out onto the street in front of your car. *He* is the one to blame."

Chris stared at her, obviously wondering how much she already knew about the whole thing. *You've got the papers,* he thought. *What do you know?* "Yeah, well, it didn't stop me from blaming myself." He rubbed his eyes. "That was the last movie I ever made. We were given a week off then had to finish up in St Petersburg. It was rough, finishing that movie. I didn't want to do it after that. And once it was done, I didn't want to act after that. I quit altogether, stayed out of sight, didn't go out and didn't do anything. Just hid out up north Queensland for seven years, building houses, herding cattle, anything to get away from what I'd done."

"I take it it was in all the papers, being on a movie set and all?"

"Front page news for two weeks," he scoffed. "Every paper, every cover, every news bulletin on TV. I couldn't escape it. I hid in the hotel for the week off and couldn't wait to get out of Moscow. Problem was, it was everywhere in St Petersburg as well, so I couldn't get away from it no matter *how* hard I tried."

"So…what did it all say?"

"Why?" His interest was piqued as he crossed his arms.

"I'm curious," I said, cocking my head. "*You're* telling me the story, of *course,* I want to know what they said." I shrugged a shoulder. "*Who* was he? *What* did he do? *Why* was he running onto a movie set at night?"

He sighed, suspicious of my answer. "His name was Grigor Yurogovnia. He was a fifty-one-year-old billionaire. Ran a multi-billion dollar industry in Russia, and was known for his charity works. Had a wife, Natasha, who wasn't in the country at the time. No children. She inherited everything. It was even said he was a descendent of the Russian Royal family, which I didn't know still existed, so all of that info just made me feel worse." He shook his head remorsefully. "God, I killed a member of the royal family, such a well-known and respected man, loved by so many, even children."

I bristled and silently scoffed at his last remark, hoping he didn't notice my brows hit my hairline at the absurdity. "Did you find out *why* he was there that night?" My brows came down quickly, and I hoped he hadn't seen them. "Billionaires generally don't go running around the streets at night on their own without armed bodyguards or something."

His eyes narrowed. "How do you know there was no bodyguard?"

My eyes narrowed in reply. "Because *in general* billionaires don't go running around the streets at night on their own without a bodyguard or something." I shrugged my other shoulder. "And you didn't mention one, so it's the next thought in the process." I thought I recovered that well.

"Mmm." He frowned. "You're right. There *was* no one with him."

I inwardly sighed and continued. "So, you finished the movie and came home?"

He slumped on the bed. "Yep, never to act again."

"You *do know* it's not *your* fault?" I sat beside him.

"Do I? I did it."

"It was *an accident* for God's sake. You *weren't* in control. Of the car, him, or the situation in any way, shape, or form. *He* made his choice. The result and consequence of that choice is *not* your fault."

Chris looked at me. "They never said *why* he ran into the street. It was never in the papers, not on TV. No one knew *why* he had run into the street. No one saw him, no one knew. So *I* don't know."

"Would it help if you did?"

He sniffed. "Probably not."

"So, what's the problem then?"

"I killed someone."

"No, you didn't."

"Yes, I did."

"*No, you didn't.* It was *not* of your control, *not* of your choosing. You need to change your mindset and stop blaming yourself for something you *did not* do. It was an accident plain and simple. *Not* your fault, *not* your choice, *not* of your doing. So dump the guilt trip you've put on yourself and get back to living. He made his choice; it's not *your* fault."

"Easy for you to say."

"Yes, it is. *You're not guilty.*"

"I'm not innocent."

"*You are.* You need to change your mindset and believe in yourself again."

He studied me for a moment. "Will you help me do that?"

I smiled. "Of course I will."

Chapter 19

The body of Natasha Yurogovnia lay motionless, unmoving, dead on the floor.

Well…almost.

Three men came into the room and looked around them. Looked around the room at the mess they had to clean up.

Her mind wandered aimlessly through the haze. She didn't know where Grigor was, and for all she knew, he'd gone to bed ages ago.

The men closed the door and walked toward the body on the floor. The body that was badly beaten, shot, stabbed, drowned and electrocuted.

She heard the mantel clock in her husband's office. Nine p.m. Its chimes echoed lightly around the room. So did she.

The men surveyed the damage. Blood and vodka mixed into a watery cocktail, slowly oozing out onto the floor around the body. The body on the floor.

She ambled along in a dream, a fog, a haze, not thinking, not seeing, not hearing or feeling. She felt dizzy and sick to her stomach, not sure if she was going to throw up or not.

They were Grigor's men. Personal bodyguards and cleaners. Cleaning up all the dirty work sent their way, and this was worse than they had ever seen.

Dimitri Yurogov had been Grigor's right-hand man for decades, and even this scene made him sick. The perverted world those men lived in, got away with, and did anything they wanted in, was the same world he had to clean up. "Sergei, get the blanket, Vladimir, the towels."

She tried to move her head, her eyes, tried to stop the pounding and blurriness. She could barely see the light was so dim. She took a deep breath and tried to move.

"We need to check body," Dimitri said. "Find her bag and clothes." The three men searched the room, but could find neither, only a negligee.

"There is nothing," Sergei said quietly as they stood looking down at the body.

The body of Natasha Yurogovnia lay motionless, unmoving, dead on the floor.

Well…almost.

"Then we check for jewellery," Dimitri replied. "Vladimir, wipe up blood." He wiped the floor around the body and Dimitri crouched down to examine it. "No earrings, no necklace." He checked the right hand. "No ring." He wiped the left hand over and saw a piece of jewellery he instantly recognised.

*****

I tossed and turned in bed. My head was pounding and full of everything Chris has told me. Was that all of it? Every *little* detail? Every little *sordid* detail? Everything he could possibly think of to tell me? Does *he* even know every detail? He was holding back, wasn't he? I could see it. I could sense it. He was holding back on me. He knew *something. Knows* something. What is he holding back from me?

God, why won't this pounding stop? It's getting worse again. I feel sick. God, I feel sick. Why do I feel sick? Why is my head pounding? God make it stop. I want it to stop. I don't want to feel sick, make it stop, make it stop, make it stop…

Chris stirred. "Alex?" he murmured, opening his eyes to see the bed light still on and Alex slowly walking for the door. "Alex?" He leaned up on his elbow and watched her open the door then close it behind her. "Alex? What the hell?" He pulled on his shorts and tank top and opened the door to see her halfway down the hall. "Alex." He didn't want to raise his voice in case he scared her.

Walking down the hall, he saw her turn for the stairs to the third floor. "Alex." Racing after her, he found Dimitri's spot near the stairs vacated and her halfway up. "Alex, sweetie, are you awake?" He saw the glazed look in her eyes and over her face. "Guess not." Wishing he'd brought her robe as she was naked, he thought about racing back for it. "Alex." He stopped to watch her.

She reached for the knob on the door and entered the sacred boudoir of the mysterious Queen.

The Queen, or was that, Natasha? One of the Natashas in the printouts? Is that *who* she is? That's who this woman is, and why Alex was involved. She must be the assistant, and that's why she has the bundle of papers. But did she know about *my* part?

He came out of his reverie to find Alex gone and the door closed. "Shit!" He grabbed the knob and twisted, but the door wouldn't budge. "Damn it!" He shoved against it, but it remained unmoving. "Shit, I…" He remembered the basement lift and tried the door one last time. "Nope, I'll have to go downstairs."

Flying down three flights of stairs and into the basement, flicking on lights so he could see where he was going, Chris ran around the corner he'd hidden behind and raced to the spot where they'd entered. "Okay, how do we do this?" He slid his hands over the ornate tiles. "There must be a trick to this." He pushed every one, moving wall sconces and knocking on panels until the wall slid back to reveal the lift. "All right." He stepped inside and hit number three. "Going up."

*****

"He has done it, Natasha. He has finally admitted what he has done."

"Why have you awoken me, Alexi?"

"Get up, Natasha. It is over, we have *finally* done it."

"Done what?" She ambled into her dressing room and threw on her see-through black silk dressing gown, leaving it open and flowing behind her.

"We have done it, Natasha. We have made him admit to what he has done."

We sat down at her dressing table and donned her black Cleopatra wig. "*It has finally happened, Alexi? We finally know what happened?*"

"Yes, Natasha. We finally know." I brushed the hair of the wig with a wide tooth brush. "Yes," I said dreamily. "We finally know. We have finally done it." I stared at her in the mirror. "We're finally free."

*****

Chris silently glided up three floors in the spacious velvet lined lift until the doors silently whooshed open. He didn't move, even though his heart pounded in his chest. He listened, even though the blood sang in his ear. He heard two female voices. Alex's and a strong Russian one.

"If we have finally done it, Alexi, finally know the truth, why do I still have this pounding in my head?"

I sighed and rubbed my own. "I don't know, Natasha, I have it too. I thought it would be gone once he admitted what he'd done. I thought the pressure would have gone away. But it seems to be getting worse. Argh."

Chris slipped out of the lift and turned left, standing…listening.

"You are right, it is getting worse, Alexi. Argh, what are we going to do?"

"God, I feel sick." I grabbed my head. "Why won't this fucking pain stop?"

We looked at each other as we gripped our heads in pain. Violent agony smashed its way through our brains and around our skulls.

I groaned. "God, why won't this stop?"

"Make it stop, Alexi."

"I can't, Natasha."

"Then we need to do something."

"We'll take a pill. Do you have those pills Dan gave you?"

"In my drawer, in my dresser."

We reached for the drawer and found the bottle of pills. Such strong painkillers that only took seconds to start working. If you opened the capsule and sucked the liquid out, that was. We opened several, sucking back the potion like it was liquid gold. Within seconds the pounding eased, and the pain subsided.

Somewhat.

Not completely, but enough for us to sit there and stare at each other. We picked up our brush and began brushing our Cleopatra hair.

Chris silently stepped forward. He'd heard the pain they were experiencing and wanted to barge right in and take over. But having never met Natasha in person, or without a blindfold, he'd held back in case she'd done something to Alex.

He stealthily headed for the door.

"Alexi?"

Stroke.

"Natasha?"

Stroke.

"Will you be leaving now?"

Stroke.

"Yes."

Stroke.

"Where will you go?"

Stroke.

"Home."

Stroke.

"And where is home anymore?"

Stroke.

"Australia. What about you?"

Stroke.

"I do not know. Russia is no longer my home."

Stroke.

"Then go somewhere else."

Stroke.

"I might just do that."

Stroke.

Chris reached the door to the dressing room and peeked through the gap. No one. But he heard the voices.

"Will you be with that blond man? The one you have taken a fancy to?"

Stroke.

"I don't know. Maybe. Hopefully. If he'll have me once he finds out."

Stroke.

"Of course he will have you. Why would he not?"

Stroke.

Chris hooked two fingers around the door and slowly slid it aside, trying to make as less noise as possible.

"Because I am as bad as him."

Stroke.

"How are you as bad as him? *He* is a killer."

Stroke.

Chris froze at the word, but didn't freeze enough for his fingers to hang on to the door. It silently finished opening, and all he saw was one naked woman in a black see-through gown sitting at the dressing table stroking her black Cleopatra hair.

*****

The body of Natasha Yurogovnia lay motionless, unmoving, dead on the floor.

Well…almost….

Dimitri stared down at the rings on the dead woman's left hand.

A huge diamond engagement ring and diamond encrusted wedding band.

He had been with Grigor when he'd picked them out and bought them in Sydney. "Natasha?" he murmured, looking up from the rings.

She ambled along in a dream, a fog, a haze, not thinking, not seeing, not feeling. But this time, she did hear. Did hear Dimitri say her name. She took a deep breath and tried to move.

Dimitri looked back at the hand in his and saw her fingers move ever so slightly. He sucked in air. "You are alive." He glanced up at Sergei and Vladimir who looked both confused and shocked. "She is alive." He squeezed her hand and leaned in so she could see him.

"I am here, it is me, Dimitri. I will help you. I will save you. I will protect you. I will do anything for you, my little Alexi. Anything."

****

Natasha sensed they were not alone and turned her head to see a tall blond hunk. "Ah, you are Chris, no? Alexi speaks highly of you."

Chris stared back and frowned. The woman looked familiar. *Very* familiar. *"Alex?"*

"She is here, beside me. You do not want to see me?"

We stroked our hair.

"Alex? What's going on?" He licked his lips and wiped his sweaty palms on his shorts. "Why are you up here? Why are you speaking in a Russian accent? What the hell is going on?"

"Alexi is not speaking at the moment." We rose from the table. "But you can talk to me. *I* am Natasha."

He stood tall and firm. "I'm Chris as you full well know."

A steely cold harshness crossed Natasha's eyes. "It is you. *You* are the one."

He frowned. "One what?"

"The one who is taking Alexi from me. *The one who took my life from me."*

His eyes narrowed. "I didn't take anything from you. I want Alex."

"You can't have Alex," Natasha screeched.

"Natasha, stop it," I cried.

"No, Alexi, I will not. This is the man who wants to take you away from me. The man who wants to ruin my life *again*. I will *not* allow it, Alexi. I *will not*." She stormed around the large, grandly furnished dressing room, flapping her arms in time to her words.

"Natasha, stop being so bloody melodramatic. It's *over* now. We can *both* get on with our lives."

"No, Alexi. *We* cannot. *I* cannot."

"Oh, shut up. I'm sick and tired of you and your dramatics, and it *needs to stop*."

Chris stood watching the woman who claimed to be Natasha storm around the room. Yet the woman was also Alex. The woman he loved. Speaking in two different accents, in two different facial expressions. *What the hell is going on here?* he thought, amazed and stunned by what he was seeing.

"*I do not care,*" boomed Natasha. "I will *not* let you go, Alexi."

"You have no choice, Natasha," I yelled back.

"I will not let him take you."

"You don't get a say."

"This, this man," Natasha pointed at Chris, "is worth leaving me for?"

"Absolutely," I replied. "It's time to leave *you* behind, Natasha."

"*Behind,*" she screeched. "No! I will *not* let you go, Alexi. *I will not*."

"Argh." We grabbed our heads and slammed into the dressing table.

"Alex," Chris yelled and took a step toward her.

"No," Natasha shrieked. *"Get away from her.* I will *not* allow you to take her from me like you took everything else. You will *not* get her, you, you murderer." She yanked open the dresser drawer and pulled out the loaded pearl-handled pistol. "I will *not* allow you to take her the way you took my husband. You killed my husband in cold blood, and I will *not* let you kill Alexi the same way. *I will kill you first."*

Chris had retreated with his hands up at first sight of the gun and now shook his head at the madness. The madness of seeing a naked Alex in a black wig and gown speaking in Russian, calling herself Natasha, and aiming a pistol at his head. He calmed his breathing. "*Your husband?* Who the *hell* is *your* husband?" he asked quietly.

She levelled the pistol at his head, and a cold, harsh wave fell over her as she went ice-cold inside. Her voice was low and lethal when she spoke. "Grigor Yurogovnia was my husband, and *you,* Mister Cameron, killed him."

"Grigor…your…" Chris could only stare in shock.

Chapter 20

"Put the bloody gun down, Natasha," I said through gritted teeth. "This *isn't* the way we wanted it, for God's sake."

Our hand wavered, and Chris took that small second to grab the gun from us.

Natasha cried out and sank into her chair. "Don't kill me. Please don't kill me," she whimpered like a small child and threw her arms up to protect herself.

Chris unloaded the gun. "Why would *I kill you*?"

"You killed our husband." We looked at him with steely determination and a massive fog of painkiller haze.

Chris stared. "Are you? I don't understand, Alex. I've seen…" he faltered and shook his head. "I've seen a picture of Natasha Yurogovnia…and it *isn't you*. It *isn't you*."

We stood, and pain exploded. "Argh! It is us. This pain, this misery. That is what we get for being the wife of Grigor Yurogovnia. Years of hell and plastic surgery after being beaten and raped to death."

"Plastic…rape…" Chris was just as dazed as the

woman before him. It was all too much for him, watching this woman, this Natasha, Alex, whatever her name was, going back and forth between accents and personalities. "Alex? I don't know what's going on, tell me."

"You cannot have Alexi," Natasha replied, picking up her brush again. "But you can have me," she purred. "We never did get to fuck because Alexi begged me not to touch you."

"I don't want *you, I want Alex*," Chris demanded.

"How dare you," Natasha stormed, slamming down her brush and standing straight. "No man has *ever* said no to me."

He remained steadfast. "Well, I'm saying no now. Give me Alex."

"You can't have her."

"Natasha, stop being stupid," I said. "This isn't the way it was supposed to go."

"Go," she shrieked. *"Go, Alexi. I will not let you go."*

"I meant the plan, Natasha." I was getting sick of this, and it needed to stop.

"Plan? We had a plan?"

I sighed. *"Of course* we did. Now stick to it, and let's get it over with. You want this to be over with, don't you? All wrapped up in a neat little package with a bow on top?"

"Yes." She crumpled.

"All right then," I said. "Like we rehearsed."

"Mister…what is your name again?" Natasha asked.

"Cameron," Chris replied, completely weirded out.

"Mister Cameron. We must thank you."

"Thank me?" He frowned.

"Yes." She stood in front of him, trying to keep her nerves calm. "We must thank you for what you have done. Grigor was not nice man. He may have started out that way, but he did not *end up* that way. He was mean, selfish and sadistic to name few things. I was… how you say…indisposed when you killed him and could not be at funeral. Or thank you personally. It has taken seven years to find you, Mister Cameron. To find you so we can say…thank you."

"Thank you," he murmured, drowning in a thick heavy sea of mad confusion.

"Yes, Mister Cameron." Natasha held out her hand. "Thank you for killing our husband."

*****

Dimitri walked around the house checking on security and found several lights on. *That strange,* he thought. *All lights should be off now.* He flicked the switches and made his way along the hall, catching sight of a shaft slicing out from under the storm shelter door. He tried the knob and found it unlocked.

"Hello," he called down the stairs. "Is anyone down here?" When he received no reply he turned off the light, but noticed others turned on down the passageway. Shutting the door behind him, he walked down the stairs and along the shelter's corridor, flicking off the lights as he went, stopping when he was standing in front of the lift.

"Now, who used this?"

*****

"Your husband?" Chris said. "You want…to thank me…for killing him?"

Her hand wavered. "Yes, Mister Cameron. He was brute of man and deserved to die. You saved us trouble. We will pay you one billion dollars for it."

"One bill…what the bloody hell is going *on*, Alex?" he shouted.

"Alexi is not—"

"I want to speak to Alex," Chris thundered. *"Now!"*

"Chris, I—"

"Shut up, Alexi," Natasha commanded. "I am not finished."

"Well, I am," Chris spat. "*No more*, Natasha. *No more* thanking me, *I want* Alex."

"Chris—"

Natasha bristled madly. "I am trying to thank you for killing our husband, Mister Cameron, and you are ever so rudely dismissing me. *No one* dismisses Natasha Yurogovnia."

"Your husband clearly did," Chris snapped. *"Give, me, Alex. Now!"*

"I—" Natasha stuttered, clearly not used to being treated this way, "I…how dare—"

"*Shut up*, Natasha," I demanded. "You've thanked the man, now it's time for you to say goodbye."

"Goodbye?" She was astounded, and her migraine was escalating. "*Goodbye? No one* says goodbye to Natasha Yurogovnia. Queen of Russia. Queen of Dracmar."

248

"Dracmar?" Chris asked.

"The name of this stupid bloody island," I told him.

"Do not interrupt me," she screeched. *"I am Queen Natasha. You do not interrupt me, and you do not dismiss me."*

"It's time you got out of my head, Natasha. Say bye-bye." I grabbed onto my head as pain exploded, sending shreds of hell in a billion directions.

"Alex?"

"I'm trying, Chris, it's hard to get rid of the bitch, you know."

"How dare you call me—"

"I dare. Bitch, it's time for you to disappear."

We lurched.

"No. I will not go, Alexi. I am owner of this island, this house, half of Russia. I am the Queen of Russia. The Queen of the world."

"You are *not*, Natasha. You are *not* anymore."

We grabbed our heads, pain seared, and we lurched into the table.

Chris stood by helplessly. He'd never seen some weird split personality thing in motion before, so had absolutely no clue how to deal with the scene before him. He could only hope Alex could sort it out. Somehow. Dimitri. What about Dimitri? Surely he must know what's going on? *But do I leave her to get him? I should stay in case she hurts herself. Stay to save Alex.*

"I am the Queen."

"You are *not* the Queen, Natasha, *not* anymore. You have *never* been the Queen, and *never will be.*

Grigor lied to you about that, just as he lied about everything else."

A tornado whizzed around in our heads, blowing thoughts and images in circles a million miles a minute. The pain was intense, more than it ever had been, more than it ever will be. The room spun, everything was out of control in the vortex that was the Alex and Natasha show. Wind howled, debris from our past whipped by, and our head was on the verge of exploding.

"Your empire has fallen, Natasha."

"No," she screamed. *"Nooo…"*

"You are no longer the Queen of your castle."

"Lies, all lies."

"And we are no longer your dirty rascals."

"Lies," she screamed.

"*Truth,* Natasha."

"Alex." Chris stepped closer, praying for the internal conflict to be over.

"Natasha, it's time for you to go." I pulled the black Cleopatra wig off my head, grabbed onto the table, and gritted my teeth for the finale.

"No, no, no," she screeched. *"Do not leave me, Alexi."*

"I was never *with* you to *leave* you, Natasha. It is *you* who must leave."

"Alex," Chris called louder, insanely worried by the wild-eyed look.

"Please don't leave me, Alexi," Natasha's childlike voice whispered.

"*Goodbye,* Natasha," I said, trying to force her out.

"No. I won't go."

"Get out of my head, Natasha. You were *never real.* You were *never me,* just a *name* that Grigor gave me as his wife. You are *not real* Natasha. *You have never been real."*

"Alex." Chris reached out to her.

"Get out of my head, Natasha," I screamed as my head exploded.

"Alex..."

"Get out." I slammed my hands and head down on the dresser and gulped in a huge mouthful of air as my brain spun out of control, and as each little piece of my life with Grigor and the seven years since blew into eternity.

"Alex," Chris called again.

I only heard Natasha's voice fading into the background along with images of Grigor, our relationship, and my life in Russia.

"Alex," Chris now yelled.

I jumped back from the noise in fright and saw a tall blond man before me. "No," I cried. "Get away from me." I threw myself into a foetal position in the opposite corner of the room.

Her actions stunned him. "Alex?"

"Alexi?" Dimitri burst through the door, past a surprised Chris, and over to the huddled figure of his beloved Alexi. He pulled me into his arms. *"What have you done?"* he thundered at Chris. *"What did you do to her?"*

"What did I...?" Chris was still stunned.

I sobbed into Dimitri's chest and hung on for dear life.

"It's all right, Alexi. I'm here now. I protect you like always. It's all right now." He rocked back and forth as he stroked my hair.

Chris watched the scene in amazement for a few minutes before finally shaking his clearing head. "*What in fucking hell is going on here?* What the *hell* is wrong with her? *Why* is she speaking Russian, and *why the hell* is she saying she's Natasha Yurogovnia when she looks *nothing like* Natasha Yurogovnia and has an Australian accent? And *why in fucking hell* was she thanking me for killing her husband?"

His words slowly, finally, cleared my own mind. I raised my head, wiped my face, and looked at Dimitri. "It's time," I whispered.

He nodded and helped me to my feet, still holding on with his Russian death grip.

"Time for what?" Chris asked, wide eyed and pissed off. *"For telling me the truth?"*

I cleared my throat. "Yes," I said, looking him square in the eye and heaving a sigh. "My name is Alex Carson. I married Grigor Yurogovnia ten years ago and had my name changed to Natasha Yurogovnia. Dimitri Yurogov is actually Dimitri Yurogovnia, Grigor's brother." I smiled up at Dimitri fondly. "My brother-in-law."

Chris's eyes flicked back and forth between us. "What…what…?"

I stared him straight in the eye. "You're right, Chris. It *is* time for telling the truth, the whole truth, and nothing *but* the truth."

PART THREE

"Hey, watch where you're going," I yelled at the skinny blond kid who barrelled into me as he ran through the 401 Café where I worked.

"Up yours, bitch," he yelled back before tripping over the foot of the well-dressed man sitting at a table with three solemn looking men.

"Hey," he yelled again, this time from his splayed position on the floor. "What'd you do that for?"

"What'd I do what for?" the man replied, buttoning his jacket as he stood. "I didn't do anything. You fell."

The kid with the blond crew cut stumbled to his feet. "You tripped me. You stuck your foot out and tripped me." He stood straight, hoping to confront the man, but fell way short in height. And weight. His skinny little arms were no match for the great big hulking bruisers who stood next to the man in the well-cut business suit, either.

I watched the scene with great amusement, giggling to myself at the audacity of some teen kid taking on a group of swarthy looking men.

"I oughta sue you," the kid yelled, making me wish

he would stop yelling everything every time he spoke. "You could have broken something."

I finally stepped in. "The only thing you'll get broken is your face if you don't shut up and get out, you thieving little bastard. Now, get out of my shop and don't come back."

"But he—"

"I don't give a fat rat's what he did, you were in the wrong." I shoved my finger in his face. "And if I see you in here again I'll smash your face myself. Do I make myself clear?" I leaned over him even though I was only a few inches taller.

He sneered in that immature 'couldn't give a fuck about you lady' way. "Fuck you, bitch," he spat before racing out of the café.

I sighed. "Bloody kids."

"In Russia, we not let our children get away with such treatment or disrespect. They would be severely punished or not do it at all."

"Kill 'em would you, in that Russian mob squad kind of way. Drown 'em in vodka, dump 'em in the river?" I snarkily asked, trying to sound smart and funny. Clearly and abysmally failing.

"We do not do that sort of thing…anymore," he replied smoothly, trying to charm me with his slick, sly smile.

"What, since the royals killed Rasputin, or the arsehole Bolsheviks killed the royal family?" I glanced at the leather-clad, sunglasses-wearing men with him.

The elegant businessman grimaced. "It is truly disgraceful way my ancestors were killed, but Rasputin was big man, he could defend himself."

I frowned at his comment. "Your ancestors?"

"Yes. My forebears were members of Russian Royal family. They were lucky enough to get out before slaughter." He took a moment of reflection. "I am truly saddened my grandmother lost her brother, but she was lucky to get out with her husband and my great-grandmother Tsarina Maria Feodorovna."

My eyes widened. "You're great grandmother was…" I had read the story of the Russian Royal family and the slaughter of the most famous, Nicolas, and his family. Wife, Alexandra, their daughters, Olga, Tatiana, Maria and Anastasia, and their son, Alexei. Tsar Nicolas ran the army, his wife and daughters worked with the Red Cross, and Alexi had a blood disorder, haemophilia, which only seemed to be fixed by Rasputin, who Alexandra asked for help. Nicolas' nephew-in-law was the one who killed him.

"Wow, I, wow." I seriously didn't know what else to say.

"Yes," he said. "It is quite a story. A very long, sad story." He smoothed his salt and pepper hair and matching grey suit. "Maybe I tell you some time."

I stood staring at him, not sure what to say or do or even think. A member of the Russian royal family in my café. Standing in my café in the heart of Sydney. Russian royal family…Wow!

"Hey, Alex, need some help here."

I came out of my royal wonderings and back to reality. "Right, coming," I yelled over my shoulder. I turned back to find the man holding out a business card. I took it. "Grigor Yurogovnia, business industrialist," I read slowly, hoping I'd gotten his name right and not made a big fat fool of myself. Again.

"Grigor Yurogovnia, at your service." He bowed his head and clicked his heels.

"Alex!"

"Coming," I yelled again. "I gotta go," I told Grigor and looked down at the card. "Thanks." I nervously smoothed my long brunette ponytail. "Thanks."

"You are most welcome…Alex."

I think my smile lit up the whole café.

"Alex!"

"I gotta go."

"Go do your job. I do not mean to keep you," Grigor said, a big smile of his own showing off even white teeth.

"Okay." I smoothed my apron. "Okay…um, bye."

"Goodbye, Miss Alex. I will see you soon."

*****

"That was the first time I met him," I said, sighing. "Where I worked, he was there, I was there. He was good looking and older." We were back in my room in the dead of night, I was in my own clothes, and we were talking about things past, things long gone, things long dead. Things that needed to be dredged up from their dark and dirty prison of angry, hateful burning hell.

"How long ago was that?" Chris asked from his spot on my bed.

I turned from the French doors. "*That* was ten years ago."

He watched me. "You were taken with him?"

I sighed again. "Yes. As I said, he was very good looking, older, obviously, but that was okay. I didn't know until later that he was twenty years older than me."

Chris raised his brows. "Twenty?"

I smiled at the memory. "Yes. He was forty-eight, and I was twenty-eight. He was nice then…" I frowned, "…in the beginning."

Chris turned to Dimitri who was in a chair by the bed. "*Was* he nice then?"

Dimitri nodded sadly. "He was nice then, but changed soon after."

"Changed?" Chris turned back to me. "Changed how?"

I shrugged lightly. "In lots of ways. He was no longer the man I'd met."

*****

The next day, at twelve on the dot, Grigor and his henchmen walked back into the 401 Café.

My heart did a little dance, and I quickly smoothed my hair and apron, grabbed a menu and walked over. "Hi," I said a little too brightly. "Back again?"

He smiled at my enthusiasm. "Yes, Miss Alex, back again."

I handed the menu over nervously. "Would you like to be seated?"

He took the menu silently and held my hand, kissing it just like in an old movie.

My breath stopped, and I couldn't get air. My heart thundered in my chest, my knees went weak, and I felt my palm slick up with sweat.

He gazed into my eyes as he held my hand delicately. "We will have same table as yesterday, same order as yesterday, and you will have dinner with me tonight. Yes? I will not take no for answer, Alex."

"Yes." My mind fogged over, and I gazed into his big steel grey eyes and swallowed. "Yes," I breathed, not even knowing what I had just said yes to.

"Good." He grinned like the Cheshire cat. "Meet me at Bella Rouse at seven. I will be waiting." He sat, and his three henchmen sat with him.

I don't know how I managed to make it into the kitchen to get the order going.

"Oh, my God, is that the guy from yesterday?" Matilda asked, jamming herself next to me to look out the one way window on the plate counter to stare at Grigor. "He's very good looking. How old do you think he is?"

"I…I…"

She stared at me. "Oh, my God, you're blushing."

I blinked and stared back. "I need to…um…get their food…"

"Oh, my, God." She followed me. "You're crushing on him, but he's sooo old, and you've gone red, and he kissed your hand, what did he say?"

"Mattie, you should get back to work. I need to get their meals ready."

"Oh, no you don't. I want to know what he said."

"Nothing, he said nothing." My face felt like it was on fire.

"Liar! Your face is bright red, and it's spreading down your neck. What did he say?" She grabbed a huge knife from the bench. "What did he say? Tell me now, or the baby carrots get it." She picked up the small bunch of carrots from the bench and held the knife to them.

I looked from her to the carrots and back again. I grinned and felt myself come down to earth. "He asked me out on a date."

"He what," she shrieked.

"Shh, keep it down." I quickly gathered their meals together. "He asked me to meet him at Bella Rouse tonight at seven."

Matilda sucked in air. "Bella Rouse. You're going, aren't you?" She munched on one of the baby carrots.

"I don't know," I whispered, feeling my face burn again. "I don't know."

"Well, he's very good looking, and if he's not wearing a wedding ring, you should go. Bella Rouse is sooo expensive it's probably the only time you'll ever get to go."

I remembered an article I'd read about the restaurant and the cost to eat there. "Yeah, I know. But I don't know the guy. I wouldn't feel right, taking advantage just to get a meal there." I chopped some lobster.

Matilda took a swig of water from her bottle. "The guy is clearly interested, so go. If nothing happens you *get a free meal. If it does, then you get another date. What's the big deal?"*

I grabbed some salad. "I don't know him from a bar of soap."

"That's why they call it dating. Do you have a dress to wear?"

I sighed and added sauce to the lobster. "The only dress I've got is that black one from the funeral I went to. It's velvet, plain, boring."

"Get yourself a new one." She hopped off the counter and grabbed a new order from the rack.

"Can't afford it." I wiped my hands. "Can you take these to them, I might drop them."

"Sure. I'll ask him what his intentions toward you are." The mischievous look in her green eyes told me she wasn't kidding.

"Don't you dare," I threatened, waving a knife at her. "Or you're fired."

Her eyes grew wide. "You wouldn't do that just coz I ask him a question, would you?"

I stepped closer. "Keep your mouth shut and you keep your job."

"Only if you let me take you clothes shopping after work."

I sighed and relented. "Fine." I threw the knife down and handed her the plates. "Just go, and keep your trap shut."

She made a big deal out of smiling. "Sure I will. You can trust me..."

"Liar," I spat and grinned at her back as she walked out the door.

For the next hour, I nervously watched Grigor and his men, wondering if they were bodyguards, as they ate their meals and drank their drinks. When I saw they were finished, I walked out. "Hope you enjoyed your meal again?"

"Ah, Miss Alex. I was beginning to wonder if you were hiding from me." He finished with the cheque and stood.

"Um, no, just busy," I murmured, taking the bill with the hundred dollar note. "Um, I think you paid…"

"No, Miss Alex, that is your tip."

My head flew up. "What?"

"The hundred is your tip for such excellent service." He took my hand again and kissed it. "Remember, Bella Rouse, seven p.m."

And with that, he left me reeling.

*****

"Oh, my God, what about this one, or this one, or this one?" Matilda held up three dresses, all short, all blaringly bright colours, and all very expensive.

"I can't afford those and I certainly wouldn't wear them." I went back to perusing the racks at Classique Boutique, a trendy upmarket store that was currently having a sale.

"Well, what are you after then?" She hung them on the closest rack.

I sighed. "I don't know. Something classy, elegant, Bella Rouse style."

"Did I hear you say, Bella Rouse?"

I turned to see the sales lady.

"Bella Rouse is a very famous restaurant. You will need something high-end for that. Come, my dear." *She led me by the arm to the other side of the store.*

I protested all the way. "I don't want anything fancy or expensive. I've only got a small budget and was hoping for something on sale."

We stopped beside a rack of very high-end dresses, and her eyes narrowed in thought. "How small a budget?"

"Mmm, one hundred dollars," I said nervously, wondering if she was going to throw me out for not having enough money to spend.

"Let me have a look at you, dear. Turn around."

I slowly pirouetted as she checked me over from head to toe.

"Mmm, oval face, green eyes, cool tones, curvy figure. Mmm," she muttered to herself and whipped the measuring tape from her pocket. "Let me measure you, arms out."

She poked and prodded, spun me around, and measured every inch of me, even my boobs, right there in the store. "Mmm, I might have something for you. Go find a dressing room." She walked off, leaving Matilda and me to find our own way to the rooms at the back.

"We have three dresses in your budget that should fit you to a T." She hung three lovely dresses on the wall hanger outside my dressing room and handed me a soft red and black velvet one. "Try this first."

I dutifully took it and flung the curtain over. After quickly pulling my clothes off I pulled up the dress.

The curtain flew back. "Have you got it…no, let me zip you."

I glanced at the dress and thought it was nice. The red boat neck, long sleeve dress with black angular bottom half made the red hints in my hair come to life under the lights.

"Turn."

I was spun around full circle.

"Mmm, not quite." She patted her bun back into shape and ripped the zip down. "Try the green one."

I grabbed the curtain and whooshed it closed then changed dresses, whipping the curtain back for approval.

"No, not that one either, not quite the right tone."

I changed it for the blue-green creation that was left and realised it was different. It was soft and luxurious, and a breeze to pull on as it flowed effortlessly over my body. The mixture of the two colours brought my eyes alive and a pink to my cheeks. The one shoulder dress started from my left shoulder with ruching and glided down to just above my knees with deepening hues.

"Well?" The curtain was flung back, and I turned. The woman and Matilda gasped.

"That is it," the assistant said. "That is the dress."

"Oh, wow, Alex." Matilda's head bounced up and down in rapid fire agreement. "That's definitely the dress."

I smoothed it down. "Really? It is nice, and the

colour is lovely."

"The colour is perfect for you," the woman said. "You must have it."

I looked for the tag to check for a price. "But is it on sale?"

"It's on sale," the woman interrupted. "Take it off, and I will ring it up for you, quickly." She pushed me back into the dressing room.

I changed into my own clothes and took the three dresses to the counter. "How much is it?"

The woman snatched it from my hands and rung it up on the register. "One hundred dollars."

"One hundred, huh?" I was more than slightly suspicious.

She bagged it and took my money. "Yes, one hundred, it's your lucky day today." She popped the receipt in the bag and handed it over. "Thank you for shopping at Classique Boutique ladies, have a lovely time at Bella Rouse tonight."

"Oh, she will," Matilda said, grabbing my arm and racing out the door.

I made it back to my place at six and hurried into the shower. Five minutes later I was taking care of my beauty routine and whipping my hair into a chignon. I didn't rush my make-up, as that could spell disaster, so I took care and went slow. Spraying half a bottle of perfume on myself, I dashed into the bedroom and pulled out my best underwear and stockings. I stopped. What am I doing? God, getting excited over a guy I just met yesterday. A guy I don't even know. A guy who is older. What the hell? I sat on the bed and wondered if I was doing the right thing. Deciding that it was just a date and I only had to get dressed up for the restaurant, I slid into my delicates and slipped into my dress.

It slithered over my body like a second skin and fitted perfectly. I took a few moments to look at my reflection and the way the colour lit up my face. I smoothed it down and glanced at the clock. Yikes! Twenty to. Better get a move on. I grabbed my purse and keys and raced downstairs to find the cab I'd ordered just pulling up. "Bella Rouse," I told him as I got in the back seat.

Fifteen minutes later I stood outside one of the fanciest restaurants in Sydney. Fanciest and expensive. I took a deep breath and walked inside.

"Madam, welcome to Bella Rouse. What name is your party under?"

I looked around. "Um, I'm meeting Grigor Yurogovnia for dinner."

"Miss Alex."

I turned and saw the man himself, resplendent in a steel grey suit and black accessories.

"Alex, you..." He grasped his chest. "You look incredible."

My breath gushed out of me, and I smoothed myself down. "Um, thank you."

"Ah, Mister Yurogovnia. I will show you and your guest to your table now."

We didn't hear the maître d', so one of Grigor's men tapped him on the shoulder.

"Yes, of course," Grigor said, holding out his arm

for me to take.

He escorted me to the table and made a big deal of pulling out the chair for me to sit. Taking his own chair, he quickly ordered, and we waited for our food, snatching quick conversations here and there between gazing out at the view.

We ate the best of everything, drank the best of everything, and I laughed at his stories and jokes. The restaurant had magnificent views of the Harbour, and we watched the sunset from our table. The three men that had come with him were seated nearby, leaving us to eat and talk in peace.

"So…you're really descended from the royal family?" I asked while sipping my wine.

"Yes," he replied. "Generations back. We are almost no more after what happened. We have died out, not passed on our name, our story."

"The fortune," I said. "I know the Kremlin got most, if not all of it."

He nodded. "Yes, they got most of it." His bitterness was evident.

"It's sad what happened to the eggs. Some collections should just be kept together." I noticed his expression and wasn't sure he even knew what I was talking about.

He nodded again. "Ah, yes, of course. Faberge's famous eggs. They are almost a family legend now. I never saw any, but know the Kremlin have some."

"So I've read. I hate what they did to the palaces, and pulling apart all that fabulous jewellery. Ugh, it gives me shivers what they did to all those gorgeous

pieces."

"Yes, yes. Let's talk about something else. Like you, Alex. You look ravishing in that dress. Is it new?" His eyes hungrily devoured me like he hadn't eaten at all.

My stomach did flip flops and my face boiled from his gaze. "This old thing," I murmured, looking out the window, down at my lap, and around the restaurant.

"Dance with me, Alex." In one quick motion, he rose from the table, took my hand and escorted me to the tiny dance floor, whirling me around like there was no one else there.

My breath left my body and dizziness overcame me.

"Alex," he whispered into my ear. "I want to see you again. I want to see you every night while I am here. Will you see me, Alex?"

I breathed hard. I didn't know what to do, what to think, what to feel let alone what to say. I was dizzy and lightheaded.

"Alex?"

I looked up into his eyes. Cold, steel grey eyes hungrily devoured me from the inside out. No man had ever looked at me that way before. No man had ever devoured me before. My jaw moved, my mouth moved, my tongue moved, but not a sound came out.

"Alex?" he whispered again.

"Yes," I breathed back.

"You will see me for the rest of the week." His eyes bored into mine.

"Yes," I managed again. "Yes."

*****

Every day Grigor and his men came into the café for lunch, and every day he left me a note telling me when he would pick me up and what to wear. The notes would send delicious shivers down my spine as I read each word then squirrelled them away into my pocket.

Every afternoon I would find a dozen red roses on my doorstep.

Every night I would be picked up by Grigor in his limousine.

We spent our nights talking about anything and everything. Walking along the harbour, taking cruises and meals on his luxurious yacht. We wined and dined, danced and romanced until the weekend.

"It's a beautiful night," Grigor said, motioning to the stars above us, floating along in their own black ocean.

I shivered. "Oooh, it is." I rubbed my arms to keep them warm.

"Are you cold? Let's go below, you will be warm there." He led me downstairs and into his stateroom. "We will be warm here."

I stared at the huge expansive bed that spread from one side of the yacht to the other.

"Here, this will keep you warm." He placed a shawl around my shoulders, turning me as he did. "Alex," he breathed into my ear. "I want you, Alex. Tell me you want me, too."

I gasped. "Grigor..." He nuzzled me, and I was immensely turned on.

"Alex..."

"I..." His lips met mine, and his tongue delved deep. I pulled away, dazed, confused. "Grigor."

"Alex..." His lips devoured mine, leaving a trail of blazing kisses across my cheek and down my long slender neck.

"I..." I pulled away. "Grigor, I..." I couldn't think or speak or breathe.

"Alex..."

He gazed so intently into my eyes I felt them bore all the way down to my vagina, which ached to feel him, hold him, come with him as it thrust into my inner core.

"Alex. I want you. I want to be inside of you, on top of you, be one with you as I come inside of you."

"I..."

"Alex, tell me you want me. Tell me you want me inside of you."

I did, oh, God I did, but I had only known him a week, and God was I aching for him. "I..." I leaned into him.

"Alex..." He kissed me again, and I didn't hold back.

It's like we were on fire. Clothes were ripped off and flung on the floor, hands touched every inch of flesh.

Grigor picked me up, and I wrapped my legs around his waist. Tongues wildly delved as we kissed our way onto the bed, falling into a heap of tongues and legs. He found his way into my inner sanctum and thrust hard.

"Ah, oh, God."

He stopped. "Did I hurt you?"

"No." I pulled him close. "No, I want you. I need you."

We rocked back and forth as if there was no tomorrow. If the world was ending, we would be going out fucking each other like crazy.

"Oh, God," I cried. "Harder, faster, oh, God."

He thrust like a wild animal claiming a mate and I thrust against him, spreading my legs as wide as I could so he could spill his seed.

"Ugh, ugh," he grunted, slowing down but not stopping.

I fell back against the pillows, and he grabbed my breast, rubbing and squeezing as he slowed further. Bringing his knees up, he used the momentum to grab both of my breasts, and as I lay spread-eagled, he squeezed in time to his thrusts till he was done, collapsing on top of me.

"Ugh," I gasped. God, my insides pounded as my blood surged to my vagina and back. "God, that was good."

He pulled his head up and kissed me. "Yes, Alex, that was very good. Let's do it again."

*****

"You had sex with him after one week?" Chris asked, incredulous and still sitting on the bed.

I stopped pacing. "I had sex with *you* after one week." I could see by the look on his face he didn't know what to think. I shrugged. "Times are different now to then. I was twenty-eight, hadn't liked sex with any of my exes. And Grigor was very…charming, very athletic."

Chris didn't like what he was hearing. "So, that's when you fell in love?"

I thought about it and sighed. "Not *in* love. It wasn't *love*. It was *lust* pure and simple. He was *very* attractive and charming. I was charmed by his charisma and very attracted to him, physically, sexually. He charmed my knickers off, and it was all about lust and desire and craving the attention he heaped on me. It was exciting and thrilling and sexually explosive. Sex with him was amazing. I'd never experienced anything like that with my exes. He was a man, an athletic, toned Adonis who knew how to make a woman feel like a woman. He knew how to please her and pleasure her and put her in charge of her own body. He liberated me sexually. He made me feel alive and free and willing to explore sex in many ways. Sex with him was incredible, and I craved *it and him*." I sat on the bed. "That's probably the problem. He made me love sex. He made me crave it and want it. He made me addicted to it. Which is probably why I've done what I've done these last few years."

"How did sex with your husband lead you to sex slaves?" Chris asked, quite disgusted at the whole thing.

I shrugged again. "With Grigor, it started off like any other relationship, full of passion and sex. After a couple of years it became a chore he forced me to do. So, somewhere inside, I probably thought I was taking back control over him by controlling other men. Making them do what *I* wanted *them* to do instead of lying back and letting him be in charge. It's all about power and control, I guess."

"Was he *that* bad?"

I finally looked at him. "He wasn't when I met him. But he changed. He was so charismatic, so charming, so damn fucking good in bed."

*****

My fingernails trailed along rock-hard abdominals and soft salt and pepper hair that was spread luxuriously across his broad muscular chest. "Grigor," I purred. "We really should get up."

He grabbed my hand and kissed me roughly. "Why? Why should we?" He rolled on top of me and entered.

"Ugh," I widened, allowing him to do the deed. "Ugh." I had taken the week off work to spend it with him on his yacht, spending the whole time in bed, or some other room we would have sex in. Grigor was sexually adventurous, and his prowess in the sack turned me on in so many ways. It's not that I had been a shy lover before I met him, but you could call it a bored lover. Positions, places, sex toys. We tried them all, and I felt more like a woman than I ever had. Sexually aware and sexually active.

He grabbed my hands, pulled out, rolled me over and entered from behind. "Ugh, ugh, ugh," he grunted, pinning me to the bed before he finished and collapsed. *"Ugh, good, is good."* We lay that way for a few minutes before he rolled off and fumbled in a drawer.

I managed to roll over and came face to face with a huge diamond ring.

"Marry me, Alex."

I gasped at the ring. The huge square-cut diamond ring in white gold setting. *"I…"*

"Marry me."

"I…" My head moved from side to side. I wasn't thinking, wasn't…

"Marry me and you will live like a queen in Russia."

"Queen…Russia…" I blinked. *"Russia?"*

"Yes, Alex. Russia. Marry me and come home with me to Russia. Live with me in my luxurious palace. You can have anything and everything your heart has ever desired and wanted. You will have no want or need for anything. I will buy it all for you, Alex."

"I…" I shook my head and breathed deeply. *"I…"* God, do I? I thought. Marry a man I've known for two weeks and move to Russia with him? Do I?

"Alex. I can give you anything and everything."

I looked at the ring. I looked at him. The man lying naked beside me in all his massive manhood glory. *"Oh, I…"* I tried to catch my breath. *"I need to think…I need to think…"*

"What is there to think about?"

I think I looked at him like he was crazy. *"Ah… everything! My job, my life, my apartment, my friends."*

He shrugged nonchalantly. "I can give you money and a royal title, Alex. I can give you a life without debt or worry. I can give you a life where you can have everything your heart has ever desired. And," he whispered in my ear. "I can fuck you and pleasure you like no other man can."

I know I went beet red at that comment. Oh, God, what do I do? What do I say? "Yes..."

Wait, what!?

Fucking what?

"You said yes, Alex." He grabbed my hand and thrust the ring onto my finger. "You said yes. We need to get married straight away." He leapt from the bed and produced a simple well-cut slimline wedding dress from the cupboard. "You will wear this, and we will get married tomorrow in the registry office and leave two days after that."

"Two days...tomorrow..." I was dazed. What had I just done? I stared down at the massive rock on my finger. What had I just done?

Fucking what?

"Yes, Alex." He was firm as he laid the dress on the bed. "We get married tomorrow and fly out two days later."

*****

I still couldn't believe it three days later, sitting in his private jet with the three-man hit squad across the aisle. I was still dazed, still in shock, like I'd been drugged. We had gotten married in the registry office and were now on our way to Russia. I hadn't even needed to do anything, Grigor had done it all, from emptying my flat to packing a bag with toiletries. I had nothing. He'd thrown everything out except for the blue-green dress I bought for our first date. I had nothing.

Grigor sat beside me. "Do not worry, Alex. I will buy everything you need when we get home."

"Home?" I vaguely said, staring at the rock on my finger.

"Yes, darling. Home." He held my hand while we taxied along the runway and flew into the air. He waited half an hour before dropping another bombshell on me. "Here is your new passport and papers, and a present for you."

I took the folder with my credentials, looked at them and frowned. "Natasha Yurogovnia? That's not my name, and why is my hair blonde in this picture? This isn't me."

"Natasha is now your Russian name, and, of course, you will use Yurogovnia. You must also dye your hair. That is what's in the box, a bottle of hair dye. You will need to do it during the flight. Everyone is expecting a blonde Natasha."

*****

"Huh," I choked with laughter as I shook my head. "I should have known something was wrong right there, but I just…"

"Why didn't you?" Chris asked.

I shrugged. "I did. I was just still dazed by

everything that had happened. I *knew* something was wrong, but he explained it away so nicely. I had to change to a Russian name to fit in. I had to be blonde to fit in; otherwise, I'd be seen as an outcast, an outsider. Oh, Jesus…"

There were a few moments of silence before I walked into the closet and dug around in a box. Walking back into the bedroom I handed Chris, who was now standing, a picture. "Our wedding. He was very attractive, very charming."

"Oh…" He looked at it and looked away.

"He'd aged quite a bit by the time you kill…ed him." I finished the sentence and let it hang in the air.

Chris scowled. It wasn't something he wanted to be reminded of. Glancing down at the photo he saw the man looked younger, less grey. Less old than the one he'd pictured for the last seven years.

"He was younger and fit then," I added.

Chris studied the photo. "Yeah, younger." He glanced at Dimitri and held the photo up to compare the two. "You look nothing like him."

"Different mothers," was all he said.

Chris handed the photo back. "I still killed him."

"And I still thank you for it."

He scowled again. "That's *not* funny."

"Didn't say it was."

"Why did you stay married to him?"

I shrugged a shoulder. "At first I loved the way he made me feel. I loved the way he touched me and kissed me and fucked me senseless. Then, it changed and ended up being what it was."

He felt disgusted. "So you loved him? You were *in love* with him?"

I shook my head. "No. I was in love with the way he made me *feel. Not* in love with *him.*

Chris threw himself back on the bed. "So, how was married life?"

"Good, for the first six months. I still thought being blonde and calling myself Natasha was weird, but I dealt with it. The sex was plentiful, and he bought me everything I wanted. I was living the high life, parties, holidays." I shook my head sadly. "The first six months were great, and then things changed."

*****

"Natasha, my dear, what will you be doing today?"

I froze. I still wasn't used to being called Natasha even though we'd been married for six months. I sighed and turned from the breakfast buffet to see him already seated at the table. "I'm going to meet up with the head of that children's charity to talk about the next ball they want to hold." I sat down at the table and felt a twinge in my stomach.

Grigor sipped his coffee. "The one you put on last month was real money raiser. I'm sure you will do well as always, my love."

I smiled and ate some eggs. In the six months of being in Russia, Grigor had matched me up with six different charities to work with, which required two fundraisers each per year. So far, it had been a hectic schedule, and I was exhausted, but Grigor had given me two assistants to help out. They were permanent Yurogovnia staff and helped me with my weekly schedule of meetings, luncheons and parties. They would also call Moscow's most famous boutiques for clothes, and every time I was photographed wearing their stock, they sold out, and sales increased.

Moscow had made me an overnight sensation. I was married to the richest industrialist in all of Russia, and it made me a star. We were on everyone's guest lists, attended parties and functions every night during the week, while the weekends were for us. Quick getaways to St Petersburg and surrounding countries, or simply staying in bed.

My life had become so busy since marrying Grigor and moving to Russia I was surprised I had time for it all. I took a sip of juice while Grigor talked about an upcoming trip. I didn't feel well and wondered if it was the eggs. The twinge in my stomach tightened, and I put my glass down with a thud. "Ugh," I gasped.

"Natasha?"

I felt his hand on mine as my eyes were closed. "I feel sick," I whispered as my head set itself down on the table.

"Natasha? Myrna, call the doctor, quickly, quickly. Natasha?" He picked me up and carried me into the living room, laying me on the sofa.

My head was spinning, my stomach was churning, and I was falling into an abyss I couldn't climb out of.

"Natasha, my darling. Natasha, what is wrong?"

"Ugh." I grabbed my stomach and doubled up. The pain was intense and searing through my entire body.

It was nothing I'd ever experienced.

"What is it, Grigor?" The doctor came through the door.

"Yuchov, it is Natasha. What is wrong with her? What is wrong?"

"All right, Grigor, let me have look."

I felt hands poke and prod me; cold metal discs lay on my chest, and something went into my ear.

"Yuchov, what is it?"

"She has a fever, tenderness of stomach and…"

"And what, doctor?"

"Bleeding."

"Bleeding? From where?"

"We need to get her to women's hospital, Grigor. Now!"

"But, I, what is wrong with her, Yuchov?"

"She is bleeding from between legs, Grigor. We need to get her to hospital. No time for ambulance, we must drive, quickly."

I felt myself being lifted and knew the scent of my husband. "Grigor?" I mewed in a tiny voice. "Oh… Grigor."

"It is all right, my darling, we will get you to hospital, it will be all right…"

My eyes slowly slid open, closed and open again. I was lying in a bed in a cold, sterile room, the curtains half closed against the light. The door closed against the noise of the world outside.

"Mmm." I shifted and grabbed my stomach.

"Natasha?"

"Grigor?"

"I am here, Natasha, I am here. You rest, just rest…"

When I finally did wake it was because the nurse was clanking my breakfast tray down on the table. "Mmm, what?"

"You are wake. I get doctor."

I watched her walk out, and Grigor walk in. "Grigor." My hand slowly reached out, and he took it, kissing it with love.

"Natasha, my darling, Natasha. How are you?" He sat beside me.

"Sore, tired, hungry."

"Of course. Let me help you up, and you can eat this delicious breakfast they have brought you." He lifted the cover and found the oatmeal and juice to be quite unappetizing. "Ugh, maybe I will buy you something."

I settled into the pillows. "Maybe you should get Olga to whip up her pancakes with eggs and bacon."

Grigor smiled and took my hand. "I will do that."

"How is patient today?" A woman in a stiff white coat walked into the room, her blonde bun tightly wound, her steel-rimmed glasses tightly fitted. She read my chart.

"Doctor, what is wrong with my wife?" Grigor demanded. "I have been left out of everything, and no one has told me anything."

"I am sorry to tell you this, Mister Yurogovnia, but your wife has suffered miscarriage. She was two months along, but clearly, uterus could not sustain pregnancy. I do not see any reason she cannot get

pregnant again, just give it time before trying. Any questions?"

I was speechless. A miscarriage? But how? Who? Why? When?

Grigor stood staring at the doctor.

"No questions? Good. Your wife can go home today. I will go sign papers and nurse will tell you when you're ready to leave. Goodbye." She exited as quickly as she'd entered.

A miscarriage? I'd been pregnant? A baby?

Grigor turned toward me, speechless from what he'd just heard.

I looked at him with a flapping mouth and burst into tears.

He took me into his arms. "It's all right, my darling. The doctor says we can try again. It will be all right. We have only been married six months."

"I didn't know," I sobbed. "I didn't even know…"

We spent half an hour like that until the nurse came with my discharge papers. Soon, Grigor was wheeling me down to his car where he gently helped me inside and took me home. We were both silent, lost in our own thoughts as we drove through the gates and disembarked out the front. Grigor carried me up to our room and laid me on the bed.

"I will get Olga to make that breakfast for you and let you rest. I will be back later."

"But Grigor?"

He didn't stop on his way out the door.

I spent the day in bed being looked after by my assistants and took my meals in my room. I looked at the door constantly, still waiting for Grigor, who finally came home around one in the morning. I stopped pacing as he stumbled into the room. "Grigor, you're drunk. What did you do? Where have you been? I wanted you here with me. We need to talk about this, Grigor."

He removed his watch and dumped it on his nightstand with his wallet and keys. "Where have I been?" he slurred. "What did I do? Where have I been? Questions you have gall to ask me, all these questions when you cannot even be wife I want you to be." He faced me.

A freezing tendril of fear wound its way through my chest.

He waved his hand around. "You cannot even have baby, and you ask me where have I been?"

"You're drunk," I whispered.

"Yes, I am drunk," he roared menacingly, moving toward me. "I am drunk because I drank. I am allowed to drink and get drunk if my wife loses my baby."

"Grigor, I didn't—"

"Didn't what?" he breathed over me. "Didn't what?" He grabbed my arms and shook me. "Didn't what, Natasha? Didn't what?"

"Ow, Grigor, you're hurting me."

"Didn't what, Natasha?" His fingers tightened.

"I didn't lose the baby on purpose, Grigor, I didn't even know I was pregnant."

"Did not know," he spat, pushing me away before slapping me so hard I spun and sprawled onto the bed before sliding to the floor.

I clawed at the sheets to stop myself, but took them with me.

"Did not know you were pregnant. That is not good enough excuse, Natasha. You lose baby, my baby. You are dirty filthy whore who cannot even have baby properly. My baby." He spat on me and stumbled his way out of the door without looking back.

I sat on the floor in shock, not moving, not breathing, not doing anything except crying. Silent hot tears poured in rivers down my face. My jaw moved up and down, but no sound came out. The door opened, and I gasped and breathed. It was Grigor's right-hand man. He closed the door behind him, and I held my breath again.

"Miss Alexi, you all right?"

I managed to shake my head, and he came over and helped me back in bed, straightening the covers over me.

"Miss Alexi, we have heard you no longer with child. I am sorry."

"So am I," I whispered through my sobs. "I didn't even know."

"Did he hurt you?"

I managed a nod.

"That is not good, Miss Alexi. Boss man must be very upset, that is not like him. He is not violent man." My ragged breath made him stop. "You go to sleep. I will deal with boss man," he said and tucked me into bed.

*****

"Things got worse after that." I slowly paced my room.

Chris shook his head in disbelief. "I am *so* sorry. No woman should ever be slapped for losing a baby. Not even one they didn't know they were having."

"No," I agreed. "It changed something in him. That was the night things changed. For our marriage, our relationship, for us. I didn't know to what degree until Dimitri told me years later."

"What happened?" Chris looked back and forth between us.

"That was when Grigor met up with some...*new* friends. *New* friends that formed a club. They drank, they fucked strippers. Although Dimitri said Grigor didn't get into it then, he just hung around and watched his *new* friends do it," I told him.

Chris shook his head again. "Did he ever apologise?"

I faced him. "I barely saw him after it. When he *was* home, it would be an icy exchange. He was always off at some meeting, and I threw myself into charity work."

"Did he apologise?" he asked again, this time his voice was more assertive.

"Yeah, did it in a big way too. Six months after it was over it was our first wedding anniversary and he made a big deal of apologising. Jewellery, clothes, cars. Took me on a month long cruise, got down on bended knee and begged forgiveness. Begged me to give him another chance. That he hadn't been the husband he should have been, and allowed the alcohol to talk for him. He was sorry."

He frowned. "Did you forgive him?"

I shook my head. "I became *wary* of him. Pretended everything was okay and lied through my teeth to make him think it was."

"Was it?"

I looked at him with a smirk. "Well, I got pregnant on our anniversary trip, so for him it was."

*****

I touched my burgeoning belly. Seven months pregnant and feeling good. The baby kicked. Soft half-hearted attempts at moving in a tiny little place it must've been cramped in.

"Is the baby kicking?" Grigor placed his hand on my stomach and felt the tiny kicks. "He is kicking." A huge grin spread across his face. "He is kicking, our baby is kicking." He hugged me tightly. "Come, see what I have bought our child. Come."

He led me into the nursery and showed me the metre long racing car. "And look, it runs on remote so baby will not be in control."

"Grigor." I smiled at his joy. "This is all too much." I looked around the spacious nursery at all the toys, books, and play things he had filled the room with. He'd gone overboard.

"This is our first child. I will buy anything and everything for our son."

"What if it's a girl?" I watched his expression change.

"Then I will have to buy more things for our little

princess. In pink." He set about re-arranging some things as I watched.

He's so certain it's going to be a boy I don't think he's really ready for it to be a girl, I thought. What if he doesn't want it? I sat in the rocking chair by the window and looked over the expansive gardens. "Have we covered all the drains outside?" The house had been made childproof, but not the outside.

"The gardeners will take care of that next week, my dear. It will be done before baby comes home."

I released a deep breath and glanced around the room. My eyes landed on my husband, happy in his little world of being a father-to-be. What if something goes wrong, like last time? I thought. What if something happens to this baby?

The dinner gong sounded, and Grigor placed the bear back on the bed. "Time for dinner. I asked Olga to prepare your favourite. Shall we?" He helped me up, and we walked downstairs to the dining room where the first course was being served.

We chatted about the day, our work, or charities and watched some TV before retiring to bed.

There was no sex. There hadn't been since my stomach had grown. Just two people lying side by side in a spacious bed. I drifted off, worried about the baby, worried about Grigor, worried about myself. Ever since the miscarriage a year earlier I had worried about falling pregnant again. It seemed easy on our anniversary, and I had been relaxed enough for it to happen. I hadn't forgiven Grigor for slapping me, and I don't know if he knew it or not. The memory of my husband's hand still resonated, and ever since I'd wondered if I had made the right choice. I'm not sure staying was, and I regretted that choice every day.

"Argh." I lurched upward, grabbing my stomach that was ripped apart from the inside out.

"Natasha, what is it?" He flicked on the bedside light.

"Argh, the baby, my stomach."

Grigor flung back the covers, and we saw a puddle of blood between my legs. "Oh, holy God, Natasha, what is it? You are bloody again."

"The baby," I screamed, "the baby is coming... something's wrong..."

*****

I woke up several days later in the same hospital I'd had my miscarriage. There was no sound, no Grigor, no baby. I felt my stomach. Bandages covered my swollen belly.

The door opened, and Grigor walked in. Solemn, dark, blank.

"Grigor, our baby, what has happened to my baby." I reached for him, but he didn't take my hand, just stood there staring at me, expressionless.

"Our baby," he corrected in a cold, calculating way.

"Grigor." I was scared by the look on his face.

"Is dead."

Fear, ice-cold fear, dread, surprise, shock all rained down on me in seconds. "No." My hand dropped, and my head mechanically moved from left to right. "No, *no, no, my baby, no."*

"Is dead, Natasha. Our baby is dead. The doctor could not save it. It was born too early and had the umbilical cord around its neck. The doctor could not save it."

"No," I screamed, "you're lying. I want my baby." I couldn't even begin to describe what I was feeling in my heart, my mind, the pit of my stomach. "You are wrong, Grigor. Our baby is not dead." I flung the covers back and tried to get out of bed, but he stopped me. "Get away from me," I screamed, fighting him off. "I want my baby."

Two nurses came in with the doctor and struggled to get me back into bed where the doctor injected me with something that acted fast.

"You're...wrong...I want...my...ba...by..."

*****

"That's what he told me," I said, biting into an apple I'd picked up from the basket on a side table.

"Isn't that what happened?" Chris asked, feeling the same coldness inside that Alex must have felt at losing a second baby.

"Nope." I stared at the apple and felt that big fat cold pit in my stomach. "It wasn't until years later, just a few years ago, that I found out Grigor had ordered the baby killed."

Silence.

"What," Chris exploded. *"What do you mean, killed?"*

"It was a girl," I said simply, finally looking up with tears in my eyes. "He wanted his firstborn to be a son, and when it was a girl, he ordered the doctor to kill it by threatening to kill *him*. They made up the story of the cord being around its neck so I wouldn't know what he'd done."

Chris was astounded, and his head mechanically moved from side to side. "A boy was *that* important that he'd kill his own daughter?"

I stared at the disgust on his face and felt it deep down inside. Eight years later I was still disgusted at losing my baby and being lied to about it. A wayward tear slipped down my face.

Chris turned to Dimitri. *"What sort of an arsehole was your brother?"*

"One I did not like," he replied, knowing it was hard for me to recount the harrowing details of my life with his brother. His own heart was heavy with my words.

Still shaking his head, Chris turned back to me. "Did you have a funeral? Something?"

Now, it was my turn to shake my head, and I wiped my face. "Nope. Bastard cremated her before I even got to see her. Kept me drugged in the hospital."

His eyes widened, and his mouth dropped. "They didn't let you see your own baby?" came out as barely a whisper.

Another head shake. "There's no paperwork on her either. No birth certificate, no death certificate. It's like she...never...existed..." my voice drifted off in sad remembrance.

"Ah, fuckin' Jesus." He rubbed his head and walked around the room shaking it in shock at the things he was hearing.

"Why do you think I thanked you? The man turned into an arsehole."

He stopped. "Arsehole or not," he turned, "I'm still responsible for a man's death."

"That man killed my baby," I spat, another tear silently whooshing down my cheek.

Chris didn't know what to say to that, so just stood there staring at the woman he loved. The woman who had suffered so much at the hands of the man whose life *he'd* taken. The woman on the verge of tears that he felt himself being burdened with. What he had done paled so much in comparison with what she had been through and dealt with.

Dimitri spoke up from his seat. "He was no man, Mister Cameron, he was animal."

*****

I pulled the final weed from around the rose bush and gave the beautiful flowers a drink. It was five months since my baby had died, and I'd planted the rose bush in her memory. It was the quiet section of the garden, furthest from the house. A place where I could come to tell her how much I loved her. How much I wished she were there with me. How much I wanted her. "Grigor, you bastard," I hissed, "taking my baby from me. Not even letting me see her or bury her. I hate you, you bastard." I touched the small brass plaque I'd placed under the flowers and read the name. Rose Grace Carson. I wasn't about to give her the name Yurogovnia after what Grigor had done. I touched my face. The bruising was finally gone, and so was the swelling. "You bastard, Grigor," I hissed again, "You are no man, you are a monster."

I hadn't even been home two weeks when Grigor beat me for losing another baby, leaving me battered and bruised on the bedroom floor. Grigor's right-hand man had sneaked in afterwards and helped me clean up.

"Why is he doing this to me?" I asked him. "Why? Again?"

"I do not know, Miss Alexi."

"I lost a baby, and he beat me for it. I don't understand, and I don't like it. What do I do?"

"I do not know."

"But you know him. Tell me what to do. Do I leave him, divorce him, what?"

"There is only one way to leave marriage in Russia, it is not divorce."

"What are you saying?"

"The only way for you to be free is for him to die, my little Alexi."

I stood and gathered the gardening tools, thinking about what he'd said four and half months ago. Those words resonated in my head every single day. Every single day I hadn't seen Grigor. Every single day I hadn't heard from Grigor. Every single day I thought about leaving and going home to Australia. I wandered back up to the house and realised something. If death was the only way out of it, then who was I to say Grigor hadn't thought of the exact same thing. Killing me to get rid of me. I had no idea what he was up to. I hadn't seen him since the beating. What if he was plotting murder, against me? My murder?

*****

"*Was* he planning to kill her?" Chris asked Dimitri point blank while I wandered back into the closet.

"My brother kept many things from me, Mister Cameron. I had no idea what he was planning until after it happened."

"So, he *was* planning to kill her?" Chris went on.

Dimitri looked at me as I walked back into the bedroom holding a precious memory. "Seems so."

"Of course, it wasn't for another year, and a lot happened in that time. I think he was building up to it by beating me down." I handed over the plaque for Chris to see.

He took it and read it, his fingers sliding over the plaque belonging to the non-existent grave of my baby before looking at me with tears in his eyes. "He beat you again?"

I blinked. "Yes." Blink. "Several times." Blink. "But not the face." Blink. "He would threaten to kill me if I didn't behave and stick to my charities. That he could do *what* he wanted *when* he wanted, because he was very rich and very powerful."

"That old chestnut," Chris murmured, passing the

plaque back and wiping away his tears.

"He had my passport, my documents, everything. He became a drunkard, pummelling me into submission, so I was his little lap dog."

"Weren't you strong enough?"

My smile was half-hearted as I gently ran my fingers over the brass plate in my hands. "I thought I was, mentally. But after losing two babies, and realising I couldn't leave if I wanted to, I fell apart. I'd made my bed, I had to lie in it. Or so Grigor kept telling me."

"You didn't fight back?" The solemness of her expression as she gazed at the object in her hands made his heart ache.

"At first I tried. But after a while, I didn't have the energy. I became a cold Russian wife who did as she was told. Although, for the most part, he left me alone."

"So, why didn't *you* do something?" Chris asked Dimitri. "You're in love with her."

I snorted as Dimitri went white.

"Mister Cameron. I am not *in love* with Alexi, but I do love her. I have from the first moment I saw her."

*****

"Watch this." Grigor stuck out his foot, and the kid went sprawling.

"Hey," the kid yelled from the floor, "what'd you do that for?"

I watched Grigor rise and front the small child that

had dared to run through café. I rose, along with Sergei and Vladimir, and watched the little rat bastard back down and run off. I also watched Grigor hit on the very beautiful waitress. Her eyes sparkled like uncut emeralds and her teeth like opals. I watched her gush over my brother as he kissed her hand. And again the second time when he invited her to dinner and got to hear about it from Grigor later.

"She looks like fine specimen does she not, Dimitri?" Grigor pulled papers from his briefcase as they sat in their limo.

"She looks fine, Grigor, if that is type you are after." He tried his best to see the sights, but the windows were too dark. She is damn good type, he thought. Womanly, beautiful, good for having babies.

"Natalia, can you reserve two tables at Bella Rouse for me tonight," Grigor told his very young and very blonde assistant who pulled her phone out from between her very large voluptuous breasts.

"Pull the limo over, driver," Grigor called out. "Dimitri, all of you wait outside for a few minutes. I need to make private call." He waited for them to alight before pulling his cock from his pants. "Suck it," he told Natalia, who dutifully obeyed.

*****

"He was fucking around on you *before* he wined and dined you?" Chris asked, shaking his head at the rampant disrespect.

I cocked a brow and smirked. "Pretty much."

"You must've seen quite a lot then?" he asked Dimitri. "Being the right-hand man as well as the brother."

Dimitri shrugged. "I see most. He was, as you say, fucking around every night. After dating Alexi, he fucked Natalia. After fucking Alexi, he fucked Natalia. He filmed it all and would show us so we would know what stud he was."

Chris blinked. "What…" He blinked again and looked at me. "He *filmed* you having sex?"

"Apparently." I shrugged. "I didn't know. Not much I can do about it now."

He aimed a finger at Dimitri. *"Why the hell didn't you do anything? He was your brother?"*

"Who looked after me and took me in when I *had* nothing. When I *was* nothing. I kept mouth shut and did as was told," Dimitri roared back.

"*Which was nothing.* You stood back and *did nothing.*"

Dimitri knew he was right and sighed. "I am not happy with myself, Mister Cameron. But that was ten years ago. I have since made up for that."

"But you could have done so much more," Chris yelled. "You could have warned her about the sex tapes, other women, what life would *be like* with him. You could have gotten her out after losing the first baby when he hit her. You could have gotten her out after losing the second baby, or the beating. You could have gotten her out and saved her life, and *you chose to do nothing.*" Chris was steaming. All the years *he'd* wasted, and here was Alex who'd dealt with a hell of a

lot more at the hands of Grigor Yurogovnia.

"Chris." I tried to stop him. "Dimitri could have done a lot, but Grigor made his choices, and I made mine. And I have *paid* for mine every single day since. Dimitri didn't make me stay. I *chose* to stay. Out of duty as a wife and her vows to her husband, and then out of fear." I walked over to him. "In the end, I was in fear for my life because we were no longer a conventional man and wife. I didn't think he'd do what he did." I touched his arm. "But it was *my* choice to stay, *not* Dimitri's." I watched his expression change from fury to sadness.

"You could have saved yourself. All the years' worth of pain and physical violence." He felt like crying at all the years of pain she had endured.

I was sad too. "I know. But my soul clearly had lessons to learn."

"And what lessons were they? How to forgive a man for abusing you?"

"I *never* forgave him," I snapped. "I *NEVER* forgave him. I *always* hated him for what he did, but I felt powerless. I *was* powerless, and that scared me." I turned and walked onto the balcony, hoping the sea breeze and black sky would help ease the memories.

"I'm sorry." Chris moved up behind me and placed his hands on my shoulders. "I'm sorry. I shouldn't be speaking to you that way."

I sighed. "It's not your fault. It's always been mine, and I have to live with that for the rest of my life. *My* choices, *my* fault." I grabbed his hands and leant against him, relaxing against his broad torso and strong shoulders. We stood there for a while, listening to the waves crash on the beach.

"Do you remember how it ended? You said something before, during your…whatever that was, about having plastic surgery after being beaten and raped to death. Is that what he did to you?" he asked softly.

"No." I breathed. "He didn't have the guts to kill me himself. He got his *new friends* to do it."

"He what?" He turned me around to see if I was serious.

I stared up into his eyes. "Yes, but that's a long story in itself. One you need to ask Dimitri about. He's the one who told me afterwards and can explain it better."

"Let's go ask him then." Chris led me into the bedroom. "What did Grigor have his friends do? Who were they?"

Dimitri looked at me, and I nodded, but he stayed silent a few moments longer. "Alexi mentioned that after first baby Grigor met new friends. They pulled him into their world, more so after second baby. It was very private, only for rich men over fifty. You had to be discreet, quiet, mention it to no one."

"What sort of club was it?"

"A sadomasochistic club."

Chris's brows flew up. "Wow. I'm surprised, but I shouldn't be. Go on."

"There are many old men's clubs in Russia dating back hundreds of years. Sometimes you have father or grandfather who was member, most times not. Grigor was billionaire industrialist who had been on their want list of membership for long time. When first baby die, it gave him excuse to get drunk and wallow like fat sow in mud pen. He drank a lot, in same club, every night for weeks. That is when they befriend him, buy him more drinks, invite him to card games and boxing ring. Except boxing ring full of women. Naked women. He was spectator most of time. Getting occasional lap dance from whore, but he did not cheat on Alexi, he held back."

"How nice of him." The sarcasm dripped from Chris's lips as he crossed his arms in front of him.

Dimitri ignored him, but inwardly agreed. "After second baby, he run to new friends and join full-time. He would join in sex parties, drug parties, whipping parties. He whip whores as he get ass whipped. His new friends were very important businessmen, like him, and became tight-knit group of own, and they, how you say, upped the ante."

"What did they do?"

"They started killing."

"What?" Chris stared from Dimitri to me and back again. "Killing who?"

Dimitri waved his hand. "Prostitutes, whores, whatever you call them."

"Wait. They *actually killed* them?" Chris asked.

"They *actually killed* them," Dimitri replied.

"Bloody hell." Chris looked at me. "Is that like what happened to you?"

I nodded. "Go on," I told Dimitri.

"It first happened on second anniversary. Grigor was at man's house, and it was full of hookers, drugs, vodka. They fuck, they snort, the drink. They took turns with whores and did things to them. Violent things, other than whipping. They used objects to fuck them with and make them snort and drink until each one pass out until last when they all descend on her and hold her down. Each one get off on it, doing what they wanted, inserting objects, fucking her senseless until she did not move. They did not realise she was dead. All of the men had bodyguards. We were Grigor's, and since we were sober, we realised what had happened. Each of us took our boss back to their homes, and the guards who were with their boss took care of women. That is how it became. The next week when they ask what happened we told them. At first, they disgusted, then they excited. They get away with sex and murder and no one would ever find out."

"Did they? Find out, I mean?" Chris asked.

"No, Mister Cameron. No one find out. When they realised they could do what they wanted and we would clean up, they did it every week. Every week we would troll streets for whores no one would worry about. And every week they would rape and murder. Every week they would use different technique to do so. Every week one man's bodyguards would have to clean up."

"That's disgusting." Chris shook his head, and his hands went to his hips. "Bloody disgusting. Did the police ever find out? What about the hookers? Their bodies would have been found; did *no one* complain about it?"

"Hookers in Russia not given fuck about. Even

police fuck them," Dimitri said.

"Great," Chris huffed, "remind me never to go back to Russia! So none of the men ever got into trouble? No one ever found out?"

Dimitri and I looked at each other. "They got into trouble," I said. "In fact, you've read all about it in that big fat file of papers I keep in the closet." I casually looked at him.

Chris's eyes widened. "How…did you?"

"I put them there to push you into revealing everything so that you could then help me."

The truth dawned in his eyes. "Those men I read about, the ones that were killed, are all part of Grigor's men's club?"

"Yep. So, you know they're all dead. They got their *just* desserts," I replied with a slight smirk.

"What are you saying? They were killed because of what they did? To the hookers or to you?"

"Who do you think?" I snarled at him before pursing my lips and blanching in regret. I glanced at Dimitri because I couldn't look Chris in the eye.

"Sit down, Mister Cameron. It is another long story."

*****

"Dimitri, we are having some guests tonight. My friends from the men's club. You will need to disappear until needed for clean-up duty."

"Grigor, you do know Natasha is home?"

"Don't worry about her. We'll be in my office for

two hours, and she never goes there. Besides, I think she's taken to those pills her doctor has given her. She won't know what is going on. Wait in the servant's quarters until I call you. I will ring bell."

"Of course, Grigor."

Grigor strode upstairs to see his wife and found her in her office on the third floor. "Natasha, my dear. I want you to entertain my friends tonight. Wear your best lingerie and get your pussy waxed for me. There's my dear Natasha." He walked out feeling the daggers in his back and went about his business stocking up on vodka, cigars, and the best blow he could buy on the streets. He also knew they'd be bringing their own.

Six-thirty came, and he led his guests into his office. They all used their home offices; it made it easier, so there were no questions asked. "I have very special surprise for you tonight, and it is one all of you get to play with on your own. I will be needed elsewhere, so you get to have fun without me."

"Why are you not staying, Grigor?"

"As I said gentlemen, I have things to do. I will go and get your surprise now." He left the room and walked up to Natasha's bedroom where he found her waiting. "Natasha, my dear, come meet my friends. Make sure you give them what they want."

"Yes, husband," she replied and followed him out of the bedroom and into his office wearing nothing but a see-through negligee.

"Well, what have we here, Grigor," the heavyset man said. "Entertainment?"

"Of course," Grigor said. "My wife is here to

entertain you. To entertain all of my friends."

"So, Grigor, is your wife up for anything?" the bald man asked.

Grigor smirked as Natasha shivered in her nightie. "Oh, she likes to think she isn't, but I know she is."

The five men laughed.

"Darling, come and say hello to Nicolai."

She walked over to the man in the chair and her husband's outstretched arm.

"Nicolai. This is Natasha, here to do your bidding."

"Grigor," she started, crossing her arms over her chest.

"Quiet," he snapped and grasped her arm tightly. "You say nothing, and you do nothing except what my friends ask of you." He leant in to whisper in her ear. "Do you understand me?"

She whimpered. "Yes, Grigor," whispered from between her lips.

"Good girl," he muttered and thrust her into Nicolai's dirty outstretched hands.

Nicolai's greedy filthy hands grabbed her and groped her, and she squealed as one went between her legs and into her private area.

"Grigor," she squealed and slapped his hands away. "Grigor, help."

"I told you to say nothing and do what they want," he snapped, stopping at the door. "I will see you, my friends, later."

"Grigor," she yelled as he pulled the door closed behind him. "Grigor."

Silence.

He straightened his tie, paused, sneered and walked away.

*****

"Each man filed out one by one and left with bodyguards. When they were gone bell rang. Bell let us know to go and clean up mess. We heard clock chime nine as we walked into room and it was mess. Blood, vodka. It was awful. Worse than ever seen. I told Sergei to get blanket so we wrap woman, and Vladimir to get towels to clean up. We could not find clothes or bag. We clean up, and I search body for jewellery. No earrings, no necklace. This woman had nothing until I saw her left hand."

"Her left hand?" Chris frowned. "What was wrong with it?"

Dimitri looked from him to me. "She was wearing wedding rings. Alexi's wedding rings."

*****

Dimitri stared at the rings on the dead woman's left hand. A huge diamond engagement ring and diamond encrusted wedding band. He had been with Grigor in Sydney when he picked them out and bought them. "Natasha," he murmured, looking from the rings to the area that had once been her face. He looked back at the hand and saw her fingers move ever so slightly. He sucked in air. "You are alive," He glanced up at Sergei and Vladimir who looked both confused and stunned.

305

"She is alive." He squeezed her hand and leaned in so she could see him. "I am here. It is me, Dimitri. I will help you. I will save you. I will protect you. I will do anything for you, my little Alexi, anything. Sergei grab blanket, we must wrap her, quickly."

They gently lifted her and wrapped the blanket around her. Dimitri took her into his arms. "Clean mess and tell no one what happened. I will dispose of body. Quickly." He rushed from the room, through the house, and into the garage where his car was hidden. Easier to sneak a body out when he needed to. Laying her on the back seat, he climbed in and headed for a very private hospital he knew where discretion was its middle name and no one asked for identification.

Screeching to a halt out the back of the small but well equipped building, where its discretion extended to no signs and no one knew it was a hospital except for those who used it, he lifted Alex from the back seat and hurried into the waiting doctors and nurses. "Help her, you must help her." He laid her on the bed, and they wheeled her into emergency. Ten doctors and nurses were on her at once.

He stood, watching. There was no way Alexi would be out of his sight any longer. His phone beeped. "Yes?"

"We have cleaned up mess and everything spic span."

"Leave and dispose of evidence. Do not talk to Grigor, understood?"

"Understood."

He watched as they worked to save the life of Natasha Yurogovnia, formerly known as Alex Carson. The woman known to him as his sister-in-law. The woman known as the Queen of Russia.

The woman he would die for.

The woman he will kill for.

*****

"They did the same to you as the others," Chris said softly. "Did they *know* they were doing that? They would do that to *you*?" He stood in front of me, tears in his eyes at the pain they had caused me.

I sucked in air trying to control the onslaught of tears I knew was fighting to break free from their tortured prison. "I knew Grigor was a bastard but didn't know he got up to stuff like that. And I certainly didn't know he had that planned for me. Otherwise, I would have killed him first."

"Do you remember any of it?" He gently touched my face.

I grabbed his hand and kissed it then shook my head. "In dreams, it's fragmented, bits here, bits there, but no whole picture. What they did took care of that."

He stepped closer. "What actually happened? How did you survive?"

I smiled and stretched my back and neck, clinging to his hand the whole time. "Dimitri got me to the hospital on time. They were able to stick me on life support, and I underwent surgery for hours. I don't remember, I only know what he told me and what my medical records say."

His frown reappeared. "You have your medical records?"

"Yes. Part of the confidentiality aspects of the hospital. All patients get their records when they leave. I was only there for a few days until they could airlift me to another hospital where I spent *years* recuperating. I was stabbed, shot, beaten, electrocuted and drowned. They pumped my stomach and got me into surgery, removed the bullet and repaired the damage. Some of it anyway."

"They couldn't fix all of it?" Chris was sick to his stomach at what he was hearing.

I rubbed my lips together. "I was raped," my voice broke, "with objects. There were some things they couldn't repair straight away." I swallowed. "I was in that hospital for four years. Getting surgery after surgery and ten plastic surgeries on top of that to fix the outside. I was either in my own coma or an induced one, and thankfully I don't really remember it."

I sat on the bed and put my head in my hands. "Whenever I read my charts, I feel sick, and images roll through my head. I don't know if they're real or not, but just seeing them makes me sick." I glanced at him and felt so sick at what I was about to say that I looked away. "I, um, had damage to my insides pretty bad. I um, can't...actually...*have* babies, but I still have my ovaries, so I may be able to use a surrogate if the time and need ever arises." I rubbed my face while that news sank in.

Chris sat beside me and rubbed my back and neck,

realising what I'd actually said. "Oh, Alex." His face crumpled. "I am *so* sorry," he said. "So, so sorry." His heart ached. Not only had she lost two babies, but now she would be able to have no more.

"So am I," I mumbled before sitting up. "So am I. I spent four years in hell and came out looking like this on the other end of it. With bad migraines and an addiction to sex and pain. Plus, some sort of split personality."

"Do you put it down to that or was it a choice?"

I looked at Chris. "I think it was both."

"How do you mean?"

"I think the assault left my brain fried. I became two people fighting in the one brain. All of the drugs I was on, the combination of everything made me think I needed to get back at him somehow, so I controlled other men sexually because he wasn't there."

"So you were the real you, Alex, and the fake you, Natasha, was fighting to be in control?"

"Yes."

"Is that why you wore wigs and negligees?"

"That came after. All of the surgeries fried my scalp, so I had almost no hair. Over four years I had the surgeries to fix it, and it's finally looking good. But Dimitri bought me a wig to wear, the black Cleopatra one. I couldn't be blonde or brunette, so black it was. It struck with Natasha. My own hair has only finally looked good in the last year or so." I ran a hand through it.

"It looks good to me." Chris ran his own hand over it. "You look fantastic."

I smiled. "I don't look like the old Alex, though. The *old* me."

"So." He shook his head. "You're the *new and improved* Alex."

My smile widened. "I don't know about new and improved."

"How about better than before. Better than ever?" He pulled me into his arms and hugged me, kissing my cheek softly. "You're *alive*, Alex, that's the main thing."

"And those bastards are still dead," Dimitri piped up.

We looked at him.

"Those men I read about in your file, it was them? They were the ones who did this? They were shot, stabbed, beaten, electrocuted and drowned too?"

"Yes," I murmured. "They were the ones." I snuggled into his chest.

Chris glanced at Dimitri over my head. "I suppose *you* know all about it?"

"Of course, Mister Cameron. I am one who killed them."

*****

"I will get revenge, Alexi. I promise you. I will do to them what they did to you, but they will not be on life support. They will be in ground." Dimitri stood by her bed, looking down at the woman who was his sister-in-law. The woman who was so wrapped in bandages she was unrecognisable. It was only two days after the assault, and the hospital was flying her to another for better care.

It was out in the mountains where no one would find her. "I vow to you, Alexi, I will kill them."

The doctor and nurses came in to get her ready for transport, and after the helicopter arrived, he waited for her to be made comfortable. "Take care of her doctor."

"We will."

The door shut, and he watched it fly away until it was a tiny dot in the sky. "Time for revenge." He drove to a small house he owned and set himself up, writing down the names of the men involved, the layouts of their homes, and where their offices were. He strode down to the basement and pushed aside a cabinet, pulled off the wall grate behind it, and retrieved his weapons stash. Knives, guns, baton and ammo. Back upstairs, he added the names of relatives named Natasha.

Oh, the irony.

They all had one.

He loaded his car with his loot and drove back to Grigor's.

*****

"So...you *did* kill them?" Chris shook his head. "How?"

"It was easy," Dimitri boasted. "I use Grigor."

Chris frowned. "What do you mean, you used Grigor?"

"I use Grigor as excuse to get into their houses, but first I took care of their relative."

"Doing to them what they did to Alex?"

"Exactly." He was so proud of his accomplishments.

Chris sighed at his show of arrogant pride. "What did the relatives have to do with it? What did *they* do?"

Dimitri's pride turned to anger. "Alexi is my relative. I took of theirs, what they took of mine."

"What I remember from the articles, the relatives, named Natasha, were assaulted in the same way, two days before you killed the men." Chris tried to remember all he had read.

"Exactly."

"So how did you use Grigor to get in?"

"By telling them I had something from him. I started with Alexander Von Blon. I told him Grigor had plans for get together and he let me in. We went to his office and talked. He was cleaning his knife at the time, and it was no problem to overpower and stab him. I took knife with me."

"As a souvenir?" Chris sneered.

"As weapon to drive Grigor insane," Dimitri shot back.

"What do you mean?"

"Listen to rest of story, Mister Cameron, I tell you." He shifted in his seat. "Nicolai Matuschewski was old man. I told him story Grigor had plans and old man let me in, and I shot him with one of Grigor's guns. It has silencer, so no one heard. Yuri Putin was different. I needed baton to bash him to death. The staff was home, and I entered through private doorway. He made sound, so I covered his mouth until unconscious then beat him. Not so bad. Victor Oblonsky was easy. He was another old man who loved his vodka because he started vodka business. Also Grigor's favourite drink. I hold him down and pour several bottles down throat. Easy. Boris Yeltonson not so. I had to make sure lamp able to electrocute when he turn on. While he not look, I screw with wires, he turn on, how you say, kerplooey, he dead."

"You killed them all yourself?"

"Yes, Mister Cameron. I'm trained KGB, we all are. We know how to kill people."

"Lovely," Chris muttered. "You obviously didn't know?" he asked me as I was still beside him on the bed.

"Nope. I was in a coma for four years. I have an excuse."

Chris turned back to the man in the chair. "You mentioned souvenirs?"

"Yes. I took from each man what they use to hurt Alexi, and after each murder, I put it in Grigor's home office for him to find. All wrapped up in newspaper with headline." He chuckled. "It drive him crazy. He tell me, *'Dimitri, how did it get here, who is doing this to me?'* I tell him it his imagination, I can't see anything, maybe he done something wrong and it is karma out to get him."

"You did that every single week?" Chris asked.

"Every week for five weeks. Knife, gun, baton, vodka, taser. All wrapped up like neat little package. It make him crazy," Dimitri told him.

"You *drove* him crazy because of what he'd done?"

"Yes, Mister Cameron, I drove him crazy."

*****

"Dimitri, what hell is going on? I can't be imagining things. You tell me you don't see that Taser in that paper." He pointed to the parcel on his desk. *"Boris is dead for God's sake. Someone has killed him, and they are out to get me next."*

"Grigor, just because someone send you same thing, does not mean they are out to get you. You are rich man, Grigor, you can find who is doing this."

Grigor paced back and forth across his office. *"Yes, yes, you are right. Why didn't I think of that? With Natasha out of way, and my friends dropping like bed bugs, I should have been doing something. You, Dimitri, look into this for me. You are not only brother, but bodyguard as well. You know the other guards, are they doing this?"*

"Why would they, it means they out of job?"

"They are out of job anyway. I need you to look into this, do that for me, Dimitri. Look into the calls I've been getting. Those ghastly calls where there's whispering down the line. It's like they're calling me from the grave, Dimitri. They're calling me from the afterlife, telling me they're coming for me. I do not like it, Dimitri, do something."

"Yes, Grigor, I will do something."

*****

Dimitri chuckled. "I call him five times every night and pretend to be dead men. He sleep with one eye open."

"Was that around the time I…?" Chris winced.

"One week after Boris drop dead, Mister Cameron. One week to the day."

"How did you…what did you do to get him there?"

"Not a lot, ironically. Phone calls, few holograms of dead men in mirror or window. Threats on paper slid under office door. It drive him crazy. That night we go out. He wanted to get out of his office so he wouldn't be next. We drive, he get phone calls. Five phone calls. I set up machine to make them as I was with him. Messages tell him I know where he is and I'm coming for him. It freak him out. He jumps from limo and goes running through streets. He far ahead and I lose him. I keep walking and find crowd of people ahead. It was movie set, and Grigor had been hit by car. *Your* car, Mister Cameron. I stand and watch. Watch paramedics. Watch you look at body. Watch ambulance take him away. I watch until there was nothing else to watch, and then I walk away."

"Wait," Chris started, realising what he'd just said. "You were there, and you did nothing… Why the hell didn't you come forward and say something?"

"Mister Cameron, it not my fault he jump out and run. It not my fault he run into your movie set. I went back to limo and went home. When police came, I told them he had not been home all night and was worried about all the killings that had been happening. They said they have killer."

"Killer," Chris spat and stood up. "I am *no* killer."

"We *all* are, Mister Cameron," Dimitri replied. "We *all* are."

I watched Chris pace the room. "You just said you weren't a killer and yet you've been blaming yourself all these years. Don't do it anymore. You really did do us all a favour." I shut up when he glared back at me.

"That was six weeks…after you…were assaulted?"

"Yes."

He softened. "You were in the hospital?"

"Yes."

"What happened after that?"

"Well, Dimitri had to handle everything. Told everyone I was out of town and he'd tell me himself. After that, I went into hiding to deal with the shock and loss. Slowly, over time, Dimitri dealt with everything. The lawyers, the property, stuff. He sold off the house, everything in it, the cars, the other properties. All that's left is this island, the plane and the yacht. Plus, all the money."

"You sold off everything?" Chris asked him.

"Yes," Dimitri said. "I knew Alexi would not want it. After baby number one we grow close. I had lost wife and baby many years before, so I knew loss. We became good friends. We're also in-laws."

I turned and smiled at him. The one man who had been the constant in my life.

"What happened after that? When did you get better?" Chris asked me.

I turned back to Chris. "I didn't. Four years of comas, surgeries, pain, living hell. And in the middle of that, somewhere, I understood what Dimitri would tell me about. As I was able to sit and speak, he told me about his plan. How Grigor had died, how he'd sold off everything. We would talk for hours so he would remind me of my life before. I didn't remember much of that time, my memory was affected, and I easily forgot. Once he was done with Grigor, he spent more time with me, and once everything was sold off, he was by my side twenty-four seven, helping with my treatment, my recovery, talking to me, walking with me through the grounds. I had to learn to walk and talk again. I was covered in bandages for years, but Dimitri made it bearable. And he made sure I had the best doctors, especially plastic surgeons. It took a year and a half to repair the damage done."

Chris moved toward me. "And that's where your migraines started?"

"Yes. My skull was bashed in, and I had brain damage. Swelling, clots, you name it, I had it somewhere on my body. I was drugged up to the eyeballs for three years, weaned off over the last. That was when we could tell what still caused pain. By the time I left, I was physically healed and looking different. Which *is* a good thing, but I was emotionally different as well."

"Did you have, *do* you have, a split personality?"

"Not technically. In the hospital, I would go back and forth. Dimitri explained who I was and the name change, and they realised it was simply because of the damage, swelling, medication. I would speak Australian one minute and then continue the conversation in Russian. By the time I'd left it had settled. I didn't realise it had taken over. Half the time I didn't know myself. I went into the hospital as Natasha Yurogovnia and came out as Alex Carson. I've been Alex since."

"What did you do when you got out?" He sat beside me on the bed.

"I saw the sights of Russia. I had vague memories of it from before, so wanted to see it again, like a tourist. Dimitri, Sergei and Vladimir took me on a holiday of Russia's most famous sights. Dimitri also made sure I remembered having money, so I could go anywhere I wanted when I wanted. We travelled for a year. Europe, Africa, the Middle East. It was amazing, and then we came here."

He was puzzled. "So why choose *this* island?"

I smiled. "*That* is another long story."

*****

I stared at the face in the mirror. Well, it was the face I had now, not the face I had before. My fingers slowly glided all over. Forehead, nose, cheeks, ears, chin. The face that was now my own. Now mine.

I wasn't sure I liked what I saw.

"Alexi?"

My eyes flicked to Dimitri's reflection as he stood behind me. His big manly hands rested gently on my shoulders, and he smiled.

"Alexi. Have you had good time on Greek Islands?"

I smiled back and my eyes closed. "Yes, God, yes. It's been so peaceful and calm. So laid back." I sighed happily. "I love it here."

"Do you want to stay on or go somewhere else?"

My eyes flew open. "I want to stay until I'm ready to leave. No timetable, no appointments, let's just spend the rest of summer here and relax."

"Anything you want, Alexi. Do you want to go out tonight?"

"Of course," I said brightly, jumping up from my seat and hugging him. "I have that new dress and must wear it. What time is it?"

Dimitri looked at his watch. "Five-thirty."

I stood at the closet of my luxurious suite and gazed at the clothes I had bought. Pulling out the dress I'd just gotten yesterday, my hand glided over the soft silky material. Brilliant blues, greens and yellows shimmered with sequins in the afternoon rays floating through the French doors. "We will leave at eight-thirty. That will give me time for a nap and bubble bath."

"Of course, Alexi. I will let you sleep."

"Thank you, Dimitri." I turned to him. "For everything."

"Of course. Anything for you, my little Alexi."

He left me to ponder my night as I matched a pair of brand-new Italian gold sandals and clutch to the dress. It was long and flowing, similar to a caftan, and suited the late summer colours of Mykonos and Santorini. After hanging the dress up so the sun's rays made it sparkle, I lay down on the bed and set my alarm for an hour. An hour nap and two hours to get ready, I knew the night would be exactly like all the others.

*****

The buzzer sounded beside my ear, and I lazily reached over and turned it off. I stretched luxuriously on the king-size bed and let my eyes open at their own pace. The early evening rays of the sun had deepened the colours of the room and, hitting my new dress, made it sparkle like a million diamonds. I glanced at the clock. Six thirty-five. "It is time for me to get ready," I murmured, alighting from the bed and moving into the bathroom.

While the bath was filling, I studied my face in the mirror. "Is good. Not as good as before, but good." I turned and stepped into the huge tub, shut off the taps, and slid under the water. Using the finest skin care products, I bathed and rejuvenated for an hour before slipping out and covering myself in body cream. "Must keep skin looking good for all young men to touch."

Finishing with the cream, I picked up my face lotion and applied it liberally. "Would not look so young without it." Once it had soaked in, I carefully applied my make-up and dried off what little hair I had. "Not thick and strong yet." I lightly fluffed the thin brown fuzz that covered the scars on my scalp. "That is why I have wig." I picked up the black Cleopatra cut wig from its foam head and pulled it on, adjusting it until it was sitting straight. Picking up my brush I began to stroke. One, two, three. One hundred strokes later I walked into the bedroom and slipped into the gold high-heeled sandals. Admiring myself in the full length mirror, I studied my body. Firm, taut, scar free. "Maybe I should go out like this tonight," I said to the woman in the mirror. There was a knock at the door. "Yes?"

"It's Dimitri. It's nearly time to leave."

I sighed at the thought of having to put the dress on to cover up my perfect body. "Just a minute." I grabbed it from its hanger and slid it over my head. It shimmered over me like a second skin, all soft and silky. Picking up my purse I flung open the door and sashayed into the living room. "I am ready. Let's go."

Hearing the Russian accent, Dimitri knew they were in for trouble and was now reluctant to leave. Natasha only seemed to surface at night, and he knew what she would want to do. "Of course, my Queen. We will go."

Winding her way through the streets of Santorini, Natasha shimmied her way up to every good-looking young man she came across. Visiting several popular nightclubs, she danced and gyrated with as many men as she could. And all realised she was not wearing underwear.

"Darling," she purred to one hot young stud. "I want to take you to my room and fuck you till morning."

His head pulled away in surprise. "You're fresh. We've only just met." The Latin American heartthrob was pulled against her.

"I want you," Natasha stated. "I want you now." She pulled him after her and stopped Dimitri with a wave of her hand. Once outside, she found a quiet spot in an alley, planted her back against the wall, hiked up her dress and demanded he fuck her.

"What? Here?" He saw her bare naked flesh and salivated.

She grabbed his hand, yanked him toward her and grabbed his crotch. "Here." She shoved his shorts and underwear down, pulled his cock out, rubbed it a few times and led it to her.

Excited at having his dick pulled, the Latin stud picked her up and shoved his dick in hard.

They ground together against the wall of the club in time to the music wafting on the breeze.

"Uh, oh, uh," Natasha groaned. "You have big dick. Uh, oh, you good."

"Is a fuck all I get?" the stud asked.

Natasha stared into his eyes. "No." She thrust her tongue into his mouth, and they mashed together, faster and faster with the beats of the music. "Uh, oh, God," she cried out as she came. "Fuck me, fuck me, oh, God, fuck me."

He slowed to a halt and gently let her down.

"I want more," she purred into his ear. "Come to my villa, come with me all night."

"That an invitation to go back to your place?"

"What do you think?" She gazed up into his big brown eyes. "Come fuck me."

"Absolutely!"

She slid off him and pushed her dress down. Taking his hand, she led him back to her luxurious villa by the sea. Private, away from everyone and everything. She led him into the bedroom and pushed him onto the bed, whipping off his pants, underwear and shirt. She admired his body while he lay back *watching her. "Muscular." Her fingers trailed along his abdomen. "Broad, masculine, manly." She pulled her dress over her head, let it fall to the floor and waited for his admiration.*

"You are good. Very, very good."

She bristled slightly. "Only good?" she purred, walking to the closet and opening a small trunk. Choosing a few toys, she turned around, displaying the cuffs and whip she had selected. "Only good?"

The flickering emotions on his face went from shock to desire. "Maybe that should be bad. Very, very bad." He laid back as she descended on him and cuffed him the bedhead.

Sliding down his body, she murmured in his ear. "You have not seen anything, stud."

*****

"Natasha had him for the whole weekend," I told Chris. "Normally they'd just last the night, or for a quick fuck in some alley. But he was good."

Chris felt sick, knowing the woman he loved was a sex fiend. And what if she couldn't stop? What if Natasha was still in there somewhere and wanted to resurface at some time? What if Alex couldn't control her, *it*, and started back on the road to the hell she had been living? "So, that was the start of Natasha and her sex slaves?"

I thought about it. "No. It started six months earlier, six months after getting out of the hospital and into our holiday. I'm not sure *how* it started after I left the hospital. I slipped in and out of personalities, slowly at first, here and there, and then when we got to Mediterranean countries it, *she,* popped out more and more. Italy, Greece…we were in these countries for months, and there were all sorts of men for her to sample."

"Were *you* aware of it?" Chris asked me, holding himself back from vomiting.

I shook my head sadly. "No. If I were, I would have had Dimitri lock me in my room at night."

"Why didn't you stop it?" he asked Dimitri.

He sighed. "Alexi, Natasha, is very strong-willed woman. I did not know what to do. Doctors said to let it happen. She needs to work things out on own. She is adult, she decide."

It was Chris's turn to sigh. "How did you get from Greece to *this* place, what did you call it before?"

"Dracmar," Dimitri replied.

"Dracmar. I know they're both islands, but how did you make the jump? And why? If you knew you had personality problems, why exacerbate them by coming to this island in the first place? Why not go and get more help? There are other doctors in the world, medications," Chris said.

"Because," I said. "I actually thought coming to this island would stop it."

*****

I breathed in deeply and opened my eyes to another Santorini morning, only to find another man handcuffed to the bed.

I froze. I panicked.

I took a quick breath, rolled off the bed and grabbed the phone. "Dimitri," I whispered. "There's a man in my bed, quick, get rid of him." I dashed into the bathroom and locked the door, hearing Dimitri, Sergei and Vladimir enter to take care of the problem. I quickly showered, threw on my robe and sneaked into the bedroom. "Oh, thank God he's gone."

There was a knock at the door, and I jumped. "Yes?"

"Alexi, I have breakfast."

I opened the door, and Dimitri came in with a tray and placed it on the round table by the balcony doors.

"Alexi, sit down. We talk."

I guiltily sat and took the cup of coffee he handed me. "I know," I whispered. "I did it again. I was her again, wasn't I?" I sipped the hot brew.

"Yes, Alexi. You were Natasha again. This must stop, Alexi, for your own good. How can we stop this?"

I looked at him, and he blurred as tears filled my eyes and flowed down my cheeks. "I don't know," I wailed. "I don't know how to stop it." I put my coffee down and wept.

"Alexi." Dimitri came around to me and took me into his arms. "Alexi, what do we do? What do we do to fix this?"

After a few minutes of being comforted, I pulled away. "There's only one thing I can think of."

"What is that?" He wiped my tears away.

"A convent."

He burst out laughing. "Alexi, a convent? Convent for old wrinkled women who have no interest in anyone but God. You have no interest in God."

"Well, maybe I'd better get some then," I said, horrified that he was laughing at me as I'd never heard him laugh before. "What else am I supposed to do? I can't keep waking up with men in my bed and no recollection of how they got there."

"There is one place you can go, Alexi. Where there is no one. No man, no people."

"Where?" I was desperate to know.

"Dracmar."

"What what?" I frowned, trying to remember if I'd heard of it.

"Dracmar, Grigor's island. When I sold everything, I kept plane, yacht and island. It in Pacific Ocean and has big mansion. May need fixing up, but should be quiet place for you to live for while."

I walked around the room. "But what if being on my own doesn't stop this? Doesn't stop Natasha? What if it just gets worse?" I faced him. "What if I become her permanently?"

He sighed and shook his head. "I do not know, Alexi. We can only try."

I thought about it as I paced some more. "How long has it been empty?"

"Ten years."

I stopped. "Is it still standing?"

He shrugged. "Grigor had maintenance crew travel to all of his places every year. I kept them on for island, boat and plane. It should be good condition."

"We will need food and stuff. What about power and staff?"

"We can stock up on food at closest city, and fly or take yacht."

I rubbed my neck and felt the lumps underneath my skin. "I don't want to be alone. I don't know if I can be there alone, Dimitri."

"You will not be alone, Alexi. We will be there with you." He held my arms. "We will be there with you."

I smiled up at him. "We'll need to hire staff and get the place up and running won't we?"

"We will. We will call agency when we get to island and have staff flown in. You will not be alone, Alexi."

I smiled again and felt an overwhelming sense of relief.

*****

I peered excitedly out the plane's window looking for the tiny island I would call home. I felt like a little kid going on holiday and couldn't wait to see what it was like. "How much longer?" I flattened my face against the glass.

"'Bout fifteen minutes," Dimitri replied, checking his phone. He had called a Sydney agency asking for staff, and the yacht would be bringing them in the next day or two. It would also be bringing a huge supply of food until the gardens could be set up for fruit and vegetables. He'd also packed several boxes of food at the last fuel stop so they would have something until the boat got there. "Yacht has left Sydney," he read from his email.

I stopped breathing at the mention of Sydney and sighed.

"Alexi?"

"I miss it."

"Miss what?"

"Sydney."

"We can always go there. Could be problem, though."

"Yeah, I know." I glanced at him and grinned. "Too many men."

Sergei guffawed, but Dimitri quietened him with his death stare.

"Leave him alone," I scolded Dimitri, straightening in my seat. "It's true. Although I happen to know the two of you haven't gone without women," I said to Sergei and Vladimir. "Possibly just as many as me." I winked. They both reddened and slyly glanced at each other.

"This is your captain. We are approaching the island and need you to buckle up. It could be a bumpy ride."

We strapped in, and minutes later landed with a bump on Dracmar. Alighting from the plane, I took everything in, and like an excited child ran around, spying the pool, the flowers, and trees. We walked the island and finally saw the house, although mega-mansion would be a better phrase for it.

Four storeys high, a football field long, and Greek Island white. Marble pillars held up the house, and a wide veranda ran around the whole building. Full balconies had French doors on every floor, and big tall palm trees swayed in front. It was like a plantation on an island.

We ran up the stairs and through the unlocked front door then stopped in the marble entrance. Expensive artwork, statues and vases were revealed as we pulled off dust cloths. We opened windows and uncovered furniture until the entire ground floor was once again on display.

"Wow." I stared. "This place is amazing."

"Wait till you see upstairs," Dimitri said.

I ran for the stairs and went room to room, floor to floor, uncovering everything in the house. I flung open the only door on the third floor and whipped open the curtains. Turning around I stared. The bedroom was massive with an extra-large four-poster bed against red velvet which covered every inch of every wall. Thick blood-red carpet allowed my feet to sink into it as I walked into the huge dressing room and circular bathroom. The floor-to-ceiling windows showed off the impressive view, and I noticed the shower nozzle hanging from the ceiling in the middle of the room.

"Wow. This is the shower?" I stood over the drain and stared up at the nozzle. "This is amazing." I looked at Dimitri. "This hasn't been used in ten years? Why did he never bring me here?"

He shrugged. "Grigor wanted to keep many things private, so you could not get it in case of divorce."

"Ugh," I groaned. "Cheap bastard." I wandered back into the bedroom and stood staring at the bed.

All that red was giving me a headache, and I massaged my head through the lovely paisley scarf I wore during the day.

Dimitri noticed. "Let's get air and have meal on terrace." He led me downstairs and rustled up a quick meal from the boxes we'd brought with us.

Munching on chicken salad sandwiches, we watched the sun go down. "Guess we'd better pick rooms and get the beds made. Did you get the power going?" I asked Sergei.

"Yes, Miss Alexi. Solar panels are clean and full. All power working."

I nodded. "Good. We'll have light, what about water?"

"Generated by solar panels," Sergei added.

"Oh, good. The place seems to be self-sufficient then."

"That is way it was built," Dimitri said. "Working at moment's notice."

"That's made our job easier. Let's go sort out the bedrooms." I chose the largest on the second floor with the others taking the rooms along the hall. We quickly made beds and unloaded our luggage. After a year of travelling, I had twenty pieces to empty. I fell into bed exhausted and didn't wake till late morning when Dimitri brought me a tray of food.

"Mmm, smells good." I threw a pile of pillows behind me and attacked the food while he opened the balcony doors. "Yum, bacon and eggs."

"Yacht will be here tomorrow, Alexi. With ten staff and more food."

"Can they set up the internet on this island?"

"Probably. There is satellite dish on back." He shrugged. "I do not know these things."

"Well, then you'd better show me around the property, and we'll make a list of what needs to be done ready for tomorrow."

"When you are ready." He nodded and left me to my meal.

We spent the day making lists and thoroughly checking the house, basement and island, and realised there was a lot that needed doing. And it was all waiting for the new staff members the next day when they arrived.

After introductions and the setting of jobs, we all got to work cleaning the house from top to bottom. I did the third floor by myself and found a headache was imminent.

I was suffocating.

Drowning in the redness of the room.

I flung open the doors and let the sea air flow in, hoping to clear my brain.

It didn't work.

I stumbled backwards and collapsed onto the bed. The pain was blinding, and I slid to the floor, grasping at the bed linen as I went.

"Alexi." Dimitri ran to my side. "Alexi."

"It hurts," I said through clenched teeth and squinty eyes. "It hurts so much. Argh." I grasped my head and gasped. I couldn't breathe, and it was getting worse.

"Alexi." Dimitri picked me up and laid me on the

bed. "Alexi. What can I do? Do you want pill? Massage?"

"Massage?" Natasha purred. "Now that is good idea."

"Natasha go away. I am talking to Alexi." Dimitri was firm.

"Dimitri?"

"Alexi?"

"Dimitri?"

"I do not want to talk to you, Natasha."

"But you are no fun."

"I want Alexi."

"Dimitri?"

"Come, Alexi." He helped me stand. "Breathe."

I grabbed my head. "Dimitri." My head violently jerked from side to side. My hands held on, but could not stop it.

"Alexi, breathe." He held my hands to steady my head. "Breathe."

I gasped, shuddered and calmed down. "Dimitri," I whispered. "That was awful."

"I know, Alexi. Let's get you downstairs."

I spent the rest of the day in my room, resting after downing high dose painkillers. Dimitri brought me a dinner tray with more meds, and I drifted off.

It was dark when I woke. Rolling over, I left the bed and found my hair in the dressing room. Pulling it on, I grabbed a black see-through dressing gown from the drawer and left the room.

The house was quiet as I glided down the stairs to the ground floor. Hall lights lit the way with a soft *yellow glow, and I padded from room to room in search of company, finding what I was looking for in the kitchen. "Well, hello," Natasha murmured. "And who are you?"*

He turned and dropped his sandwich on the counter at the sight of the naked woman in a flowing open gown. "Well..." His voice cracked, and he cleared his throat. "Hello, there." His eyes devoured her shapely body, perky breasts and brunette thatch. "Who are you?" His sandwich was long forgotten as he stepped toward her.

"I am Natasha, Queen Natasha. This is my island, and I want man to fuck. Are you married?"

He blinked at her blatant honesty. "Um, no," was all he managed.

"Are you sure?" He was close enough for her to grab his hand. "No ring does not mean you not married."

"I'm not, I'm not," he blurted, now standing toe to toe with her.

"Good," she said and planted his hand on her right breast. "Squeeze." He jumped in surprise, and she grabbed his right hand and shoved it between her legs.

"Hey," he cried. "What the hell?"

"I want to fuck," she said. "You want to fuck me?"

He stared at her luscious lips and moved his fingers. She was moist and hot inside, and her breast felt right at home in his hand. "Fuck, yes," he whispered, all hard and horny.

"Good." She pushed his shorts down, and he lifted her onto the kitchen bench where he entered her hard

and hot.

"Oh, uh, oh, fuck…me…" She flung her head back and braced herself on the bench as her legs held him in place.

"Oh, God," he groaned between sucking her breasts and groping them. He touched her all over until he felt himself escalate, then held her tightly as he grunted and thrust into her to the point of ejaculation.

"Oh, God, oh, God, oh, God," they groaned together.

"Roddy?" The main light flicked on, and a woman was standing there, shell-shocked. "Roddy? How? What? Bloody?"

"Babe," he gasped, trying to get out of Natasha's leg lock. "This is not what it looks like."

"Of course it is," Natasha said, understanding the situation. Unwinding her legs, she slid off the bench and smoothed her hair. "We were fucking."

The woman's eyes were wide, and her lips were in an o shape.

"Babe, listen, we weren't…we were…" He shoved his dick back into his shorts and straightened himself.

"Roddy?"

"Bloody hell," he muttered.

"What were you doing?" she yelled.

"He was fucking me," Natasha replied, watching the idiotic young girl trying to comprehend two people having sex on the kitchen bench.

The girl turned to the Cleopatra wannabe. "Not you, whore. I didn't ask you."

"Whore?" Natasha spat. "Who the fuck are you to

call me whore, you vile little toad. I own this island, and I will do what I want on my island."

"Big fucking deal," the girl spat back. "You were fucking my husband."

Natasha's left eyebrow rose, and she turned to the brunet stud she'd just fucked on the kitchen bench. "Husband? You told me you were not married, otherwise I would not have fucked you."

"Well…I…" He went bright red as he stammered. "I…uh…"

"Roddy, how dare you! I don't want to be married to a man who'd so easily cheat on me with a whore."

"Again with the whore," Natasha murmured. "I am Queen. Queen of Russia and you will speak to me with dignity, or get off my island."

"With pleasure," the girl yelled and turned on her heel.

"Babe," Roddy called, running after her. "Babe?"

Shaking her head at the scene that left the room, Natasha straightened her gown and spied the untouched sandwich on the counter. Picking it up and munching on it, she went back to her room on the third floor, dusted off her hands, flung the thick red comforter back, piled up the pillows and settled back on them.

Dimitri burst in. "What have you done?" he bellowed upon seeing her.

"What do you think?" she replied. "What I always do."

"This has got to stop, Natasha. Now we must send them home and pay them off, so they don't talk."

She dismissed him with a wave of her hand. "Then get new staff and bring back men for me."

"This will not happen, Natasha."

She sat up straight. "This will happen, Dimitri. I want men. I want men to fuck and be fucked by. I want men. Lots of men who will do my bidding when I want them to. I want men, you get me men. You dismissed." She lay back and closed her eyes.

"When will this stop, Natasha?"

"When I say it stops, Dimitri."

PART FOUR

"And that is how I ended up here, on this island, three years ago, with a sex problem," I said, kind of disgusted at the whole thing. I stretched the tight muscles in my back and neck.

"So, your split personality became worse due to being on this island?" Chris asked.

I shrugged nonchalantly. "I can't explain it, and don't fully understand it myself, but the doctors said one day it could just go."

"And that's why you've had such bad migraines for so long?" He was trying to understand everything he'd heard over the last few hours.

"Yes. First, they were from physical injuries and then developed into emotional ones. Apparently, I had to deal with my *issues* to get rid of them. Looks like I've done it."

Chris frowned, unsure if that was the case. "Because you found me?"

I shrugged slightly. "Looks like." I prayed he accepted me after everything he'd heard.

He stood and stretched before walking onto the

balcony and leant against the railing to watch the first changes of colour in the sky.

"I don't expect you to understand. I don't really myself. I just know I needed to find you to find out what had happened. To hear the story myself. Unfortunately, Natasha was in control half the time and what she got up to disgusts me." I stood beside him and shook my head. "I am *so* disgusted by my behaviour. It's disgusting and gross, and I can't believe I did it." My shoulders shrugged limply. "I can't explain it, I can't. I *can* ask *you* to accept me the way I am *now*, though." I bit my lip and held back tears for the man I had come to love with all my heart.

"She thanked me."

"I know."

He looked at me. "*You* thanked me."

I nodded. "Of course."

He shook his head. "All this time I haven't coped or dealt with killing a man and his wife thanks me for doing so."

"Weird, I know."

"More than weird." He straightened and stared hard at me. "I don't know how to deal with this, Alex. I really don't." His head shook side to side, and he sighed and moved for the door. "I need a walk."

I waited for the door to close before bursting into tears.

Dimitri came to me and held me in his death grip, willing me to be better.

"I love him."

"I know, Alexi, I know."

Chris didn't come back to the room, so I tried to fill

my time. Grabbing boxes from the storage lockers, Dimitri helped me pack all the things in Natasha's room. He packed up her sex toys, and I packed the wigs and clothes.

I picked up the black Cleopatra wig from the floor, sighed, and glanced in the mirror. No Natasha. No migraines. "Thank you, God," I whispered and finished loading box after box until nothing was left. Drawers empty, shelves clean, closet void of any and all person. Real or imaginary.

Dimitri, Sergei and Vladimir carried the boxes downstairs and transported them around to the fire pit. I was going to burn them later, and I hoped Chris would join me. I called up Jenny and some of the other girls, and we got the room cleaned. They had never been up there before and oohed and aahed at its opulence. They did ask where her majesty was, but I just brushed it off by kind of suggesting she was in my room so we could give it a good clean up.

Walking out the door, I took one last look, a look at my past, a look at the pain, a look at what once was and never will be again.

I closed the door on so much more.

*****

The next day I set out for the fire pit.

It was twenty-four hours since I'd finished telling Chris the whole story. Twenty-four hours since he'd walked out of my room. Twenty-four hours since I'd seen him.

Staff had reported his whereabouts, and I told them to leave him be unless he needed something. He needed time to think first, like I needed the time to say goodbye.

Dimitri stood by my side at the pit, flames already soaring into the air, greedily licking at the oxygen keeping it alive. He opened a box for me, and I pulled out the sheer black dressing gown I'd worn two nights earlier. I threw it on the fire and watched it be eaten alive. Piece after piece followed. Lingerie, silk and satin, sex toys, bondage play things.

Even the blue-green dress that I had bought with Grigor's hundred dollar tip back in Sydney. The one thing of mine he'd kept after throwing everything else out.

The one thing I'd kept to remind me of my past.

A past I no longer needed.

A past I definitely no longer wanted.

The wigs came next. Red, blonde, brunette. I left Cleopatra for last as that was the one we wore most.

I heard breaking twigs and saw Chris walk up beside me. We said nothing, just stared at each other. I swallowed the painful lump in my throat and threw the wig onto the fire. "Goodbye, Natasha," I whispered as the flames melted it into a puddle of black goo. After a few moments, I motioned for Dimitri to leave us and waited for him to be out of sight.

"You've burned all of her stuff."

I nodded. "Yeah." My eyes and throat burned from the heat.

"I watched the whole thing from over there." He

nodded toward a leafy area of the garden. "I didn't want to disturb you."

"I wanted you here." I sniffed and wiped my tears.

"I was."

We spoke at the same time. "Alex/Chris." We smiled. "I love you/I love you."

"I don't want you to hate me." I burst into tears.

He took me into his arms. "I don't hate you. I hate what you've done as Natasha. I hate what Grigor and his friends did to you. I hate what you had to go through the last ten years."

"I hate what you went through," I murmured into his chest.

He sighed. "Yeah well, looks like we both went through our own version of hell because of that man. Although I'm not sure I can deal with Dimitri being the mastermind behind all their deaths. I don't agree with what he did to their relatives either. That's just..." Another sigh escaped from between his lips.

"Yeah well, it's not like I could stop him. I was in a coma. I had no say in the matter."

"I know," he said quickly. "Doesn't mean I like it."

"Yeah well...I'm glad he did." I pulled away and turned toward the fire.

"Still?"

I looked at him, and anger rose to the surface. "*After what those bastards did to me I'm glad Dimitri got revenge. I was left for dead.* I was shot, stabbed, drowned, beaten and electrocuted by my *husband's friends.* I'm *glad* they're dead. And if Dimitri hadn't've done it, I sure as fuck would have!"

He sighed again. "I can understand that. Doesn't mean I like it."

I was still angry. "You don't *have* to like it," I snapped and then softened when I saw his face. "But can you accept what *has* happened?"

He frowned. "What do you mean?"

I softened. "Can you accept what happened to me? What Dimitri did *for* me?"

He stared at the woman he loved. "I don't know."

*****

To give Chris some space, I didn't get upset when he slept back in his old room. It gave me time to think about things and make plans. I gathered the staff together for a meeting. "Okay, long story short, I'm shutting up shop and leaving."

Gasps and words of 'what' went around the room.

I put my hand up and shook my head slightly. "Now, don't worry. I told Jenny days ago there's always a plan and there is. We're going to get the place cleaned and shut up by the end of the week. Then you can all have three months paid leave. You'll get three hundred thousand dollars each, one hundred thousand a month, to go and do what you want, how you want. Go to the places you've always wanted to go. Do what you've always wanted to do. Party like you've never partied before." That definitely cheered them up, the prospect of being rich.

"What's going on?" Jenny asked. "You said we still had jobs."

"You do," I said. "After your party hard three months are over, be prepared to come back and work if you want to, because the place will be open as a holiday resort and spa, and you lot," I pointed both forefingers at them, "will be in charge."

Oohs and aahs went around the room.

"So, you'll all have to decide who's in charge because I'm moving on and taking my Russian mob squad with me." I waved my hand at Dimitri, Sergei and Vladimir. "So you can either choose one of *you* or hire someone else. And the third floor," I picked up a colour brochure I'd made on the PC, "will be the luxury suite."

"Nice!"

"Fancy."

"Fantastic."

"So, let's get this island cleaned up and closed, and we'll all go off on holidays and new adventures. Dismissed."

They all exited the room full of surprised comments and bubbling with excitement except for Dimitri.

"Alexi. Do you think this is right decision?"

"Yes, I do." I gathered my papers and turned to him with a sigh. "It's time to move on, finally. She's no longer a part of my life. I know what happened to Grigor and…" I shrugged. "If Chris wants to be a part of *my* life, great, if not, I'll have to deal with it."

"You will not deal with it alone, Alexi."

*****

Over the next few days, we cleaned the house from top

to bottom, shut up rooms after covering the furniture with dust sheets, and shut all of the storm windows. We put away outdoor furniture, mowed the lawns, and cleaned and covered the pool. I didn't see Chris, but had been told he was staying out of the way, doing laps of the island and cove, and I hoped all that running and swimming would clear his mind. He took his meals in his room, kept to himself, and had been informed of our departure date.

I'd called in the Yurogovnia yacht again, although more of a luxury liner that could hold one hundred guests, to take everyone on their three-month sojourn. It sailed into the bay and moored at the wharf.

The plane was fuelled and stocked, the hangar cleaned and closed up. All that was left was to transfer any leftover food to the yacht and get everyone and their stuff on board.

The last day came, and that's what we did. The yacht staff came and collected our five fridges full of food for a big beach party goodbye, and the girls cleaned them and turned them off. All electricals were unplugged, and the staff went off to pack their belongings.

I walked up to my room, wondering about Chris and whether we'd make it or not. We hadn't spoken since the fire, and I didn't know what to think, or what *he* was thinking. I packed my clothes and toiletries then stripped the bed. Our rooms were the last to be cleaned and closed down, and the linen washed and packed away.

I stopped and stared at my empty room.

It was just like the first day we'd arrived.

Dimitri took my bags to the plane. He, Sergei and Vladimir would be flying with me and so, I hoped, would Chris.

We all met on the beach at three for a barbeque feast. The house was locked and loaded, the staff quarters shut down, and the island was ready to be deserted.

The boat staff did an amazing job of cooking just *some* of the leftovers, the rest went into the yacht's fridges, and we enjoyed juicy meats, crisp salads and fresh fruit topped off with ice-cold sodas and cheesecake.

I stood and held up my drink, spying Chris sitting alone and away from the crowd, looking forlorn and lonely. My heart ached for him and hoped we could sort it out. I focussed. "I just want to say thank you, to all of you, for everything you've done for the last few years. It's time to say goodbye and get a life. I thank you for your hard work and dedication. Cheers."

We partied until the wee hours of the morning and until the staff could stumble on board to their rooms. I watched the yacht staff clean up and tidy the beach, making sure the barbecue pit was extinguished. They retired to the boat, and I sat watching the sun come up with Dimitri.

"So, this is goodbye, Alexi?"

"Yes, Dimitri, this is goodbye." I leaned my head on his shoulder and waited for the sky to go through its rainbow of colours to get to blue before I moved. Letting out a deep sigh, we got up and walked arm in arm to the runway with sadness in my heart. I hadn't seen Chris since the afternoon before, so didn't know if he was coming with us. We boarded, and I spoke to David. "We're looking at nine sharp after showers and breakfast."

"Where to?"

"Sydney, Australia."

"I'll map the flight plan."

"Have you seen Chris?"

"I think he's on board."

That surprised me. I went to my room and found him there. "Hey."

"Hey," he said from his seat on the bed.

"I—"

"It's okay. I didn't know which room to take, and I recognised your luggage, so I had a shower, hope you don't mind."

"God…no…of course not. I'll—"

"Why don't you have a shower and…we can talk over breakfast."

His lack of enthusiasm worried me. "Okay, I'll be back in a minute." I quickly showered, dressed, and had breakfast brought to the room. We sat at the small table, and I waited for him to start.

"I want to fly back to Sydney." He ate some cereal.

"Okay." I couldn't eat as my stomach was doing flip flops.

"Hope you don't mind."

"Of course not." He wasn't looking at me, and I worried.

"Alex…"

"Chris…"

"I—" He finally looked up from his food.

"Yes..." I waited with bated breath.

"I can't accept what *I've* done, even if he *was* a monster. Because what *I've* done is kill someone."

I held my breath.

"And I can't accept what Dimitri has done, even if it *was* justified. Because *he* killed someone. Not just someone, but five someones and assaulted five more."

I died inside.

"And I can't accept what *you've* done as Natasha. Because it's highly gross and disgusting and degrading."

I was dead.

"And I don't expect *you* to accept *me* and what I've done either."

I swallowed back pain and misery.

He rubbed his forehead as if a big weight was sitting there and he wanted to get rid of it. "But, I love you. And I want to spend the rest of my life with you. So, I think, I think that even if we can't accept what *we* have done, or what the *other* has done, we should forgive ourselves and each other so we can be together."

My heart soared at the news, and I flew into his arms. "I love you. I want to spend the rest of my life with you and make babies with you, even if it's with a surrogate, and be your wife." I kissed him. "So much."

"Wait..." He pushed me away. "Did you hear me? I can't accept what's happened, but I can forgive."

I stared into his eyes, a bit confused as to what he was really saying, so I went with it. "I don't *need* your forgiveness," I said, puzzled by his attitude. "I don't want it. I want to forget everything that has ever happened to me where Grigor and his friends are concerned and move on with my life. I just want *you* to love *me* and accept *me* for what and who I am *now*. Not what and who I *was*. And I really do believe that Natasha is gone and I'm back to my old self again, which means no more behaviour like before." I stared into his blue eyes as they registered what I was saying. "The *only* forgiveness *you* need is your own for what you did, and what happened to me is *not* my doing." I kissed him. "We both need to accept each other for the person we are *today* if we plan on having a life from this day forward. Can you do that?"

He stared back before pushing me away and standing, thinking about what I'd said. "Let me think about it."

I was disappointed. Disappointed in him, disappointed in myself. That I could put so much into one man and be left with nothing.

Again.

I checked my watch. "We leave in an hour," I said and walked out the door.

I wandered back to the yacht to make sure everyone was on board, and everything was in working order.

"We're ready to go when you are," the captain informed me.

I checked my watch. Half an hour left. "Nine a.m. we fly."

"We'll be ready."

I said goodbye to those I came across and disembarked for my flight. I hoped and prayed Chris would be as willing as I was to put our pasts behind us and start a new life together. I made it back to the plane and found my Russian mob squad already seated and belted in.

"Alexi."

"Dimitri."

"Ready to go?"

"I am. Is Chris still here?"

"Was he ever?"

I gave him a death stare and checked my room, finding Chris still there. "We fly soon."

He looked up from his reverie. "Okay."

I found a double seat away from the others and buckled in. The door was closed, and Chris made it to the seat beside me as we started taxiing to the runway. He smiled and took my hand in his, waiting until we were in the air to speak.

He sighed. "You were right, and I was a bloody idiot. We've both done things we're not happy with *or about*, and I can't *not* accept you because of all the shit that we've done or gone through. That would be unfair to you and the wrong thing to do. Not to mention hypocritical. I love you and want to spend the rest of my life loving you, and making a life with you and making babies with you, even if it's by surrogate."

A slow grin spread across my lips. "I do."

Surprise lit up his face, and he realised what I meant. "I haven't even asked you yet."

"You don't need to. The answer will always be yes."

"Will you?"

"Yes."

Our lips met as we flew into the sky for our journey home.

About the Author

L.J. has been writing since 2006, when her first of many novels, ***The Road To Vegas,*** was born. In 2016 she created the ***Porn Star Brothers*** series about three sizzlingly hot Australian born Greek Island raised brothers who became the hottest porn stars in '70s America.

L.J. lives in Australia, loves '80s music, disaster movies, and collecting Jackie Collins books as Jackie is her inspiration and mentor.

L.J. Diva is the adult pen name for author Tiara King. You can find more about Tiara on her website; follow her on social media, or visit her publishing house, Royal Star Publishing.

Socials

tiaraking.com.au/ljdiva

royalstarpublishing.com.au

Sign up for *Tiara's* Newsletter…

Make sure you're always in the know and never miss free exclusives, the latest news, book updates, and so much more with newsletters from…

tiaraking.com.au

Have you read these?

Or these?

NOVELS

Burning Desires
Anything for You
Falling for London
The Road to Vegas
Hollywood Dreams
The Billionaire's Dirty Little Secret

SHORT STORIES

The Body
The Perfect Plot
The Star of Your Own Crime Scene